The
Red
Doorknob

E. FRANK

PublishAmerica
Baltimore

ISBN: 1-4241-0705-9
PUBLISHED BY PUBLISHAMERICA, LLLP
www.publishamerica.com
Baltimore

Printed in the United States of America

To Dale, whose patience was sometimes tried but who stood by me all the way.

Acknowledgements

I wish to thank Dale, my wonderful wife, for her help and her encouragement on the final proof; Denise Nielsen, for her proof reading; and Mary Lou Werlich, for an excellent title.

Chapter 1

In the Beginning

The morning sun is shining through the window casting its rays across a very traditionally decorated room. The room is located in the back of an old lodge overlooking a small valley in the foothills of the mountains in Austria. A light scent of mountain flowers is wafting in the window and I lie here in bed with my arm around the most wonderful person in the world. I wonder how, after so many years and so many turns of fate, we have finally arrived at what can only be simply described as happiness

I guess the best way would be to start at the beginning. The beginning for most people is as a kid and I am no exception. I was born at home on our family farm. My mother named me William, Will for short.

Typical for most kids, my mother had a great influence on my early life. She was very strict and a stickler for something she referred to as deportment. Her version of deportment was based on manners as applied to eating, drinking, and cleanliness. Boy, did she impress these lessons on me as she believed if you behaved at home you would not need to be disciplined when out in public. Another thing sacred to her was being considerate of other people. I did listen and heard whether I wanted to or not. When repeated enough it eventually sinks in. Her examples used some of the less desirable persons in our area, particularly the smelly and boorish types. She was right; after all, who can battle the obvious, and the results of her lessons turned out to be a pleasant and useful asset for getting advancement and, to my pleasure, attracting girls.

I was raised on our family farm, which helped my direction in life and my love of the outdoors. I was given the freedom to roam in the nearby forests and typical for a kid of that age I had an active imagination. I was attracted to rivers and creeks, usually under the disguise of fishing, and built dams to help the fish in the heat waves of the summers. One could say I moved a lot of stones to make fish happy and when I read of a device called a fish ladder I moved even more stones so the fish downstream could move to the safety of the deep water. I had the skills to enlist the help of a number of my friends to assist me with my various projects.

A natural lean towards mechanical things helped me enjoy life around the farm. My father was very mechanically minded and helped me learn problem solving techniques. He taught me to sit back and get an overview of everything that was involved with a problem. He was proponent of the idea that when the true problem was identified the problem was eighty percent solved. I was a good student of his techniques and tried to copy his abilities. Any farm is loaded with mechanical things and the best ones had tons of pulleys, belts, chains, shaker arms, and other moving parts. I loved to find out how they worked. Sometimes my never-ending questions drove my father to distraction.

Even at an early age I tended towards analyzing problems in my own way. At seven I figured out the Santa Claus thing by counting the kids in our school and considering the time to go between all of their homes and put all the presents under all of the trees and realized it was simply not possible as no one person could stop at all of the places on the same night no matter how magical he was. Also since none of their homes had fireplaces, the "down the fireplace" story wouldn't work either. I decided to test the waters by asking how Santa Claus got into our house and was told the door was left unlocked. I knew that would never happen because Grandfather, who always stayed with us at Christmas, was paranoid about leaving any door unlocked. My older sister and younger brother were still into Santa Claus, so I smugly kept the whole thing to myself.

In high school I tended to drive my teachers into total frustration by not working at anything I didn't like, so languages, plant and animal stuff, and chemistry plummeted towards lower marks. That

8

resulted in teachers' comments on my report card like *He has far more potential than these marks indicate.* My parents somehow never really appreciated the comments and I heard about it. My marks in mathematics, physics and history lifted my averages into the more acceptable area.

Friends tended to vary from year to year. I never had the so-called lifelong friend. In the early years most of my friends left school before finishing and went to work. At the end of high school we all went off in every direction and I never attempted to keep in touch. I presumed their lives were busy enough that they didn't attempt to keep in touch with me either.

I discovered very early in high school that there was a definite social stratum in small-town Canada and one could go down the levels very easily but the climb up was very difficult. You could get to the highest level only by birth. I made enough of the right friends to smooth my entrance into the parties and functions to which I wished to go and avoided the difficulties of maintaining a fixed social status by being independent but thoughtful to all. Girlfriends were short lived, as I was oblivious to anyone who was interested in me and anyone I was interested in was oblivious to me. The logistics of a date before I got my driver's license were impossible as we lived ten miles out of town and there was no way I was going to be driven anywhere by my parents when a girl may be involved.

My marks were good enough to get into engineering school and since this was 1942, I felt that going to university and joining up later would be more beneficial. At university life was good, with lots of girls available, especially since most of the potential competition was sitting in England or North Africa waiting to go into battle and they had been long forgotten by the girls. I had an absolutely fantastic time and lived by the philosophy of *So Many Girls and So Little Time.* I did not have a lot of money and to keep up the social pace I had to resort to a little ingenuity. I seemed to look slightly older than most of my classmates and managed to convince the clerks at the beer store I was of age. I bought all the beer for a bunch of underage drinkers. I retained the empties and when they had been cashed in I got enough money to keep my car in gasoline and me in beer. The gasoline was quite often appropriated from the tractor

9

when I went home for the weekend and bonus—that left more money for beer. I think my favorite course was the evening version of applied anatomy.

By second year my school marks suffered and towards the end of the school year I got called for The Interview. On the way to The Interview I passed the recruitment office, conveniently set up on campus, and thought, *One always needs options.* I backed up and went in to have a discussion with the recruiter. He was especially good at his job and allowed me to determine that the Engineers needed engineers and directed my thinking to the fact that one was less likely to get hurt building or fixing things like roads and bridges than charging around with a gun and shooting at a guy that was shooting back. I bought it because the recruiter did nothing to persuade me to think otherwise. The interview with the university guidance department was short because I had my recruitment papers and all I got was a good luck, maybe we will see you after the war. I then went to see the dean of engineering. He looked at my marks from both first year and the second year to date. He then sat quietly for a while. Staring over the top of his glasses he asked, "What happened this year?" I smiled and told him that I had somehow got sidelined with girls and beer. He asked me a few questions about engineering and then told me that I would get my second year as a result of my experience in military service and added that when I returned after the war I would be able to start in third year. He left out the part that said, "providing you get back alive and not screwed up too much." I thanked him and left his office feeling quite proud of myself.

I had a week before I was to report to basic training so I went home. When I appeared on our front doorstep, with all of my belongings, I was met by Mother, who didn't look very pleased. Father had a few even less complimentary comments when he returned from the backfields. I did not want to let her know about how low my marks had plunged, so I concocted a story about how the military had forced some of the better students into service because they were in dire need of good officers. I don't think she believed one word but at least it made me feel better. The day before I was to report to Basic Training Mother gave me a signet ring that she had bought at the engineering school. She had planned to give it to me when I graduated. She asked me to wear it as a reminder that I had a commitment to finish school when I returned. I promised her I would.

Basic Training was as bad as it is portrayed in the movies. I worked hard to make sure I got into the Engineers and not the Infantry. I fudged the aptitude and medical tests. My end results showed a person with high mechanical ability and lousy peripheral vision. My upper body strength was good because of my summers working on the farm so the physical part of training was easy. I devised ways to beat many of the obstacle courses by having several pulleys and ropes in my backpack. Why go hand over hand along a rope when you can do it twice as fast with a pulley and a handle!

When we were sent over to Europe I was assigned to the Engineers. As fate was smiling, I just missed the D-Day landings. I acquired the job of checking out the English pubs and girls. Again my luck had held out as most of the competition had just left for the Continent so there were lots of girls available.

I arrived in France with a group of Engineers who were assigned the job of improving the routes that the convoys used to move equipment and supplies to the Front. Our projects mostly involved rebuilding bridges that had been destroyed or damaged by either the Germans to prevent us from pursuing them or by us to prevent the German supplies from reaching them. After being in France for a short time I discovered three things, in order of importance; French girls really did appreciate having the German soldiers being driven out, French wine was superb and French cooking was indeed exceptional. I did discover Engineers do get shot at but we will get to that later. The French girls, in demonstrating their appreciation, contributed much towards my schooling of practical social interaction. They were definitely much more passionate than the English girls and I did my best to be a good student. My high school French improved very quickly to the point of fluency.

Materials were required by the Front and the quickest way to bring them from the harbors was by road. Roads have bridges to cross over rivers. My main projects were concentrated around bridge repair and improvement so the supply trucks could get to the Front.

The best part was most bridges were located in towns with girls, restaurants and taverns. I had access to many products from our supplies that the restaurants could not get so a little bartering allowed me to eat and drink well at little cost. I developed an appreciation for fine wines, excellent cooking and good sex.

Life was grand.

I acquired quite a reputation for collecting admiring females and exceptionally quick ways of getting bridges into useable condition. I also became quite an expert in using Bailey bridges in unique ways that speeded up the bridge repairs and river crossings in record time. The first reputation did not put me into good standing with most of the other officers in my group. They preferred to stay in each town a little longer and they wanted less competition for the charms of the local girls. I think there also was a little jealousy around my obvious superior treatment by the local restaurants and bars. I had no desire to stay in any one place for an extended period of time. After all, I had no plans for any permanent relationship. A new set of girls in each new town presented a completely different set of challenges, not to forget an entirely new collection of good wines and local foods that had to be sampled. Both reputations accelerated my posting to the Front, where the real bullets were flying.

I wasn't impressed that I had let my enthusiasm get in the way of common sense and vowed to be really careful at my new posting. I don't think very many of the other officers in my old regiment made any effort to keep me from being posted closer to the Front. In a letter, I informed my mother of the posting. I think she was probably smarter than I gave her credit for and, with her practical side showing through, gave me some sensible advice, "Keep your head down and don't be stupid."

I think she left out the word "again" and was chastising me for getting myself out of a comfortable situation into what she considered a dangerous one. At my age I thought I was immortal so I wasn't afraid of getting shot. I was just upset that I was going where the girls were scarce and, probably, the wine even more scarce.

Chapter 2
Will at the Front

There I was sitting in the back of a rather shot-up store. The store must have been a bakery in better times because what remained of the front window had a bunch of twisted racks and in the back room there was a large oven and a large number of rusted, bent-up bake pans scattered all around. My perch in the bakery allowed me to see across the river to a German flag without being seen by the enemy. I felt some form of energy in the air and wondered if I was really stupid or if something exciting was coming.

The Engineering Regiment where I had been posted had mixed feelings about me having joined them. The officer whom I was replacing had been killed while inspecting what was left of the bridge that crossed the river. He had stepped on a landmine near the bridge approach and lain on the ground in a mess. One of his legs had been blown off and the other leg had been shattered. His internal injuries must have been massive but he had survived for over an hour, calling for help all the while. Nobody could get to him because of the covering gunfire from the Germans on the other shore and subsequently he died from loss of blood. Two of the medics who had tried to get to him had been shot; one just a nick, the other somewhat more critical. The officer's body was then removed under cover of darkness.

The Engineers had no concern about the local girls as they had long since cleared out for safer places or had been herded by the Germans to the other side of the river, where the town had remained intact. The wine had been either consumed by the Germans before we got there or taken with them when they retreated across the river. If there was any left it had been broken when our side of the town had been destroyed by the Germans as they pulled out. I was an unknown to them and replacing a very good friend of theirs, whose death and mode of dying had shook them all severely. My reception was cool. I understood their feelings so I made no effort to push myself on them and let them come to me. I had introduced myself and then reported to my quarters.

The river was a difficult obstacle to our advancement and everyone was working on some method of getting the troops across the river. The tanks had to be gotten across to support the troops as fast as possible. They then would be followed by supplies to keep the troops moving.

The river gorge was deep and the current was moving fast.

There existed an old path, mostly overgrown and suitable only for foot travel. The path had a twin on the other side. It had originally led down to a ferry that had been in use before the first bridge had been built. The only use the paths had now was for the occasional fisherman to get to the bank of the river. The connection across the river had been by a bridge for at least the last two hundred years. The latest bridge had been a suspension bridge approximately two hundred feet long and had been destroyed by the Germans when they had crossed over the river three weeks before. The bridge looked rather forlorn with the bridge deck long gone into the river. Most of the suspension cables were hanging with miscellaneous parts of the supports still bolted and hanging in pieces. The rest of the cables still held some remaining parts of the side rails for the bridge deck.

I then realized that the bridge was basically intact and reusable. I quietly left my bakery and went and got one of the other engineers. We arrived back at the bakery and I asked him what he saw. Most people would look at the mess and think, *How could you believe the bridge is intact?* The other engineer was not any different. I asked him to look again at the bridge and imagine it was a new bridge under construction with the bridge deck not yet installed. A few sketches and he then could see what I was talking about. We both went back to headquarters and got the colonel. The three of us went back to the bakery and I again explained what was sitting in front of us.

The colonel was elated.

The suspension cabling system could support a tank, because it had already supported the German tanks before the bridge deck was destroyed and they were heavier than ours. All we needed was a new deck and the time to install it. I knew that the deck was just one of the finishing touches to a bridge. The cables and support towers were the hardest parts in the construction of a bridge and they were all intact. For a bridge of this size it would normally only take several weeks after the bridge cabling had been prepared and drawings made for the deck fabrication and delivery to the site. We didn't have an engineering office or a metal fabricator available and we had no one to set up the cranes to swing the metal into place. Even if we did, the Germans would find the bridge workers great for target practice. We had several meetings to try to sort out the problems and the pressure to find a solution became almost unbearable. Our project meetings became extremely argumentative with all the naysayers in full swing. I went back to my bakery and stared at the bridge as it stared back at me. I realized that we had a bridge deck sitting in the back part of the town in the form of several Bailey bridges. If we could consolidate several suspension cables at the end of each section of the Bailey bridge we could then swing the bridge section into place. With support beams underneath the deck and fastened to the ends of the cables, we could support the bridge deck. I got out my slide ruler and with some basic assumptions, and a few sketches, mathematically proved to myself it could be done. I went to the next meeting where the military commander happened to be present and explained my solution to the problem. Nobody else had any solutions except to say it could not be done. I got the go-ahead.

The first thing we did was to build a stone and earthen wall across the area where we were going to work to protect the workmen and hide what was going on. The bulldozers also cleared a wide area just behind the wall, using part of the destroyed buildings as material for the wall. The tanks then had to be dug in behind the wall. They kept up a regular schedule of firing to keep the Germans occupied.

We organized the Baileys that were in storage at the outskirts of the town and moved them much closer to the bridge. At night we had

crews on the bridge preparing it for the new bridge deck. The
infantry kept a steady fire at any area where the Germans could spot
the workers on the bridge. We even brought in some mortars to make
sure the Germans kept their heads down. The Germans tried to rig a
search light to light up our side of the river and blind us or at least
find out what was going on and illuminate some targets. One of the
mortars made short work of it. We only had to move four bridge
sections into place for the center section of the bridge. One more
section at each end of the bridge was to be used to fasten the bridge
to the shore and ease the tanks on and off the bridge. We then set up
a system by which the first bridge would be slid out and supported
by the suspension cables that were one cable past where it would be
fastened. The first section would be fastened to a section that was on
the roadbed on our side of the river. The second bridge section was
to be slid out on a dolly which we made out of several trailer axles
and lowered into place using the suspension cables as anchor cables.
The whole procedure was simple on paper but with the Germans
objecting to any work, they made life anything but fun. We figured
that we could do the final work in one night. As soon as we were
ready the Infantry would plan to have a raid two nights before and
they would place as many troops on the far shore as required to keep
the Germans very busy. Our job was to get the bridge ready for the
tanks to cross at first light. This meant we had one day to get
everything as close as we could to the bridge and one night to place
the sections in position.

The big night came. The troops went across the river by boat that
night with plenty of covering fire and scrambled up the overgrown
path on the other side. They had installed a cable which was fastened
to each shore to assist the boats when a larger body of troops went
over later that night. The path brought them up to a spot just below
the road behind an embankment, which must have been a loading
area many years ago. The tanks and mortars on our side kept a steady
fire on the German positions just as they had for a week of
successive evenings. The Germans must have thought we were just
doing our standard evening and daytime "keep you on your toes and
your head down." We managed to land several hundred men and
took control of the area facing several buildings directly across from

the bridge before they figured out what had happened. The greatest surprise we got was the lack of heavy guns on their side and not one tank showed its nose. There was a lot of action all of the next day but our troops held their position and by evening we went into high gear with the new bridge deck. We had several hitches, all of which slowed us down. The trolleys kept going off track and the further we went across the bridge the worse it got. We lost two bridge sections into the river when the cabling attached to the suspension system either slipped or broke. We had to use our last section as the sixth section to complete the roadbed on the far shore. The troops had set up a heavy smoke screen to hide our progress with the bridge from prying eyes and by eight that morning the first tank was ready to make the crossing.

The first tank driver was not too impressed about being the first across. Actually he raised quite a fuss and kept mumbling about the suicide bridge. I got very upset and opened my big mouth and somewhere in my tirade I stated I would have no problem taking a tank across.

Big mistake!

There I was riding on the first tank across the bridge. I was not driving it because we would never have made it with me driving. I suspect the driver thought if the bridge let go I could swim and drag him ashore. I didn't tell him I was a lousy swimmer. The first tank rolled up on the far shore and promptly fired a few well-placed shots at the German defenses. They were strangely very silent. The tank was followed by a large number of troops with machine guns and then the remaining eight tanks were followed by the rest of the troops. When the men approached the German defenses nobody fired back. Upon arriving at the defenses we found them vacant. This put our forces more on edge as they now expected an ambush somewhere in the town.

Chapter 3
Dieter on the Other Side

I was the reluctant German commander Oberleutnant Dieter Hess and I was sitting in the old clock tower across the river with my binoculars, trying to figure out what was going on. I had withdrawn the troops across the river when the Allies arrived. There had been five tanks and a number of field guns as part of my defense line to stop the Allies at this bridgehead. The general, whom I refused to acknowledge as anything that resembled a leader, had inspected my positions. He had congratulated me on my ingenuity over a glass of wine, which I had to pay for, in a local hotel later that day. He thought my scorched earth policy on that part of the town, on the far shore, had been a brilliant move. Forcing all of the residents over to this side had depleted the Allies of any local knowledge. He laughed at any possibility of the Allies crossing the river after the bridge had been destroyed. I wasn't so sure. The general felt the Allies could be stopped for months and added the bridge was to be held at any cost. The tanks and field guns would remain to back up my troops.

That lasted two days. The field guns were pulled out on the morning of day three. I was furious at the broken promise but that was mild compared to what I was like when the tanks left at five that same afternoon. All telephone protests fell on deaf ears, if I got through at all. I was left with about one hundred and fifty very tired soldiers with small arms and four machine guns. I mulled over the general's comment that the bridge was to be held at any cost. It wasn't hard to figure out at whose cost. Without the tanks the crossing was much harder to guard because the bridge approach was open to the riverside, except for a low wall along the river embankment. There was an old overgrown path leading down to the river but it hadn't been used in years except maybe by some fishermen. I knew none of our men had ever ventured down there. The river current was very swift and there was no visible path on the other side for the Allies to use. The tanks had been partially buried in dugouts along the river facing the other shore. They had provided excellent cover for troop movement and had been effective as a means to preventing the Allies from getting at their side of the bridge. With the tanks we could hold up the Allies' advancement for weeks. The tanks were now gone and I wasn't sure if the Allies had seen them go. The distance across the river was not great and even my worst soldier could keep the Allies' heads low.

Then it started.

A nonstop bombardment, nothing very heavy, just a nonstop fire.

First the field guns took out the lights that had been placed to illuminate the area around the bridge. They concentrated on the area where the tanks had been placed and now contained the machine guns. After four days of bombardment only one machine gun was in a working condition. The rest were scrap metal. The troops that had manned the machine guns were dead and the inevitable letters were written every night. I then called headquarters to demand assistance. The general, who had promised me that the tanks would remain at the bridge, was busy in meetings and I was told he would call back. He never did. I placed another call to an old friend in the tank corps and found the tanks were en route to the general's estate. The general was following with several trucks and a staff car. I was furious. Give me the possible task and then take away my tools to make it the impossible task.

The view from the clock tower allowed me to see over the wall the Allies had built along the riverbank. It was hard to determine what was going on because the old clock tower was in the center of town and at least one hundred meters from the bridge. It seemed that the Allies were assembling some form of bridge. I could not see how it could be used because the old bridge consisted only of a bunch of cables. We had planned to destroy the suspension cables but the charges did not go off. Now we could not get near the bridge to plant new ones.

Several days later the bombardment increased and morning brought us a small contingent of enemy troops on our side of the river nicely tucked in behind the wall. I had planned to fill in the depression behind the road but the Allies had started shooting back before the job could be started. We had one machine gun and as many troops as we could place in the old buildings adjacent to the road. The situation was not good but we had lots of ammunition for the machine gun, as the other three had been destroyed and required none. We would hold on as long as we could.

The local townspeople were already upset with me for destroying the part of the town on the other side of the river. They were upset enough that all of my men felt rather uneasy when they walked about in the town. We were thinking we might have to watch our back as well as our front if the Allies started shelling the whole town rather than the area just adjacent to the bridge. I knew that we could hold the enemy behind that wall as long as they did not get any heavy support.

Last night was worrisome as there seemed to be an oily fog all night. There was no meteorological reason to have any fog so I assumed it must have been created by the allied troops. This was confirmed in the early hours of the morning by one of my sergeants, who had seen it used before as a screening method. I doubled the guard at the riverfront, much to the displeasure of the troops. The Allies continued a steady fire on us all night so our troops had to return the fire whenever possible. Luckily nobody was hurt by gunfire but the night was anything but quiet. Amongst the firing we could hear men giving the odd shout, scraping of metal on metal and a couple of very loud splashes in the river. We tried to use one of the remaining lights to find out what was happening. It lasted much under a minute until it was destroyed by mortar fire, along with the two troops that had manned it. The first two mortar shots had weakened the support so quickly that if the third mortar hadn't made a direct hit the whole structure would have fallen down but at least the two soldiers would have had a chance to get to safety.

Two more letters to write tonight. God, I hated that part. My mind drifted off as it wondered if any of the letters that I had already sent had ever made it to their destination.

I was anxious that daylight would return so we would be able to at least determine what the Allies were up to. When daylight did appear the Allies had somehow moved an even larger compliment of troops across the river. They were safely tucked in behind the wall at the river edge with the few troops that we knew were already there. They quickly began a steady fire, which forced our troops to keep their heads down. We desperately needed tank and artillery support but I knew that was not going to happen. I decided to reduce the casualties by pulling most of the men back, leaving a few to create some return fire to at least let them know we were still there. I went back to the bell tower because one of the men had sent a runner to get me. Looking through that horrible oily fog, the field glasses proved my worst fears. Last night the Allies had rebuilt the bridge deck and a tank was starting across. It was time to pull the men out of all positions and get them to a safe place. We did not have any hope of getting away from the town because the Allied aircraft would soon stop any traffic or troop movement on the roads. Strafing was not the way to die. For us, the war was over. If we fought, we would lose many more men before we were defeated and if we retreated we would be strafed to death. I sent a runner to gather what was left of our troops and arranged to meet them at the local beer hall. The German Mark still had some value, so when I got to the hall I arranged to have as many kegs ready as I had money. As the troops arrived, the sergeant told them to stack their guns outside in the center of the square and come in for a beer. When all of the soldiers had arrived I realized we had lost twenty-five of the one hundred and fifty men all for that useless bridge. I explained our situation to them.

It was not good.

I calmly thanked all of the men for all of the support that they had given me over the last few months; some of them several years. I explained we could stand and fight and a large number of us would probably die or we could surrender now and live to see our families sometime in the future. If we decided to surrender we should have a beer or two to kill the time waiting for the Allies to arrive and maybe even invite them in for a beer. After all, are not the German people hospitable? All of the men looked around at each other bewildered and hesitated before expressing their feelings with a rousing cheer. They'd had enough of this lousy war. They agreed it was time for a beer. After all, one really did need to celebrate the end of a war.

I sat alone for a while as I had just made the rounds to the various tables the men were sitting at and wondered if I looked as worn out as they did. The strain of the last four years had been enormous. We had started out elated at the German victories. We then proceeded to having a slight feeling of sickness as the rumors of the concentration camps worked through the ranks. Then the Allies landed and subsequently, we were abandoned as a pawn by the rest of the military. We had been left to die. This stark realization slowly surfaced in the faces of the men as they sipped their beer.

After several beers, I thought it would be interesting to meet the guy who could build a bridge overnight. He deserved an ovation for figuring out how to rebuild that bridge. I also wondered if they had found the explosives that had not gone off.

The tanks rolled into the town on our side of the river. The Allied troops quickly followed and as I found out later were quite surprised at having met no resistance. They could not figure out where we had gone until they got within earshot of the beer hall. We had been at it for over an hour when they arrived.

Did you ever figure out what shape a group of lonely and worn-out soldiers can get into when they surmise that the beer in their hand may be the last one that they will see for a long while coupled with someone else picking up the tab?

Imagine the shock when the first tank, with the troops following closely behind, arrived in the square and saw a small mountain of rifles, pistols, ammunition and other accoutrements of war and all that breaks the silence is a bunch of drunks singing their hearts out.

They had the decency to at least knock on the door and when it opened we met them with a great big tray of mugs of beer. They all rushed in, each grabbing a mug of beer. They were as thirsty as we had been.

When their commander arrived, the allied troops were now in the same condition as we were. It was obvious that they too had a dry time on the other side of the river and it was time to catch up. When the colonel walked through the doors the singing stopped abruptly.

He looked disgusted at the bunch of us drunk as skunks at ten a.m. He approached me and demanded we surrender. My English was acceptable so I looked at him and said, "Not as long as the beer holds out." He looked quite like he didn't know what to do so he told me to give him my gun. I laughed and said, "It's out in the yard with the rest of them." I needed to get the pickle out of his ass so I reached for a mug of beer and handed it to him and motioned for him to sit at a table. He looked very hard at the beer, at me, and at the rest of the troops, who were all watching him.

The air grew very tense. The silence was deafening.

He took the beer, shrugged, grabbed the handle, held the beer up and threw it back as fast as any German. He then motioned for a refill. The troops cheered and the singing restarted in earnest.

The word soon reached the rest of the Allied troops and by noon we had run out of beer and no more was left in the town.

Later that morning, I mentioned to the colonel that I would like to meet the fellow who had built the bridge overnight. He said that could be arranged as he was sitting three tables from us. Together we walked over to him and the colonel introduced us. I joined the infamous bridge builder at his table.

I was quite surprised how young he was. I told him that after the war I would be working for my father's engineering firm and if he ever needed a job to give me a call. We discussed how he had rebuilt the bridge in such a short time. I rather admired his ingenuity. We then exchanged names and I gave him a card with my father's engineering firm on it and wrote my name on it.

Three days later I was shipped out with my troops to a POW camp and spent the rest of the war there. We were among the first to be released when the war was over, probably because of the beer. As soon as I went home to Frankfurt I went back to work for my father's engineering firm. We were not lacking for work because of the rebuilding of Germany as it had been destroyed in the war.

Chapter 4

Will Now on the Other Side

The Infantry, correctly believing I was not the best shot with a rifle, let me stay behind as they followed the tanks into the town but not before they made sure I was not armed with anything more substantial than a hand-gun. I stayed low listening for the action in the town. Not a shot was fired and all I could hear was the tanks rumbling through the streets.

Curiosity got the better of me and thinking it would be interesting to explore, I started into the town. Not being a total fool, I carefully followed the tank tracks. The streets were narrow and deserted and since I wasn't following at tank speed I soon caught up with our troops. Our brave guys were following very close behind the tank. The tank came to a corner and a square slowly poked into view. The street that we were following had come out into the square in the center of the village. The tank stopped for a moment and everybody listened for there was a beer hall across the square and the racket coming from it was something to behold.

Between us and the beer hall was a small mountain of military hardware. There were guns, ammo belts, helmets and all sorts of military stuff. The pile had to be at least six feet high.

When people have too much to drink they seem to believe that they are God's gift to the singing world. If there is more than one person singing, they try to outdo each other. None of the drunks have any idea or even care how bad they are. This was the substance of the racket.

Some of our more daring guys worked their way along the wall until they were on each side of the door to the beer hall. The tank moved into position for a clear shot of the door of the beer hall. One of our troops, who was positioned beside the door of the beer hall, in desperation for something to do knocked on the door.

The door opened shortly and a soldier with half a German uniform walked out slowly with a tray of beer mugs. The four troops at the door looked at each other, shrugged, and grabbed a beer. The beer man took the tray, tucked it under his arm and, with a flourishing bow, motioned them inside so in they went. The singing never faltered. It did not take long for the rest of our troops to arrive at the door and get into the liquid action.

You must remember that we had been across the river in a destroyed town with no beer or wine. Since we were at the Front, no beer came up with our supplies. Our soldiers had been dry for far too long and this opportunity was not to be missed.

I joined them as fast as my legs would let me without looking like a dry alcoholic. I walked into the hall and was greeted by a room half filled with drunks. They were hanging over each other around a piano, where one German soldier was pounding the keys and belting out drinking songs. Everybody was in great humor. A beer was stuck in my hand, which I gladly accepted, and I started on my first real German pub-singing lesson. Our other troops filed in as quickly as they could. Then someone sent a reluctant runner to bring in everybody else. One hour later the colonel arrived. He quickly became totally furious when he saw his troops mixing with the German soldiers and everybody totally drunk. His bellow caused a silence in the room and the tension was thick enough to cut with a knife. I wasn't sure if he was mad because our troops were totally drunk or because he missed an hour of drinking. I suspect it was the latter. Our commander demanded to see the German commander. He wandered over with two beers in his hand. The German commander was a tall, good-looking, distinguished soldier, with a good physique. He was probably about three years older than I but command had aged him. I felt young compared to him. Our commander was at a total loss for words, probably the first time in his life. He blurted out an order demanding the German commander to hand over his gun. He laughed and in good English told our fearless leader that he had a choice. Go out and dig it out of the mountain in the square or sit down and have a beer. Our commander looked around and accepted the beer, clinked glasses and downed it. The tension collapsed and the singing resumed. I collected as much money as I could from everyone and bought as much beer as the hall had. The German commander got up from his table and came over to me. He sat down and asked me if I was the fellow who created the bridge from nothing. I said I was and thanked him for leaving the cables in place. I then heard about the explosives that didn't go off and were still in place. I made a mental note to get our demolition experts to get rid of them as soon as possible.

He offered me a job at his father's engineering firm, which I had to refuse with the excuse of having to finish engineering school when the war was over. He gave me a business card and went on to another table.

By noon all the beer in the hall was gone and everybody was starting to crash and sleep off the combination of beer for breakfast and the tensions from the last several weeks.

During the next two days we worked on the bridge to strengthen it and improve the approaches. Diet, as I called the German commander, came down to see how the repairs were progressing. We had several talks about the war and our varying points of view. He was a pleasant sort of a guy but he wore a maturity that comes with fighting men. I wondered if I might be developing that same sort of look. I considered him lucky to have his future somewhat organized when the war was over. We talked about life before the war, about the girls, of the war, and what our plans would be after the war. He again offered to hire me if I was ever looking for engineering work.

Three days after the beer hall party, they loaded Diet and his troops onto a bunch of trucks and took them somewhere to a prisoner of war camp. It was sad to see them go, sort of like seeing a baseball team that you defeated dragged off to jail.

I busied myself with the bridge and other road repairs that were required to move the equipment and supplies to the Front. This time I took my time so we could stay put longer. I felt I did not need any more people taking shots at me.

Chapter 5
Will Hanging Out in Town

Since I had decided to stay put for a while I had to create reasons why my work was required here and not elsewhere.

Our trucks were starting to create havoc with the main road they followed through the town so a rework was in order. This rework gave me the opportunity to frequent some of the sidewalk cafés and restaurants. In the weeks following the departure of the German troops, the business of the town came back to life, and much to my pleasure, the local girls reappeared. I made a point of being in the same cafés where the girls tended to meet for coffee and morning sun.

I was back in business, but this time I made sure that the others in our division got introduced to the girls as fast as I met them. Somehow I felt that I did not need to make any enemies at this time. Believe it or not, I do learn from my mistakes. Besides, there were more than enough to go around. I had money and was willing to part with it for coffees and wine. I also made sure that the other officers assisted me in sharing the drinks and girls.

I became very friendly with one particular group of young ladies, all either my age or slightly younger. We had a wonderful time, me improving my two years of high school German to the point of usefulness and they either learning or practicing their English. We solved most of the world's problems and boosted the local coffee and wine economy, all the while going hoarse with laughter.

We were having our usual afternoon meeting when one of the girls, a real sweet one and very pretty, named Gisele, mentioned that her cousin Hanna from Vienna was going to be visiting. She was arriving the next day and Gisele asked if it would be all right if she could join us. I had no problem with a new member to our crowd. The more the merrier. A couple of the other girls made some side comments to me about forgetting about having any interest in *her* as she was a bit snooty. Naturally I got very curious and asked a few questions, none of which got an encouraging answer. Apparently she seemed to have nothing more than a cursory interest in any of the men to whom she had been introduced. I was told she had shut some of them down so fast their heads were probably still spinning.

The next afternoon the whole crowd was there as usual with only one empty chair; lo and behold, it was beside the snooty cousin. Apparently, I was being set up for a crash for the amusement of the others. They had planned this set-up the day before, after I had left to go back to work. While I walked up to the chair—or should I refer to it as the hot seat—I could hear the tittering of some of the group. I approached the table and coming from behind her, I quickly noticed she had short blond hair, a slight build and, from what I could see, flawless skin. I sat down as the waiter was bringing me my coffee and said hello to everyone. At this point the cousin had not said anything or even acknowledged my existence in any way. All I could think of was the friends were probably correct in their evaluation and I might as well ignore her and at least minimize the joke on me. Gisele turned to me and said, "I would like you to meet my cousin, Hannelore Erfurt, more simply, Hanna from Vienna."

She turned to me, seemingly slightly embarrassed, and all I could see was the most beautiful girl I had ever set my eyes on. Hanna was lightly tanned, with a flawless complexion and the brightest blue eyes, that just danced. I was lost for words and sort of stammered my response to the introduction. She smiled at me with a smile that totally melted me. Her eyes locked into mine and started to soften. They simply said, "Welcome to my heart for ever." My heart began to pound with an intensity I had never known before. I thought it might burst. We both stared at each other and all the sounds from the rest of the table floated away as we entered our own world. I was jolted by someone and sort of came to, as did Hanna.

The voices of our friends talking about us came out of a blue mist and they were saying, "What the hell happened to those two, we think they just left us."

One of the other engineers started to laugh and spoke out saying, "The impossible has happened; he's just met his match." We sort of weakly joined the conversation with the others and when her hand found mine under the table I was finished.

Hanna had heard about the bridge and mentioned it. I picked up her lead immediately and asked if she would like to see it. We quickly left the others and as soon as we were out of sight we joined hands and, saying very little, walked not to the bridge but out into the country. As we walked little was said at first. When the conversation did get started, I felt I was a fourteen-year-old on his first date and became tongue-tied. She wasn't much better. A couple of stammers and all of a sudden our conversation was easy and genuine. Within a few moments it was as if we had known each other forever; everything felt so comfortable and natural.

There was a small hill just on the outskirts of town that had a beautiful view. I directed our walk towards it and when we got to the top, where the view of the river and the valley could be seen, we halted and sat down. We had made some small talk as my German had become quite workable and her English was certainly much more than acceptable, at least in my opinion. Hanna turned to me and said that she had been here before with Gisele and some of Gisele's friends for a picnic but that had been before the war. I looked over towards the hills at the end of the valley and could see a thunderstorm. It seemed to symbolize the times we were in. I turned slightly away and told her that, yes, war definitely causes one to grow more quickly. I turned and looked into her eyes and again they welcomed me. I leaned over and kissed her. She returned the kiss with a passion I never thought possible. Hell, she made the French girls look like rank amateurs.

When we came up for air, I looked at her and with a gasp said, "What happened?"

She looked at me and said in a whisper, "I don't know but there is something about you that seems so right."

I looked straight at her and said, "Ditto." I never have seen such a perplexed look, so then I had to explain what *ditto* meant. This brought on a laugh that was so pleasant and genuine that I had to join in. We sat and stared at the view for a while in silence. Hanna broke the silence by telling me that she had been out with a number of men, mostly German officers, and had found them more concerned with conquests and honor, whatever that is, than getting to know her as a person. She told me that Gisele had tried to set her up with a number of men but they were mostly duds. Gisele had called her stuck up when she had told her to stop with her matchmaking. She turned and laughed and with a twinkle asked me if I had been set up too. I laughed and told her that I had been but I didn't intend to be a dud.

I looked at my watch and jumped up with the explanation that I had a meeting with my boss in thirty minutes and asked her if we could have dinner that evening. She said, "I would love to." I smiled and told her I admired a person who did not play games and said what she thought.

Hand in hand, we walked back to the town. I was about two feet off of the ground. She was about five foot five and walked easily with me, sort of tucked in beside me, a natural fit. I left her at the café, where Gisele was still chatting with some of her friends. We kissed good-bye and out of the corner of my eye I caught Gisele's shock at our responses to each other. Hanna smiled and turned and sat down with her cousin, looked at her, and with a pleasantly mocking tone asked, "What is the matter?"

I hurried to my meeting, arriving about five minutes late to a very stern glance from the colonel. He stared at me and looking carefully at me asked if everything was okay. I said, "Definitely."

He smiled and said, "That is obvious, wipe off the lipstick and let's find out how our projects are progressing." I blushed, choked down the frog in my throat, and opened my files.

I think I managed to keep my mind on the business at hand but I do confess, when things got slow, I quickly drifted off to the kiss on the hill, only to abruptly return when out of a blue haze I heard the colonel speaking my name sharply. I think that everyone at the meeting got a chuckle at my expense but I was in no shape to respond.

Work for the rest of the day was a total loss. My attention span was about five seconds and what was in front of me was a total blur. The only thing I was successful in doing was making dinner reservations for that evening and that was easy.

How could one short meeting create such a mess in one's heart and head?

As soon as I could, I rushed back to my quarters and washed, scrubbed and changed my uniform to a fresh, clean one and then grabbed a jeep from the motor pool. I got lost several times before arriving at Gisele's home as it was just outside of town in a small estate. Although I had never been there I did have a good feeling of where it was located. Nevertheless, I still arrived about thirty minutes early. Gisele's mother, Ingrid, met me at the door. She looked me over, smiled, and under her breath told me that Hanna had been dressed for about thirty minutes already. I blushed and then she added that the curfew was 9:30 and she did not want Hanna to spend the night in jail. I promised her we would return on time.

I heard a rustle and Hanna and Gisele walked into the foyer. Hanna was radiant, with a kind of funny grin from ear to ear. She was wearing the most fantastic white dress I had ever seen. It was form fitting but loose and was made from a material that glowed. With her tan, looks, and her smile she would have taken over any function in the world. She wore a simple strand of pearls around her neck, again standing out because of her tan. I was totally speechless and probably had the same stupid grin on my face. Gisele looked at me with a mischievous smile and asked, "I have known you much longer than Hanna, how come Hanna gets to go on a dinner date before me?" She had given me the time to get some composure back by diverting my attention from Hanna, so I was able to laugh and told her it was because she had arranged it that way. Her mother looked quite interested in that statement. With that I offered my arm to Hanna and we started to walk to the jeep. Ingrid took one look at the jeep and asked if a Mercedes might be more in order for a dinner date. Hanna quietly said that the Mercedes had a bench front seat. I smiled and thanked Ingrid and told her that I hoped it would not present any inconvenience for her and that we would find it more appropriate. I added that I would be able to bring the car back full of

31

gasoline, a rare commodity for civilians and very much appreciated. I opened the door for Hanna and by the time I got into the driver's seat and the door closed she was snuggling up to me.

Dinner was a waste, at least as far as nutrition. We should have just ordered two glasses of water. Our food got cold as we talked about family, friends, early years and what our individual future plans might include. I told her about having to finish engineering school when I got home. She told me her father owned an engineering firm in Vienna called Erfurt & Hess, GMBH—Ingenieure and I should work there. I laughed and told her that was the second job offer I had in a month. She thought that she was closer to her father than her mother. She felt her father had the most influence on her; although her mother was very strict and very proper she still thought she was great. She thought she enjoyed driving her mother to distraction. She told me that she had told her father that she wanted to go to Technische Universitaet Wien, the engineering school in Vienna, but her father had absolutely forbidden it. After a long, drawn-out battle he had relented enough to let her go to the business school Facultaet fuer Wirtschaftwissenschaften und Informatik, Universitaet. She had no other brothers or sisters other than an older brother, who had been killed early in the war.

The waiter had taken our untouched food from us and brought coffee. It too was untouched. He came over to us and inquired if everything was all right, then looked thoughtfully at our dazed expressions and said, "I think everything is more than all right." I had told Ingrid where we were having dinner and at 10:30 she phoned. I was asked to come to the phone and by this time, Ingrid had become more than a little concerned. She proceeded to instruct me on some of the finer points of punctuality.

I went back to the table and told Hanna about my lecture. She laughed and I paid for our non-meal and we departed. We first drove to the motor pool, where I filled the gas tank, knowing that Ingrid would check that and it would be very much appreciated.

I needed to stay on the good side of Ingrid.

Next we drove to the Military Police, who gave me the pass to get Hanna home and not in the brig.

I got her home at midnight and we sat in the driveway for about thirty minutes, not wanting to part. We heard a gentle knock on the window and we separated. I got out. Ingrid was standing there with her arms crossed and a silly grin on her face, a sort of I-caught-you look. I laughed and told her she need not look because the tank had been filled. She gave me a big hug, complete with a kiss. I went around to the other side of the car and opened the door for Hanna. I walked with her up to the door with Ingrid in tow. We hugged and I gave her a gentle parting kiss, turned and slowly walked to the jeep, looking back every other step. Hanna was watching me from the front door. I was in such a total daze, I was lucky to find my way back to town.

We had arranged to meet for dinner again the following evening and when we walked in the waiter asked if we were going to eat that night or let the food go to waste. I laughed and he suggested a simple glass of wine for each of us might be more appropriate and maybe a coffee later. He then led us to a very private booth in the back of the restaurant.

We did drink the wine and later the coffee.

The coffee was good as I had liberated it from the stores earlier in the day and had taken it to the restaurant. They were very pleased with the gift.

I was at a total loss as to how two people could talk as much as we did and still have more to say.

Every evening that week we did a lot of talking but had little to eat. The drives home were very passionate. The restaurant seemed to understand us.

I told Hanna I loved her and she replied she had been unsure of what love would be until she met me and now she knew. She looked deep into my heart through my eyes and told me she loved me with all of her heart. If I wasn't a mess before, I certainly was then.

Work was a disaster and I wasn't much better. All I could think of was Hanna. Thank God I had all of my projects in a stage that was well in advance of the work being done. On the second Friday, the colonel called me into his office and asked me to sit down.

I figured I was in shit.

He informed me he had seen me twice in the restaurant and added that he thought she was quite pretty, no, actually very beautiful. I had not even known he had been there. He told me he had done some investigation to find out who she was and discovered that her family was well respected in Austria and had not been a Nazi supporter. He checked my records and said I had not had any leave since arriving on the Continent and a two-week leave would hopefully put my head back into some form of useful thinking shape. He smiled and said, "You are kind of useless the way you are right now. Will, you had an interesting reputation when you arrived here. I think that reputation has just changed. I only hope the war will let you continue on your present course."

I sort of stammered an agreement. He dismissed me after giving me the location of a small hotel in the mountains along with the comment, "If I know where you are, I can locate you if I need you."

I went back to my office to finish up the work on my desk.

I was elated and called Hanna as soon as I was free. I suggested that if it was possible I would like to take her for a two-week trip to the mountains. I told her we would need at least two days to get there and two days to get back. She was excited and said that she would ask Giselle to help her work on Ingrid for permission. I hung up and thought, *I'm glad I'm here and not around for that negotiation session.*

Later that afternoon, I went to see Hanna and was met by Ingrid. She gave me the protective mother lecture and I insisted that my intentions were honorable and if she would let us go away for a short holiday together we would have separate rooms. I think Ingrid wanted me to sweat for a while so she invited me for dinner that evening, then stuck me into the drawing room and left me to sweat while she went to check on dinner. Dinner was excellent and I used my very best manners, almost to the point of being gushy. Hanna was seated across and down the table from me, just out of reach. Talk about torture.

I later found Hanna had already packed. She and Gisele had been pleading with Ingrid using every reason in the book why it would be all right for Hanna to go with me. Ingrid had relented and all she wanted to do was watch me sweat and see how I handled it.

We left early in the morning with the Mercedes and a pocketful of gasoline chits.

We drove up in the foot hills of the mountains to the small hotel that had been suggested by my colonel. We stayed one night in a hotel on the way. True to Ingrid's request we slept in separate rooms.

The hotel was set in a narrow valley with a view overlooking a small fast-flowing river. It had not been damaged by the war. The owner was quite old and welcomed us with open arms. He had not seen a lot of business since the German army had pulled out. There was only one other couple in the hotel and they were quite elderly. We found out later they were celebrating their fiftieth wedding anniversary.

We walked up to the front entrance of the hotel and the first thing I noticed was that each of the front doors had a bright red doorknob.

I checked in and asked for two rooms. Hanna spoke up and quietly suggested to the owner that one room would be sufficient because he might require the second room for other guests. She gently took my hand and squeezed it, all the while looking demurely straight ahead. The hotel owner did not question her rationale or our marital status.

I booked reservations for dinner at 8:30 and carried our two small bags up to the room. Hanna went into the room first and I followed, setting the two bags on the bench near the door. The room was old in a quiet, elegant manner, reminiscent of a period around the turn of the century. The furniture did not seem to fit the room. It did not look that old or of too high a quality. Hanna went to the window and opened the drapes to reveal a set of French doors leading to a small balcony with the most romantic view one could imagine.

The vista looked over the valley that had been carved by the small river. The valley had a forest climbing up its sides. Looking down the valley, in the distance, you could see a patchwork of farm fields all green and rolling in the haze. I followed Hanna out on the balcony and when I got there put my arms around her and gently kissed the nape of her neck. We floated back in, she turned to me and we kissed forever.

In a very husky voice she said, "I hope your intentions are anything but honorable."

At that point they became anything but.

We fell on the bed and clothing was discarded in every direction.

So much for neatness.

I was her first. She was a true blonde and I had never been so happy in my life.

Afterwards we lay exhausted in the bed and I admired her perfect form. Her skin was as flawless as any Greek goddess's. Her breasts were not large and not small, firm and round. Her body seemed to be perfect, thin but not overly, toned but not muscular. She was fine featured with a softness in her whole persona. There was nothing about this girl that was not perfect. Pulling up the duvet, we lay in bed cuddling as close as physically possible and talked about our feelings toward each other. She stroked my chest and her hand went exploring. She found me and within seconds I was alive again. I carefully rolled over and this time there was no hesitation.

She accepted me easily and completely.

Her passion flamed far higher than our first round of love.

She was anything but a silent lover.

My training by the French girls was very helpful but they couldn't hold a candle to Hanna.

Afterwards, as I lay on my back, with her on my chest as close as she could, she glanced over at the clock and asked if I knew what time it was. I told her I didn't care and hoped time could stop. She told me that we had been in bed for more than two and a half hours and it was 8:00. I smiled and asked, "Are you hungry" She smiled and said, "Famished and maybe this time we may even eat our dinner."

We both had a good laugh and jumped out of bed. We had a quick shower together, dried each other off, gathered up our clothes and got dressed arriving at the dining room five minutes before closing. The look of the owner was of a knowing surprise that we actually made it.

Dinner was incredible but with our state of mind and appetite, stale bread and water would have been wonderful.

After dinner we went out for a short walk in the moonlight but since it was cool and we did not have heavier jackets, we soon retired to our room.

We got undressed and climbed into bed. She crawled into my arms and we quickly fell into the sleep of love.

The morning sun woke us as it shone across the room and onto the bed. Our hands went exploring again.

The result was morning delight.

We had breakfast. As there was an excellent hiking trail that led up the valley, we dressed in more comfortable clothing and headed up into the hills. I had brought a camera and took many pictures of the scenery, making sure Hanna was in every one. She even got a few pictures of me. I promised that I would give a copy of all the pictures to her. The old couple from the hotel came up the same path and stopped for a chat. They asked if we would like them to take our picture together. We gave them a resounding yes. They took several pictures before continuing on their hike. They seemed like a lovely couple and we realized how lucky they had been to go through two wars and still be together, with one not lying in the ground somewhere.

We slowly worked our way back to the hotel and had a light lunch. We retired to our balcony, sipped a glass of wine and watched the world go by, talking quietly to each other.

We returned to our room, followed our instincts and dealt with the first thing that popped up.

Dinner was amazing again that evening.

The whole two weeks went the same way with some side sightseeing trips to many of the small local towns. We met the old couple several more times and had some pleasant talks with them. They could tell that Hanna was not from the area and was probably from Vienna. My accent was much more confusing until I told them I was from Canada. They told us they had relatives who had gone to Canada in the early twenties and lived in a place called Kitchener. They were very excited when I told them I lived in a nearby city and they gave me their relatives' address and made me promise to visit them when I got home. They stayed away from any discussions about the war and I appreciated that.

I bought Hanna a small necklace in gold and a very nice shawl. The shawl was white with a fine gold line through it. She loved the shawl and promised me that she would only wear it on special occasions and only with me.

We did a number of other hikes and had meals in different

restaurants in the area. I was pleased with her physical ability as she had no trouble keeping up with me and at times I think she may have even been waiting for me.

We were exceedingly sad to have to leave and go back to reality. I told her I wanted to marry her. She burst into tears and said, "Yes," many times between the tears. I wasn't exactly the most composed person in the world. We hugged and kissed and held each other as tight as we could. She pulled away and said I should come to Vienna as soon as possible to meet her family. I agreed with her, secretly hoping her father and mother would approve of me. I gave her my signet ring as a sort of engagement ring and promised her I would have the perfect one for her as soon as I could. She told me no other ring could ever mean as much to her as the signet ring. I thought Mother would approve, especially after her lecture of it being a symbol of commitment.

When we got back to Gisele's house we were met by Ingrid, who quickly told Hanna to pack the rest of her things as soon as possible. Her mother was not well and Hanna needed to get back to Vienna as soon as possible. Her father had called the evening before and Ingrid had covered for her by saying that Hanna was in town and Ingrid would not be able to arrange a train ticket until late the next day. Hanna packed quickly and I drove her to the train station in the jeep.

It was a sad departure. She cried all the way to the station. We stood on the platform kissing each other good-bye and holding each other as long as we could. As she got onto the train she gave me her address in Vienna and I gave her my address in town and we promised to write. I promised to come to see her in Vienna as soon as possible.

The drive back to town was the most depressing time of my life. I felt totally empty.

Chapter 6

Hanna's Part of the Story

I decided that it would be fun to visit my cousin Gisele for a short break. Mother had a bad cold that had been lingering on for a long time and suggested that it would be best that I got out of the house so I didn't also catch it. I called Gisele to see if it was all right and she was excited that I was coming. I took the early-morning train, knowing it was the simplest way to get there because the roads were plugged with military trucks with numerous checkpoints all along the way.

Gisele was there to meet me at the train station when I arrived. I was quite surprised because the train was three hours late and as it was so late, I expected I would have to telephone her to come to get me. Gisele's mother, Aunt Ingrid, was with her and greeted me with open arms. Aunt Ingrid was my father's sister and had always been my favorite aunt. She was fun loving and had always been, according to my father, the wild one of the family. Aunt Ingrid had married Uncle Gerhard. He was never at home as he was also an engineer and worked on mining projects. He had been in South Africa when the war broke out and had been unable to get home. The family stories assumed he had stayed there to keep out of the army. At the beginning of the war most of the family was disgusted with his actions but now they were admiring his foresight. Gisele and I joked around all evening and had a great time as we usually had with each other. As we were getting ready for bed she told me that she was going to introduce me to a Canadian stationed in the town. Apparently he was in the Engineers. She had become aquainted with him and some of his friends at the local coffee shop. I was slightly annoyed at Gisele's matchmaking again and told her so. All of the previous introductions had been total duds. I could not believe in her selection of men and told her that I was truly concerned with her future marital situation.

She laughed at me and said, "This one is special because he is very good looking, smart, kind, considerate, fun to be with but doesn't take over." I asked her if she had a date with him and she said that she was saving him for me. I told her no thanks but added that since she had not had a date with him it was probably a good sign that he might be "just fine." We both had a good laugh and went to sleep.

Aunt Ingrid's house was actually a small estate that had been in Gerhard's family for at least four generations. Gisele and I hung out all morning. I checked out the gardens and the small stream that ran through their property.

After lunch Gisele and I went into town to pick up some bread for Aunt Ingrid but I thought it was just an excuse to get to the coffee shop.

Sure enough, we ended up at the coffee shop and sat down at two of the empty chairs with a group of Gisele's friends. Gisele's Canadian friend was not there.

So far so good.

One of her friends got up and moved across to another chair to show somebody something. That left one empty chair beside me. I now knew they were all in this together and could only think that this guy was going to be worse than even I had feared.

About ten minutes later I started to relax, assuming that maybe "Mr. Real Dud" would not be coming today.

Somebody came up behind me and sat down. My heart sank and all I could think was *Here goes nothing.* He greeted everybody with an enthusiastic hello, in plausible German. He then switched to English with a very pleasant tone in his voice. Gisele introduced me to Will using my full name, yuck, but at least she confirmed what name I really like to be called. He turned to me and stared straight into my eyes.

I melted.

I stared straight back not knowing what to say and the more we stared at each other the more I melted. There was something there that told me he was special in every way. I think I fell in love in all of ten seconds.

The more we stared at each other the further we seemed to drift away from the rest of the group at the table. Someone said, "What the hell happened to those two, I think they just left us." We sort of joined into the conversation with the others. It was clear he was as uneasy being there as I was so I touched his hand under the table. I melted all over again at the simple touch of his hand. The energy from that touch was almost unbearable.

We had to get away from there. Gisele had told me something about a bridge he was sort of famous for so I inquired about it. He offered to show it to me; I accepted. Anything to get away from our audience. We left the others and as soon as we rounded the corner out of sight of the others, he gently took my hand. I was totally tongue tied, probably for the first time in my life. I noticed we were heading away from the river and used it to start some conversation. His German was quite good and my English was acceptable so we started to make some light conversation. As soon as the ice had been broken our conversation became easy and natural. We walked up to the top of a hill, where I had gone on some picnics with Gisele and her friends several times. We sat down and stared at the river and countryside below. I told him I had been there before with Gisele and some of her friends but that had been before the war. I had lost a number of friends in the war, some because they had been sent to the Front and never came back and some when the Russians came through Vienna. He became sort of wistful and commented that we all grow up much too fast during a war. He turned and looked at me, staring straight into my eyes, and slowly leaned over and kissed me. I think a bomb went off and my whole body became a flame. I returned his kiss because I wanted to give back a little of what was happening to me.

When we cooled slightly and broke the kiss he quietly asked, "What happened?"

I looked at him and said, "I don't know but there is something about you that seems so right."

Will looked at me and said, "Ditto." I did not have any idea what *Ditto* meant and only hoped it was good. When he explained it to me I couldn't help but laugh partly, because his method of explaining was funny and partly because I was relieved to find out it really was good. We sat and stared at the view for a while in silence. I decided to break our silence by starting a conversation. I still don't know what I was thinking but I told him that I had been out with a number of men, mostly German officers, and had found them more concerned with conquests and honor, whatever that is, than getting to know me as a person. I also mentioned that Gisele had tried a number of times to set me up with several different fellows but they were mostly duds. I thought, *I hope he doesn't think I am calling him a dud.* I asked him if he had been set up too. He laughed and said that he had been and added that he hoped he wasn't a dud. I assured him he was not.

Suddenly he jumped up and said he had a meeting he had to go to and we had better get back. He took my hand and asked me if we could have dinner that evening. I told him that I would love to and hand in hand we walked back to the town. I have never been as comfortable with anyone as I was with Will. It was as if we had been together for years. We walked back to the café. Gisele was still with some of her friends. She looked at me with a question mark all over her face. We kissed good-bye and you should have seen the shocked look on Gisele's face. I smiled and turned and sat down at the table, and asked her what was the matter, all the while thinking, *Got You!*

When we arrived back at the house, Gisele made a big point of telling Aunt Ingrid about Will and me. I was totally embarrassed but that would not change the fact I had accepted an invitation and was going out to dinner. Aunt Ingrid tried to persuade me to invite Will for dinner with them. I was not having anything to do with that idea. I did not want family around on our first date. I went through the things I had brought and selected a long white dress. I thought it would be striking with my good tan. It was a fairly plain dress, which showed off my figure. Gisele lent me a shawl in case it got cool later. Gisele went to work on Aunt Ingrid to see if we could use the Mercedes and she relented, provided Will could meet with her approval.

I must have been excited because I was all ready to go an hour before Will was supposed to pick me up. I guess the theory requiring men to wait for the lady was not on my mind that evening. I had to stand or walk around, as I did not want to sit down and crease my dress. Actually that wasn't hard because I was too nervous to sit still and needed to keep pacing just to keep my nerves in check. It drove Giselle nuts. I smiled to myself and thought, *Serves you right,* but I was certainly not complaining.

Will must have been excited too because he showed up thirty minutes early. He arrived in an army jeep that was a little dusty. Aunt Ingrid took one look at the jeep and then at my white dress and frowned. I knew our lobbying for the Mercedes had not been in vain. Aunt Ingrid met Will at the door and he introduced himself to her with a big smile. Gisele and I were peeking in from the next room when he arrived and walked into the front hall as he was talking with Aunt Ingrid. I felt like a schoolgirl on my first date and could not help the foolish grin that was stuck on my face when I first saw him. The grin did not match the butterflies that were bouncing around in my stomach.

We had some small talk but I haven't a clue what it was about. He took my arm and started to walk out the door towards the jeep when Aunt Ingrid suggested we use the Mercedes. Will looked a little hesitant so I quietly told him it had a bench front seat. He accepted and volunteered to fill it with fuel. He could not have used a better winning point, as gasoline was very hard to come by for civilians. Aunt Ingrid suddenly looked very pleased.

We went to a small, good restaurant in town, where Will had already made reservations. He ordered wine, which we sat and looked at as we talked. I think we only had two sips each. The waiter arrived and we quickly ordered something from the menu. I cannot remember what it was. Our conversations continued as we held hands and the untouched food got cold. The waiter looked concerned when he found we had not eaten anything but after a quick glance at our glazed eyes he knew what was happening and left us alone to continue in our little world. I had promised Aunt Ingrid we would be back before 9:30 and at 10:30 she called, all worried. I think she was relieved to find us there and not in some military police office. Will suggested that we should go and I agreed, although I felt we could have spent the rest of our days sitting in those same two chairs. We first went to the military police to get passes and then to the motor pool for fuel. I was quite surprised that he filled the car as it had a large tank. I knew that Aunt Ingrid would be most impressed. We got home quite late and we stayed in the car very close together sharing lots of wonderful kisses. Our time was ended by a knock on the window by Aunt Ingrid, who suggested it was time for Will to go home. We walked into the house where he kissed me good-bye and slowly walked back to the jeep, turning to wave several times. I quickly got cornered by Gisele, who had twenty thousand questions. She laughed at me and said, "I told you he was special but I did not think you two would fall head over heels in love at first sight."

I didn't sleep much that night as I spent the whole time tossing and turning. The next morning, I was famished at breakfast but food was not on my mind. All I could think of was Will.

The next week we spent every evening in the same restaurant but this time the waiter gave us a quiet booth near the back corner of the restaurant and suggested if we were not going to eat just to order wine, then coffee later. We laughingly agreed. I have no idea what we talked about that week. All I can remember is that I had never been so happy in my entire life. On the way home on the second evening, Will told me that he loved me. I was in heaven.

One day the next week Will called and told me he had two weeks' leave and asked if I'd like to go somewhere with him. He told me it was a little hotel that his commander had suggested. I told him I would love to but had to get permission from Aunt Ingrid.

Gisele and I went to go to work on Aunt Ingrid. She finally relented with the stipulation that we must have separate rooms. I agreed, which let her off the hook if my mother ever questioned her. She knew where the small hotel that Will had suggested was located and told me it was quite nice. She said it was in a beautiful setting and had good hiking trails, which would give us something to do during the day. I think she was really telling us to wear ourselves out by taking long hikes. She gave me the directions in case Will got lost and told me we could use the Mercedes providing it came back full of fuel. Will came for dinner that night and we were very happy that our plans were falling into place. Aunt Ingrid had put him on pins and needles before giving him her final approval. She had also subjected him to her big mother-type lecture while I stood by listening in total embarrassment. The next morning he arrived in a jeep with a driver, who dropped him off. Aunt Ingrid again gave him her lecture in spite of my earlier protests and my embarrassment. We left shortly thereafter.

The drive up to the hotel was wonderful. Just to get away and be with him was all I wanted. I was trying to figure out what might happen during the next two weeks but didn't say anything. He noticed I was quite quiet and asked me if everything was all right. I laughed and said nothing could be better than being here. He smiled and agreed. The drive was not fast and we had not gotten away too early in the day so we stopped for the first night in a hotel on the way. I was not too impressed to end up sleeping by myself in a separate room and vowed that would not happen again.

We arrived at the hotel and it was as nice as Aunt Ingrid had described. It was in an out of the way place and was lucky enough to have avoided damage during the war. We parked the car and went up to the main entrance, which was airy and protected by two large, very sturdy doors, each with an enormous red doorknob. We checked in and Will requested two rooms. I quietly spoke up and said one would be sufficient. I gave some lame excuse, I cannot remember what it was. Probably something like "My aunt will not be able to come until much later in the week." Will smiled and signed the register.

We went up to the room. It was beautiful, with French doors that opened onto a small balcony. I opened the drapes and doors and walked out to admire the view. Will came out on the balcony and put his arms around me, gave me a gentle kiss on my neck and we walked back into the room. I turned to him and he gave me the longest kiss in history. I was on fire. I told him that his intentions had better be anything but honorable.

I was certainly glad they weren't.

We discarded our clothes in a sort of frenzy and he gently laid me on the bed. He was the first man that I had made love to and he could not have been more considerate. I do not understand how anyone that was in our state of arousal could take such time and be as gentle as he was. I think he was surprised when he realized he was the first.

Later as we lay spent on the bed I got to really see him without any clothing. He had an excellent build, well developed with no extremes. We lay in bed under the duvet cuddling as close as I could get and talked about our feelings toward each other. I went exploring with my hand and to my surprise and joy he was suddenly ready all over again. I thought, *This is wonderful.* I now had none of my first-time hesitations and holdbacks. I could not believe the feelings that were going through me. As I reached my next orgasm I couldn't help but cry out. I hope nobody was in the hall close to our door.

Afterwards, as I lay with my head on his shoulder, I glanced over at the clock and was surprised to find we had been in the bed for more than two and a half hours and it was 8:00.

We had a short shower together, dried each other off, got dressed and went down to the dining room.

The meal was excellent and we actually ate dinner. After dinner we went outside for a walk to catch some fresh air. The moon was bright but it was cool so I suggested that we go back inside.

I went into the bathroom to get ready for bed and when I came out I crawled into the bed and cuddled up tight, right next to my guy. I quickly fell asleep knowing I was the happiest girl alive.

The morning sun woke me up by shining across the bed as we had forgotten to close the inside drapes. I woke up first and as I studied his face I decided to go exploring with my hand again. He awoke with a silly grin and with a gentle kiss we repeated yesterday's performance.

The whole two weeks went the same way with some sightseeing trips to several of the small local villages. We met the old couple who were staying at the hotel and had some pleasant talks with them. I was totally surprised when Will bought me a gold necklace and a very nice shawl. The shawl was white with a fine gold line through it. I loved the shawl and promised him that I would only wear it on special occasions and only when he was with me.

We did a number of hikes. I had been active in a hiking group in Vienna so I was in good shape. Will was quite fit and I had to work hard, at times, to keep up with him. I wasn't letting him get too far away from me. Aunt Ingrid's idea of us wearing ourselves out by hiking was only wishful thinking. We had several meals in other restaurants in the area. All of the meals were excellent. The two weeks were the most natural, carefree and content period of my life to that point.

I was very sad to have to leave the hotel and head back home to reality. On our last evening Will asked me to marry him. I was so excited that I burst into tears and kept saying, "Yes," between the tears. I was certainly the happiest person in the world. He hugged and kissed me and we held each other as tight as we could. I realized he would need to meet my parents. I had no concern with what they would think of him so I asked him come to Vienna as soon as possible to meet them. He took off a signet ring from his small finger and gave it to me as an engagement ring. I thought it was the most romantic thing he could have done.

We sadly left the next morning stopping one night on the way back. When we arrived at Gisele's house, Aunt Ingrid met us at the door and told me to get the rest of my belongings packed as Mother was not well and I needed to get back to Vienna as soon as possible. Father had called the evening before telling her that Mother's cold had gotten much worse and he wanted me there. I packed quickly. Will had called for a ride to town so he was able to drive me to the train station in the jeep. Aunt Ingrid had arranged a ticket for me on the overnight train back to Vienna.

I was so sad that I cried all the way to the station. We stood on the platform and Will held me tight as we exchanged kisses for as long as we could. Just before I got onto the train I gave him my address in Vienna and he gave me his address in town and we promised to write. He promised to come to Vienna as soon as possible.

The ride to Vienna was the most depressing trip of my life. I alternated between staring out the window and staring at my ring, both through tears.

47

Chapter 7
Will Back to Work

The colonel welcomed me back with open arms and a list of items on my projects that required answers, as long as those arms. I'll swear that no one had lifted a finger since I had left on my leave. Our first project meeting was busy, starting with lots of comments by the other engineers about my leave, along with questions looking for details as to what I had been up to. The colonel put a quick halt to anything other than business when he arrived. He certainly did not look happy. He glanced around at us and said we had three days to get everything wrapped up as we were moving out to a location that he could not reveal to us until later.

I realized suddenly that any mail coming to me from Hanna could not arrive before I left so I would need a forwarding address for any mail coming to my billet.

The colonel was of no help.

That afternoon I went to the coffee shop to see Gisele. She wasn't there.

That evening, after I had cleaned up my work, I drove out to Gisele's home to see her and get the address problem straightened out. The only person there was the gardener who told me no one was at home. The family had gone somewhere with the car and they had taken luggage. I left a note with him and hoped Gisele would get it.

I wrote a new letter to Hanna telling her of our relocation and said I would write again with a new address as soon as I had one. I told her I would write a letter every day and finished by telling her how much I loved her and that I would be in Vienna as soon as possible.

The next three days consisted of a whirlwind of little jobs to get the various roads in a good enough state to take the abuse of military trucks on their way to the Front.

We pulled out on the morning of day four. The previous evening I had made one last trip to Gisele's house with no better response from the gardener and so I left one more note.

We left the town with all of our equipment and the townspeople waving us good-bye. Gisele was not amongst them.

Four days later we arrived at our new location and, much to my displeasure, it was within range of flying bullets. This time there was no town on either side of the river for protection. The area around the bridge was relatively flat so we had to set up camp some distance from the site. This required much travel to gain information on how to get the bridge back into operation.

The bridge was an old multi-arched bridge that spanned a relatively shallow, fast-moving river. The riverbank was soft and would not support any new structure without substantial rebuilding of the bank. I felt it would be best to use the pillars of the old bridge as a base for Bailey sections.

The colonel confirmed our thoughts when he decided that ours was the best solution. I got the job of obtaining the necessary measurements from the old bridge with the assistance of several other engineers in our regiment.

I was in a real dilemma. I was not in a place where mail could reach me in less than three weeks. The mail out wasn't any better and I was still writing my daily letter to Hanna. The letters just piled up in my pack waiting for an opportunity to mail them.

We had most of the measurements, but since the majority of them had been taken at night we needed some conformations and some photographs. I was being sent with two other engineers out on what was remaining of the bridge to get correct measurements so we could determine how the Bailey sections would fit.

Some soldiers were brought in to keep the Germans busy and make them keep their heads low enough so they couldn't see us out on the bridge. I scrambled out on the bridge with two of the other guys in the Engineers. We had a long tape measure which we were going to use to get the measurements we needed. We carefully worked our way along the bridge top, keeping as low as possible, and hiding behind any stonework that was available. We had to bring with us a long ladder to cross over the sections where the arches had disappeared completely.

There was minimal fire from the Germans that afternoon so we were feeling a little safer than we should have been. Then we heard a high-pitched sort of scream and realized that some mortars were coming our way. There was nowhere to hide so we just lay down behind anything that was handy and waited. We hoped that they were either going to miss us or were actually not heading our way. Charlie and I dove down near a stone block, lying side by side, hoping the mortar would miss us.

They were actually heading our way and they did not miss us.

I was the only one who lived.

The mortar had landed on the other side of Charlie and he had unknowingly protected me from the majority of the blast.

I came to three days later in the bridge camp medical tent and I was a mess.

I had a concussion, my left arm was broken and my right leg was badly bruised. I couldn't hear anything. My vision was almost nonexistent and I drifted in and out of consciousness. When I was conscious I was talking nonstop and totally incoherent.

They transferred me to a hospital in eastern France, where I was being scheduled to return to Canada on the first available hospital ship.

The war was over for me. I tried to locate my bag especially since all my letters to Hanna were in it along with the addresses for Gisele and my previous billet. The bag was nowhere to be found.

While at the bridge camp I had regained consciousness enough to straighten out another small problem. When they had dragged all three of us off the bridge they had assumed, because I was covered with blood from both of the other two guys, that I was also dead. They had mixed up the dog tags and it was several days before I was able to become me and not Charlie. The letters home had not yet been written so Mother and Father did not find out I had been killed. That was a bonus!

My mind wasn't working very well and I could not remember

much of anything. I was lucky to remember my own name. I had only two things on my mind, Hanna and how to get in touch with her. I could not remember her last name, her address, or Gisele's address. I couldn't even remember my address at home.

I had tried to convince the doctors that I would mend best in Vienna but they took my ravings to be a result of the injuries and ignored me. I was then sedated again.

Two weeks later the doctors figured I was well enough physically to travel and so they placed me aboard a hospital ship back to Canada.

The transfers to and from the ship hurt like hell and the train ride to Toronto from Halifax was an ordeal.

By the time I arrived to Toronto my mind was starting to recover. Mother and Father came to see me the morning after I got into Toronto. They must have left home long before dawn to be there at that time in the morning.

I was elated to see them. Mother had the most relieved look on her face. She knew that I was at home from the war and more or less in one piece. That was far better than the sons of some of her friends.

I had one picture of Hanna and me that had been in my wallet when I was on the bridge. I showed it to Mother and she was amazed how beautiful Hanna was and said she would love to meet her.

Chapter 8
Will at Home, Now Recovering

I was in the hospital in Toronto for about three more weeks before they transferred me to a hospital in London for further recuperation. Two weeks later I was sent home to finish my recovery. The best part was I was still receiving full pay and I had no way to spend any of it. My head was slowly coming back to order, including an address in Vienna. I sent off several letters to Hanna at the address, as I had remembered it.

About two months after I got home my pack arrived. I grabbed it and ripped it open in a mad frenzy knowing that my letters to Hanna were in it, as well as the remaining pictures.

All of the letters were missing and there was a note from one of the guys in the Engineers, who had been a close friend, telling me they had been mailed. The rest of the contents consisted of a smelly, dusty, dirty mess of mildewed clothing. My address book, Hanna's letters to me and other personal paper items were a soggy mess of mush. Obviously the letters from Hanna were totally unreadable, which left me very frustrated. Two of the photos that had been in a plastic bag were still in reasonable condition. Only the edges were damaged. The negatives from our trip were destroyed by the water. Where the bag had been was a mystery. The only pictures I now had of Hanna were the two from the plastic bag and the one that had been in my wallet. Her address in Vienna was gone and I could not remember the name of her father's company.

I felt I was in good enough shape to go back to engineering school so I made a trip back to the university to visit the dean of engineering. He looked over my records from my previous stint in school and frowned. He asked me to give him a good reason why he should let me back into the school and asked what I thought my chances were of finishing engineering.

I cleared my throat and told him that things were different now as I had a very fast growing up, being shot at on the Front while fixing bridges and roads. I left out the parts about the French girls, the great coffee shops, the wine bars and the great restaurants. He was very old fashioned so I also left out the part about Hanna.

They let me back in and honored their agreement to give me credit for the completion of second year because of my military service.

I was a little perplexed as to what type of engineering I should major in. I had difficulty picking between mechanical or civil. I solved the problem by taking both as a double major. Everybody including the dean thought I was crazy but I later got the last laugh when I graduated with honors in both degrees.

I sent several more letters to Hanna and received no replies. I used the university research facilities to search out any engineering companies and engineers in Vienna. Our records were all dated from before the war, some as far back as the early thirties. The library staff told me that the turmoil caused by the war would make it even more difficult to get any information that was even remotely accurate.

I buried myself into my studies and sent a letter once a week to Hanna. The only response was a visit from two MPs, who had three of my letters asking who this Hanna was and what my connection to her was. I invited them in, offered them a coffee, told them the whole story and then showed them the picture of her. They seemed to believe me so I asked them if they had stopped any of my previous letters. They said they only knew of these three. They said they would mail them in the morning. I thanked them and they left.

Back to the books, long and hard, resulted in excellent marks. I had two job offers from Europe, one from Dieter and one from Hanna, and I needed the degree to accept one of them.

I continued to send one letter a week, I think it was my way to keep sane for those two years that were required to finish third and fourth year and get my degree.

The local girls whom I had known probably thought I had lost my mind because I ignored them as well as most of the pubs that the other engineers frequented.

I needed to save my money for my trip to Europe after graduation. I was going to go to Vienna and find Hanna so that we could pick up where we had left off.

After graduation I got a job for the summer doing survey work in the bush up north. My reasoning was simple; it gave me the most experience, with the best pay and a short-term commitment. The first round-trip ticket to Europe that I could afford was in September and that fit perfectly with the end of my summer survey job.

Chapter 9
Will to Europe

I was on my way to Europe after an eternal wait. I had to take the train to Halifax and wait two days before I could get onto the ship. The ship was delayed two more days while cargo was loaded. Talk about frustration after all this time and now more delays! I spent the time pacing around town and the evenings pacing around my hotel room.

The ship sailed and I was finally ready to settle down. That lasted two days and there I was trying to figure out how to speed up the old tub.

This trip was much different than my last one. We did not have a destroyer escort and I felt better that we no longer needed it. I was glad that mess referred to as World War II was over.

We arrived in Portsmouth, England, and I grabbed a combination of trains to get to the channel ferry. The rail cars were in poor condition and very shabby. Nothing but minimal maintenance had been done since 1939 when Britain diverted all funds to the war effort.

I made a detour to my old billet near the base where I had stayed during the time I was waiting to go to the Continent. I had taken the time to find out what would be most appreciated and when I delivered the ten-pound smoked ham to my old landlady she was in tears. I had found out that meat was still heavily rationed and hard to find even if you did have the appropriate cards. I stayed overnight with her, headed for the ferry the next morning, and caught the afternoon ferry to France.

In France I decided not to visit any of the girls I had previously known and caught as direct a train route to Vienna as I could. We had many delays as the train schedules were being affected by the major repairs being done on all of the train tracks and on the infrastructure. I am afraid I was not very patient with the progress. My lack of patience certainly did not help my humor. I was quite short with a number of rail and restaurant employees, which I later regretted.

I got to Vienna and checked into a small, inexpensive hotel, grabbed a telephone book and started to check out Hanna's last name and, as best I could, engineering companies.

The next morning I took a taxi to the address where I had been sending the letters. The house had been very large but had been totally destroyed by fire. Only some of the outside walls remained. My heart sank. I could only hope that Hanna had not been around when the fire broke out.

I went to the homes adjacent to see if I could find out any information. The people on one side were totally unfriendly and of no help. The people on the other side said that they had only moved in two years ago and the house had been in the same condition at that time. The lady said that she had heard that there had been some people killed in the fire but did not know who they were. My heart sank lower.

I next went to the post office because I wanted to know if my letters had been forwarded or had they just gone into some sort of dead letter box.

It took some time to find out where the post office that looked after the area was located. I found an old gentleman who had worked in the post office all of his life. He remembered my letters and said that they had been stamped undeliverable and sent to the main post office facility. He said in theory they would be returned but in actuality they would probably go into the boiler to help heat the place in the cold weather. He remembered at one time a bunch of letters that all came at once but that was before the fire.

I was somewhat relieved to know that it seemed that I had the correct address.

He dug out the old records and located the original forwarding address. It was in a rural area just outside Vienna. I thanked him and left. It was too late to go searching around the countryside so I went back to my hotel.

I had a dinner with a couple of beers, my mind racing with excitement.

I was in Vienna.

I had kept my promise to come as soon as I could and was going to meet Hanna the next day.

I went to bed early, as I was tired from all the walking I had done that day. I thought I would get a good night's sleep. Big mistake, I saw every hour on my watch as I tossed and turned all night. A good cold shower in the morning got me going.

I had a light breakfast while waiting for my taxi. Thank God I had gotten a map, as the taxi driver knew as much about the area around the outside of Vienna as I did.

We finally located the correct area, which was the address that I had gotten from the old man at the post office.

It was a small estate with a large stone gate in a wall that went down along the road in both directions. I got out of the taxi to take a look and heard a roar.

A small Mercedes was coming down the driveway at a dangerous speed. I ducked around the gatepost as it came out of the driveway and tried hard to turn onto the road. It didn't make it and promptly rolled over landing up against the wall across the road and caught on fire.

I ran over to see if I could do anything but the flames were too hot to get very close. I ran around to the other side of the car and tried to pull at the door. It was jammed closed and I burned my hands slightly pulling at the door. I could see someone in the car. She was a young blond female who was slouched over the steering wheel. Blood was running down her face, which was partly covered by her hair. The windshield had a large bulge in it. She had hit the windshield with her head. I ran back to the taxi to get a cloth or something to get the car door open. The taxi driver was all over me screaming for me to get in the car and leave before the gas tank exploded. We ended up in a wrestling match on the ground. I scrambled free and headed back to the car, taking off my jacket to use as a glove to get the door open and get the girl out. The taxi driver was still screaming like a madman that we had to get away before the police came as he did not want to get involved. Later I found he was still paranoid about anything to do with the police, a real fear learned during the war. The car exploded and knocked me to the ground. He picked me up and shoved me into the backseat of the car, slammed the door, jumped in and drove off.

I regained consciousness a few minutes later and looking on the seat beside me saw a small purse clutched in my hand. I picked it up and looked in it. It must have been blown clear of the car or fallen out when it rolled over.

I knew it was Hanna's purse because the picture of us taken in the old hotel was in it. I took the picture out of its little leather case and tore it in half, leaving my half in the purse. I took the half with her picture on it and stuffed it in my pocket.

The taxi driver by this time saw that I had come to and also saw the purse. He grabbed it from me, did a very quick U turn, drove back to the flaming car and pitched the purse out the window near the car and kept going. He yelled that we would be arrested for stealing it. He drove back to Vienna at high speed and dumped me off at my hotel. He had made lots of noise about payment during the drive. He wanted to be sure he had his money before we got to the hotel.

I had found her, only five minutes too late.

I was heartbroken!

All my plans in life had included Hanna.

All my dreams had been crushed in a flaming instant.

I simply became stunned.

My reaction to everything was numbness; it was as if I was in a trance.

I think I paid my hotel bill and went down to the train station to wait for the next train to somewhere.

I do not think I started to function, on anything but some sort of autopilot, until I was on the ship and on the trip back home. I spoke to no one unless they asked me for something. I did see the ship's doctor to get some salve for my hands. He bandaged them and asked how long they had been this way. I did not reply, I just shrugged.

I had not slept until I was on the ship and then it was the sleep of the troubled exhausted. It was not a restful sleep as all I could see were flames destroying our lives. I spent my days on the deck staring at the sea, always questioning how it could go on and on, while Hanna and I couldn't. Sometimes I quietly cursed the water for not being available to put out the fire.

I ate very little in spite of the efforts of the steward. The captain, probably acting on the concerns of the steward, invited me to the bridge. I think he was worried that he might have a suicide on his hands. We had coffee with black milk, which is what he called rum, and I softened up and told him my story. He told me he had lost two sons and a brother in the war and could understand my feelings. He told me that I would probably never forget her but I should find another outlet to channel grief rather than let it destroy me. I said that I would probably direct all my energy into my work, as no one would or could ever replace Hanna.

Mother and Father picked me up at the train station. I had wired them from Halifax when the ship landed telling them what train I would be coming in on. I never told them what to expect so when I got off the train by myself with an extremely long face Mother knew things had not gone well.

I said very little until I was home and when we sat down in the living room after dinner, I told them the story of Hanna and showed them the picture. They wisely offered little more than a quiet sorry but I could see in their eyes how sad for me they really felt. I went to bed and cried myself to sleep.

I had finally broken down.

Chapter 10

Will, Now It's Time to Work

It took me a week to regain some semblance of composure and after much pleading from my mother, I started to send out résumés for a job.

I had several interviews and took a position with a midsized engineering firm in Toronto. The firm was active in a number of areas including roads, bridges, land development and mining.

I worked very hard as I had few interests outside of my work. My bosses loved me, while the other guys in the office thought I was somewhat nuts to put in as much time as I did. They had tried to introduce me to a number of girls but none of them came close to Hanna. I went out on several dates but I felt I was cheating on Hanna so I guess I wasn't much of an escort. The girls in the office all gave up on me. I was labeled nice but a little strange.

Work was the only real outlet I had for my energy, so when I was asked to do some site work I was even happier. As time progressed, I did more and more site work until I eventually became a site supervisor. I hardly went into the office and since I now lived wherever the construction projects were located, I no longer had any need of a home. I didn't even spend my salary because I lived on expense money. A few years of that and I was quite comfortable. What holidays I did take consisted mostly of outdoor activities such as skiing, hiking or canoe trips.

I worked on projects all over Canada and USA as well as South Africa and Central America.

Most of my friends now were people whom I met working on the projects that I worked on.

My extensive traveling enabled me to develop a liking for all kinds of foods and I became an accomplished cook. My tastes for good food and wines would have led to a weight problem if I had not also worked on construction sites and had a rigid exercise program. I was ahead of the time as far as fitness was concerned as my workouts had become part of my daily routine.

I visited my parents as often as I could and made a point of being home for Christmas. Some years I had to come home from the tropics to the cold. Other years I came home to get warm from the way up-north country. My mother became very concerned about my lack of female friends, specifically a wife. I tried to pacify her by telling her I had not yet met anyone. She knew I was still tied up with Hanna and wished I could let the past go and get on with my life.

I was quite happy with the way things were although it was getting harder to have a date with a girl who was not looking at me as a prospective husband. Breaking off the relationships that had gotten too serious for me was getting messy and I did not enjoy the conflict. Whenever there was a difficult time with a girl, I always felt very upset and when I went to bed that night I would hear whispers in the night, which sort of told me eventually all would be all right. I always felt very comforted by them. The same whispers would appear whenever I had conflict at work and would comfort me ever so slightly.

Every time I was home Mother would attempt to introduce me to another girl. I humored her by showing some interest in some of them. None of them could even come close to Hanna.

I do not know if Hanna would have grown better as time passed but I was quite happy to keep her image as perfect as I thought she was.

One Easter when I was home Mother was up to her usual antics of finding Will a wife. She invited Judy over. Judy was a friend from high school who had hung out in the same crowd as I had. She had gone to university and had completed her degree in science and then went on to get her master's of science. She was working in a research laboratory in Toronto.

Judy had come over with her mother, who probably had the same matchmaking ideas as my mother. Our mothers probably thought they could get two people with one stone. Judy was about as interested in a serious relationship as I was. She did not want restrictions placed on her work by a home life and that included children.

I had recently been promoted to a senior project leader and was now spending more time in the office. I was in charge of more than one project so there was a lot of travel but of shorter duration. I was now forced to be in the city so I had bought a house but had done little with furniture. A couple of chairs, bookshelves—you remember the brick and board ones—a TV and a mattress on the floor all were my version of furniture. My house was close to where Judy worked so she offered to help me pick out some living room and kitchen stuff. I thought that was great as I did not have a clue and was too cheap to hire an interior decorator.

Her taste turned out to be similar enough to mine and I thought she did a great job. In appreciation, I invited her over for a good dinner with some great wines. She accepted.

We saw each other on a rather irregular basis as our work allowed it. We became comfortable with each other and used each other as a sounding board for work headaches.

One evening after a pleasant dinner I told her the story of Hanna. She looked at me carefully and said, "I don't think you will ever get over her, will you."

I turned away and quietly said, as I turned back to her, "No, I don't think I ever will. Maybe there really is something to finding your one and only soul mate."

I was away at a jobsite for the next few weeks and while I was there I got a call from Judy. There had been a fire in an apartment in her building and since she had a key to my place would it be possible for her to stay at my place until they got the smoke damage cleaned up. She said the smell was horrible and she was getting tired of spending nearly all her time at the office so she could avoid going home to the smell. I did not care, as I totally trusted her and what were old friends for if not to lend a hand to each other when needed.

I was delayed a couple of weeks more and when I got home Judy was still there. I joked with her telling her not to get too comfortable as I would soon be booting her out the door.

We were forced to spend a lot of time together that week and I began to think that the house would be much better with someone in it when I was away. I asked if she would like to move in and become a flat mate. She offered to share all the costs. I suggested we could just throw some money in a pot for utilities and food. I told her I couldn't ask her to help pay any part of the mortgage because I would then need to share the gain in value when I sold the house and I had no intention of sharing the wealth. We both chuckled and agreed that flat mates we would become. She would share the utility costs and purchase the food and I would look after the rest. Judy moved her things in over the next two weeks.

I was happy that Judy took over the job of wine selection and purchase as she had developed a taste for good red wines. Since she had some good contacts in Europe she had arranged for deliveries of wine in case lots. I had to build a wine cellar in the basement of the house to keep up with her purchases.

Judy used the guest bedroom and when she answered the telephone one time when my mother called she got the third-degree. Mother appeared to be horrified but I think she was quite pleased that her match making finally was panning out. Judy moving into my place caused quite a stir with our friends as this was the fifties, not the eighties.

For the next six months I spent a lot of time away from home. I was either working on projects in South Africa, Colorado or in Western Canada. Judy was deep into some sort of drug research. By this time Judy and I had become very close, sort of best friends, and the subject of Hanna never came up. We mainly discussed work-related subjects. The next six months I spent mostly in the office as the senior project engineer on the South African and Western Canada projects. In both cases the owners of the plants had some of their staff in our offices so I did not need to travel as much to the job sites.

Somewhere in that period Judy and I became more than just good friends.

Hanna had slowly slipped into the back of my mind as the relationship with Judy had developed. The relationship between Judy and me had grown slowly and we had become comfortable with being around each other. Our lovemaking had started because of too much wine and good food followed by a warm fire with another glass of good wine. One thing had led to another and we ended up in my bed.

Judy never went back to the second bedroom.

Three months later we were married in a quiet family celebration. Our mothers were very pleased with themselves and made some quiet inquiries about grandchildren. Both Judy and I shot that one down in flames. After all, we did have careers.

One month later I spent four months in South Africa on site for start-up. One of the engineers who were on site was from a German company that was supplying some equipment. He had brought his wife, who also was from Germany, and very good looking. I spent a lot of what free time I had with them. She had some of the features and mannerisms of Hanna and succeeded in bringing Hanna to the forefront of my mind.

I felt some pangs of guilt that I had betrayed Hanna by marrying someone else. I knew this was impossible because Hanna was gone. I had watched her die in the flames of the car crash.

I finally returned home, when the plant was running, leaving some our staff to turn the plant over to the owners.

I was glad to be home and promised myself that I would not be away for as long a period of time ever again.

Judy was very glad to see me, as I had only written her a letter every two weeks or so. Some letters may have been as much as a month apart. We quickly fell into our old routine of long hours and late dinners. Our lovemaking seemed different now. I brought work home and now would spend less time with Judy and more time working. I also had joined some work-related associations and spent several evenings working on that, when I was not out to meetings related to the various associations.

Over the next two years Judy and I very slowly drifted apart, mostly because I was too busy to spend any time with her. She had responded by either working more herself or developing outside interests. Most of our conversations were related to our work or our new outside interests.

This slow downward spiral continued for two more years. I still spent a lot of time away, even though I had promised Judy that I wouldn't.

Now don't get me wrong, we did take vacations and did have some wonderful times. We had gone to New York City for a week and stayed in the Waldorf Astoria Hotel and had a ball. We went to some live theater, danced a lot and took in a number of the tourist attractions. Other vacations consisted of trips during the summer to lodges or cabins in the lake area north of Toronto. We also took a train trip across Canada. Winter holidays were ski trips to New England or the western USA with a group of friends or our local ski club. We did enjoy ourselves and having the money to do as we wanted certainly did not hurt.

We were happy enough together. We just did not see what was happening to us, as the drift was so gradual. We were as comfortable as we thought we always had been.

One day Judy asked me what had happened in South Africa. I could not comprehend what she was talking about. She told me that our love life had abruptly changed after that trip. She said it had taken her a long while to realize that all was not right and to look back and discover when the problem had started. She felt that love had sort of taken a backseat in our relationship, almost as if I had a lover.

I looked at her, shocked at this accusation.

She told me not to worry as she knew that I did not have a lover because there was simply not enough time between work and running between associations and functions. She laughed and said, "Hell, you are lucky to find the time to sleep."

Judy looked at me and asked if Hanna had come back. I thought for a minute and realized what had happened. I then told her of the other engineer's wife in South Africa and how she had looked and acted so much like Hanna.

I apologized and thanked her for being so patient with me and promised to spend more time with her. I then made a point of being home in the evenings. It was a grand gesture but Judy was now deep into the development of a new drug and was as busy at work as I had been.

I now sat at home alone. I spent my spare time working on some new proposals for projects in Mexico and the southwestern US. The time change of three hours to the West Coast made this easy to do.

One evening, Judy and I sat down and decided that we had better do something to get our relationship back on track. We both felt that most people experiencing martial problems have a relationship that deteriorates into a conflict. Ours was simply wandering away because of lack of contact. We still considered each other as best friends and enjoyed our discussions whenever we could find the time.

I suggested that we should have an extended vacation where we could be together without interruptions from work.

Judy was very enthusiastic about my idea.

Both Judy and I had difficulty to arrange the time off. We both got the sob story from our bosses about how will your projects survive without you. Our companies had gotten used to controlling our lives and knowing that we would deliver whatever they demanded. I was very upset because all we wanted was four weeks off, to be together. I had six weeks accumulated holidays coming to me and Judy had five weeks owed to her. After much persuasion our holiday plans became a reality.

I purchased two tickets to Europe and set about to make some initial reservations.

Our plans were to arrive in Europe through Amsterdam, rent a car and tour around, staying at small hotels and bed-and-breakfasts.

We were both very excited.

Chapter 11
Will and Judy
Off on Vacation

We had three weeks before we were to go on our European vacation and we had already started to pack. Neither of us had ever gone on an extended vacation so we spent much time trying to figure out what to take and what not to take.

My boss came to me and told me that we had a major problem in one of the projects that was located in Mexico. I did everything in my power to find someone else to go. No one was available who had the expertise that I did. I was told that I had better go. The only guy who did have some knowledge was now in South Africa and would not be able to get there in time.

I went home and told Judy.

She was furious with me for agreeing to go. I told her that it would not take more than a few days and I would be back long before we were to leave on our trip. Judy said that she would believe that when she saw it. She then made a point to tell me that our tickets were non-refundable and were only good for the dates we had arranged.

I left the next morning and spent one week fixing the problems and three weeks trying to get back home. The mine site was in the mountains and a landslide closed the pass and our small airstrip was flooded out because of the blocked river. I was considered excess baggage and could wait until it was convenient for them to get me out.

Judy left on our vacation without me.

I sat on my ass in the mud in Mexico.

To say the least, she was very, very upset with me.

Actually she was far more than furious, and hung up on me when I was finally able to get through with a telephone call.

I flew home and after a screaming match with my boss he relented to supply me with a ticket to Amsterdam, where I would attempt to catch up with Judy.

His only comments were his usual "I haven't had a vacation in five years" and "My wife goes to the cottage alone with the kids, what's the problem?"

I was so upset I flew first class. Screw the company! They had just screwed me!

Judy and I had developed a sort of plan where we would go so I rented a car and followed that route. I never did find Judy and I did not see much of the countryside because my concentration was on the hunt for her. I did manage to locate a couple of places she had been or at least someone who looked like her had been there.

The lady fitting her description was traveling with a German gentleman driving a very big Mercedes. I decided the lady could not be Judy even though two people had told me she looked exactly like the person in the photo I had shown them.

The longer I looked for her, the more frantic I became. I realized that all I was doing was just spinning my wheels. I decided to quit the chase and headed back to Amsterdam to wait for her at the hotel where we had reservations to spend our last night before flying home. I spent some time checking out Amsterdam and did wander around the red-light district. I was in no mood for the services sold there.

That was an interesting area. There was only one girl who was at all good looking enough to be inviting, that is until I looked at the chains and whips hanging on the wall behind her. Maybe I should have introduced my boss to her. Well, maybe not, he might get some new staff incentive ideas.

As planned, Judy arrived at the hotel the evening before we were to fly home.

The minute she saw me she became totally unglued. I tried to tell her about the landslide but she wouldn't listen to any explanation.

She told me that I had destroyed our last hope for our relationship by deserting the time that we had planned together. She suggested that I should move my things into my office at work. I reminded her it was my house.

That comment did not help my position.

Judy asked me how I was getting home. I looked strangely at her and told her I was going to use the return half of my ticket. She looked at me and said, "You will find it in many little pieces in the garbage at home, and furthermore, since you did not use the first half of the ticket, the second half would be deleted from the airline system as a dead ticket.

I flew home two days later when I could get a flight.

Judy and all of her things were gone from the house.

I had another screaming match with my boss. He was very indignant about the first class ticket. After all, he did not travel first class!

It took me a week to locate Judy. I tried her office but she had educated the receptionist to screen all of my calls. I finally was able to arrange a meeting with her to discuss the situation. She was very upset when we met and between crying and anger she told me she could not go on as we had been because my work was so much more important than everything else.

The bombshell landed near the end of our talk. Apparently she had been sitting in the dining room of the hotel in Amsterdam and met some people from Europe, whom she had met at one of the chemical trade shows she had attended. They invited her to join them when they found out she was alone. She did and about a half hour later a man came in and walked over to them. He was a senior engineer in an engineering firm located in Germany who was working on a process plant for the company that they worked for.

Judy looked at me and asked if I could remember the story that I had told her about Hanna when I had first met her.

I asked, "Which story?"

She said, "The story that I thought was cute but totally unrealistic and maybe bordering on bullshit. The one about love at first sight. I thought no one could fall that hard, that fast."

She continued and told me about how the German engineer had

looked over at her and somehow both of them forgot the rest of the group existed. The others had left and he stayed with her in the bar for the rest of the evening. He had picked her up the next day early in the afternoon and took her sightseeing around Amsterdam, including the red light district.

She looked hard at me and said, "Will, we are best of friends and always will be. We should never have gotten married. We are too much alike and both of us are way too driven. I am sorry things have worked out this way." We both had a good cry, lots of hugs and I sadly left to go home.

Six weeks later Judy called me and asked to see me. I had some meetings that evening so I came over later and as always with her, I was late.

She handed me some papers. I did not need to read them to know they were our divorce papers. I placed them on the table and asked what the terms she wanted were. She said, "Only my freedom to marry if I ever want to. Everything else I might want I already have, including your friendship, I hope."

Maybe it was foolish but I signed them without reading a word. I kissed her good-bye and told her she would always be my best friend. Two weeks later she phoned me at work and asked to see me that evening. I went to her place and she told me that she was leaving for Europe the next day and would probably be back only to visit once in a while. I wished her good luck and asked if it was the German engineer. She said it was and they would be getting married later in the year. I smiled and told her that at least she was keeping with the right profession and wished her good fortune. She burst into tears, thanked me and wished me good luck.

It was a long time before I saw her again although we did exchange Christmas and birthday cards every year. Her letters that were enclosed with her cards indicated she was very happy. I only wished I could be as happy. The biggest surprise was the picture of the first baby and even more so the second. She had always told me she had no interest in a family. I guess love has a strange way of changing one's ideas of what one wants out of life.

After Judy moved away, Hanna came back to my thoughts very regularly.

I became very busy again at work but my boss and I never saw eye to eye again. He was no longer a friend, he had become an adversary.

I was approached by several of the other engineers in the company with a proposal to leave and form our own company. I jumped at the chance, knowing that I probably was on limited time with the company. My boss was for sure out to free up my future for other endeavors.

Chapter 12
Will Continues with Life on His Own

We set up shop in my house for the first six months until we could get sufficient work and generate some backlog.

I had no home distractions so I buried myself in the development of the company. Our projects were closer to home so I spent a lot more time in the office, even if you did not include the late nights and early mornings.

I had some friends who were female but none that you could call a girlfriend. They might have thought so but I was more married to the company. I wouldn't give these relationships the room to develop into anything. I never did find a friend who was like Judy or a person who could come close to Hanna. Mind you, I wasn't really looking very hard.

It had been close to twenty years since I had seen Hanna and I still felt like she was with me every morning when I woke up. Perhaps it was an illusion, but every girl I met was compared to the one in my mind and all were pale in comparison.

When I went home for Christmas or for any other visit for that matter, Mother always brought up the subject of Judy. She always mentioned to me how happy Judy's mother said she was and how I had blown my best opportunity. She left out the part about the opportunity would have been hers to have some precious grandchildren to fuss over. Father just shook his head at my situation. He used to try to convince me that a balance in life was important but finally gave that up as a lost cause.

Our company progressed, slowly at first, and then picked up as clients from the old firm began to use us for some of their small projects. Their thinking was sort of *I know you but can you handle our needs on your own?*

We could and the staff grew.

We had a lot of good people, most having been stolen from our old firm. The working conditions at our place were much better and we did our best to keep the best employees between projects.

I still received my yearly cards from Judy and I was happy to find that she had met the man that I could never have been. In one of her notes she told me she had met her version of Hanna. I completely broke down with that one. Thank God I only read her letters at home when I was alone. She also sent pictures of her two little ones. They both were growing up so quickly and both were very cute.

I had submitted many, many proposals for projects. Our hit rate was about ten to one. That means for ten proposals presented we would get one project. I was good at getting a proposal as part of a study that allowed us to squeeze most of the costs of proposals into the studies, so they were not all overhead as it was with most firms.

Our firm expanded from just working on civil engineering type projects to development of industrial sites. We then started to work with the clients in "design build" of process plants. We managed to pick up a couple of very good process engineers and made good use of them.

We were successful in getting a contract for a small chemical process plant that was being built in a city about fifty miles from the office. The process was not overly difficult but it contained a number of pieces of equipment that were supplied by an engineering and process equipment firm from Germany.

We had received a number of drawings both preliminary and final. There were a lot of questions on how the equipment was to fit into our process and how the control system was going to react to the process. We were also concerned about how some of the materials used in the equipment would survive in our application. We were using standard off the shelf equipment in a non-standard application.

After several meetings with our clients, I was volunteered to go and meet with the supplier to resolve the difficulties. I had also noticed some minor modifications that, if incorporated into the equipment, I felt would enhance the throughput of the process.

I sent a letter to the German company requesting them to set up a series of meetings because I would be coming over to discuss our concerns.

They responded, thanking us for showing enough interest in identifying and eliminating problems before they became irreversible. The meeting schedules encompassed a whole week and they suggested that I plan to remain after the meetings for the weekend as their guest at the company's fifty-year anniversary banquet. If I did not have a tuxedo, it could be arranged when I got there. They probably thought I would arrive in a snowsuit and mukluks, still wondering what a tuxedo was. I faxed back and thanked them, accepting the invitation. I felt attending the party would help generate a better working relationship between our two firms. I had two reasons for getting the tuxedo in Europe. The first was a North American tuxedo would probably look out of place and the second was that I did not have one, nor the time to get one.

I gathered up all the drawings and specifications that I needed and indeed a few I felt that wouldn't be needed, but better to be safe than sorry. I booked a ticket so I would arrive one day ahead of the meetings and leave two days after the party. They had suggested a hotel and I asked them to make the necessary reservations for me. I felt this gave me time to get over the jet lag, a short holiday and time at the end to clean up any loose ends. Any items that would be required to be handled quickly could be faxed to my office. I was truly very excited about going on this trip. I had not been this excited about going anywhere since Judy and I planned our disastrous European trip. There was something in the air and I could not figure out what it was. All I knew was it felt good.

Chapter 13
Dieter's Story Starting at the End of His War

I think that our liquid surrender, or maybe it was the singing, must have helped, as we were shipped out to a very lightly guarded POW camp in Belgium. We were released within a couple of months after the German defeat in Berlin. I was very pleased to have the release form telling the world that I, Dieter, had been released as a free man and could return to normal life. I think we must have gotten priority because most of my other friends who had been captured took much longer to be released than we did. Some were stuck in North Africa for three years before getting home.

My father was very pleased to see me arrive on the doorstep of his office. He rushed me home to see my mother, as she had been very upset when she had heard that I was in a POW camp. I guess she was concerned about the quality of food and how often I got clean sheets. Mothers!

She was very tearful. I got chastised for not giving them some warning of my arrival. I laughed and told her that I had only been released late yesterday afternoon and in my documentation I had found a train schedule. I took one look at it and realized that if I hurried I could get the all-night train to Frankfurt and there I was. Mother burst into tears again and hugged me, telling me how happy she was that I was now home and safe. My younger brother had not made it. He had been in Stalingrad.

I hung around home for a few days and started to get restless. I accompanied my father to the office and took a look around for something to do. Father quickly put me to work, doing a job similar to what I had been doing before the war.

Father owned a small engineering company that specialized in design and manufacture of automation equipment used in industrial plants. I had worked for him for a short while before being called up by the army. We had supplied a lot of equipment for the German war effort and the expertise that the company had developed was very helpful in getting postwar Germany back on its feet.

I had made some friends with guys who were staff in the prison camp from the US and I made good use of those contacts to ensure that our firm got more than its share of the US money that was being used to rebuild Germany.

Our firm expanded significantly and we developed an excellent reputation for our work, particularly in complicated process automation.

A few years later, Father developed some heart problems and decided to retire from the company. His version of retirement was only coming to work five days a week. I had to think of something to get him to slow down and, more importantly, out of my hair in the running of the company. He was a little old fashioned in his ways and it was not sitting well with many of the staff.

The answer came in the form of a visit from a lawyer. The lawyer was a representative from an engineering firm in Austria that was wishing to expand into plant automation as a method of completing the design packages that they were offering to their clients. They wished to purchase our company. The offer included the condition that I stay on for five years to run the company. After that time they would renegotiate the contract with me.

Father looked at the amount of money they were offering and jumped at it. He had quickly forgotten about his five days a week. I had always believed that Father was the sole owner of the company but unbeknown to me, he had transferred forty-nine percent of the shares to me. We both became financially quite comfortable. Part of the payment was in shares of the firm that purchased ours. Father was quite happy with the cash part of the settlement and decided that the shares that were to come to him would be in my name. I ended up with an eight-percent share of the parent company. I decided that if I was to make a good go of it I should purchase as many shares as either my money or the firm regulations would allow me.

Father settled in a small estate in the country that he had purchased with part of his money and I worked as hard as before. I think I was a little jealous. I had as much money as he did but he got to enjoy his.

After the purchase of our firm was completed I met the principals of the company that had purchased us. The president was a woman and my first impression was *She is beautiful.*

Over the next couple of years I traveled to our head office in Vienna for meetings many times and became good friends with the president, Lore, as I called her. She was as much a workaholic as I was and our times together were spent discussing business. We had also attended a number of social functions together and had a delightful time. I had even kissed her, after which we had both been somewhat embarrassed. After all, an office relationship was not what either of us had wanted or needed.

Her father was still involved in the business as the chairman of the board of directors and, as some of the managers called him, "chief meddler." On one of my trips he called me and asked if we could have a meeting later on that afternoon. I was concerned at his unusual request to see me and thought hard to figure out what I had done wrong. I finally settled in my mind that it would be a discussion concerning my future employment contract. I went to his office at the appointed time. He asked me to sit down and offered me a drink. After pouring two drinks he then turned, looked straight at me, passed me my drink and asked why I was not married. I almost dropped my drink, and so I just stared at him and then answered that I had no good answer other than I was too busy at the office to get seriously involved with any ladies.

I had gone out with a number of lady friends but none of the relationships had ever materialized to anything serious.

He told me he was concerned about his daughter, as she seemed to have no interest in anything except work and her two children from her first marriage. I was quite surprised by the existence of the two children because Lore had never mentioned them to me, nor had

I ever heard any mention of them around the office. I also had never heard, nor had she ever told me, that she had been married before. He told me that the children's father had been killed during the war and he was concerned because he believed she still could not accept the loss of her husband. He added that he had spoken to her and had suggested, for her own good and for the good of the firm, that we should get married.

I was totally in shock.

He picked up the telephone, called somebody, and Lore walked into the office. When she saw me standing there, a little red faced, she turned to her father and demanded to know what he had done. He laughed at her and said, "I am proposing for you two, as you are both too stupid to see how this relationship would be good for both of you and, of course, the company."

In unison we said, "We are not in love."

He laughed and said, "Love has nothing to do with it. It is the company that counts. He then said he was arranging an engagement announcement at the next company function in one week and added that we had better get our arrangements in order including a replacement for me in my office. We both stammered a list of useless words. He waved us off like two children being sent back to their rooms.

We obeyed.

My father and mother were very excited, as they had both given up hope for an heir to the family name.

The wedding was the big event in the neighborhood that year, and I moved to Vienna. I now spent as much time traveling to my old office in Frankfurt to keep it running as I used to spend traveling to Vienna for meetings.

Lore stayed at our new home in Vienna. It was quite large and beautifully furnished but not really our style. Lore's father had provided it along with the furnishings. I felt slightly overwhelmed, and for the first time, totally under the control of someone else. I think Lore felt the same as I did.

We made a fearsome pair in the engineering world. She looked after the overall management of the company and I kept a close eye over the engineering side and the business development of the whole organization. I was on the road more than ever before. We had agents working for us in North America, South America, the Far East and of course all over Europe.

Lore ran the company with a velvet iron hand and nobody, and I mean nobody, caused problems. New people coming into the company would look at this beautiful, slight, soft-spoken lady, and try to flex their muscles. They usually ran back whimpering to their office, with their tail between their legs, and if not, out the door on their ass.

Our married life was pleasant, although most of our conversations centered around the company.

Lore's two children from her first marriage were twins. They were ten years old when we married. The girl, Stefi, was the spitting image of her mother and Lore said the boy, Wilhelm, was the image of his father. He certainly did not look German, and as he grew older, even less German. I got along very well with the children and we had a lot of fun, as a family, when I was at home. There was enough money to provide for a full-time nanny, so the home life education such as manners, sports, and study habits were well looked after and both the twins did very well in school. Not surprisingly, they were both interested in going to engineering school. Lore and I both thought that they may change their minds as they grew older and more independent.

We had some problems in my old company and I had to go there to straighten them out. I started by firing the guy who had been hired to replace me and was supposed to be running the day-to-day operations of the company. I was now stuck there running the company while we recruited a replacement. I went home on the weekends and as time went on, it became easier just to stay in Frankfurt some weekends. Lore and I saw less and less of each other.

Our life together was at best described as formal. As a husband and wife we got along very well. Although our sex life was good, it was sporadic and we had no children of our own. It is hard to be passionate when you are always dead tired when you arrive home. Lore would often drift off into a dream world and I always felt she was thinking of her first husband. I did not learn the entire story of him until much later. I always found it hard to compete with someone as perfect as he was and I told her so many times. She usually burst into tears and told me she was very sorry but she could not help herself. I never told her to stop acting like a kid and get on with her life. I felt that was too harsh for her. To me, she was just too gentle and nice for that kind of treatment. We slowly drifted apart, as I stayed longer and longer in Frankfurt. When I went home it now felt like her home and I was only a visitor.

One day I got a call from her asking me to come home that weekend and I said I would. I was quite interested in what was up.

I arrived in Vienna Friday evening and went to Lore's home, as I now called it. She was sitting in the library waiting for me with a glass of wine for each of us. It was one of our favorites. I accepted the glass and we clinked a toast. She asked me to sit down and said there was something she wished to discuss.

She started by telling me that she considered me her best friend and wished it to remain that way. This got my mind in the questioning mode. I said, "Thank you and I believe we will always be, no matter what gem you have waiting for me." She took a few moments and collected her composure and continued. She asked me to hear her out before making any comments. She then told me, as her best friend, she felt that she was being unfair to me. We were married on paper only. I lived in Frankfurt, not Vienna. She lived in her past with Will and could not ever see letting him go. She told me that he was a Canadian and had been in the Engineers. They had never actually married, although he had proposed and she had accepted. She showed me a signet ring that he had given her as an engagement ring. I never got a close look at it as she clenched it and started to cry. Her father had created the story of the wedding as it made her family situation much more acceptable to Vienna society. I asked her if she had ever gotten proof of his death. She told me that one of his friends had written her telling her of his death and had enclosed a copy of the letter that was being sent to his family. She shuddered, saying that it was the worst day of her life. She showed me his picture and there was no doubt that Wilhelm was his son.

She continued and said she wished to release me from any obligations with her, so I could continue my life without her and maybe marry if I found my Will.

Now it was my time to try to regain composure.

Our agreement was easy to work out, as both of us were financially very comfortable. We agreed to remain best friends, which we did. I moved the rest of my things to Frankfurt.

The twins were sad to see me go but I had not been around very much for the last few months so it did not significantly affect them. The lack of conflict between Lore and me made everything easier for them.

Mother was totally upset as there were no grandchildren for her to spoil. Father was upset, as there was still no heir to the family fortune.

I was too busy at work to care about their lack of grandchildren problems.

Chapter 14
Dieter's Life Goes On

The company in Frankfurt kept me very busy, as I doubled the size of the organization. I continued to see Lore during visits to the head office and we remained the best of friends. I understood her world and she understood mine.

The company was somewhat shook up when we separated but the rumor mill quickly and disappointingly settled down when it discovered we did not have a big fight when we separated and that we were on very good terms with each other.

I went over to Amsterdam to see some clients and the meetings dragged on as they usually do. I decided to stay over and finish the meetings the next day. I checked into what I call a standard commercial hotel near the airport. I was hungry so decided to go to the dining room. There was a bit of a commotion when I walked in, so I looked over to see what was going on. A number of people from another company that I had supplied some chemical process equipment were sitting there. They motioned me to come over and join them. I complied. I did not know everyone there, so someone proceeded with the introductions. There was a female Canadian chemist there, who was known by a few of the group. Her company used materials produced by the rest of the group. I sat down beside her in the only spare chair.

I looked at her and thought that I would love to get to know her much better. One by one the rest of the crowd drifted away and I continued to talk nonstop to her. She was interesting, smart, good looking, knowledgeable, nice figure, well dressed and, judging from her ring, married. Dammit!

We were finally the last two sitting there and I asked her if she would care to join me for dinner, as I did not feel like eating alone. I left out the part that was how I usually did dine.

We had a pleasant time. She appreciated good wines and knew what she was drinking. I found out that her husband was an engineer and they were supposed to be on vacation but he was stuck in Mexico and would not be out for at least a week. I told her that was too bad, not really meaning it. She laughed and said that was normal. We talked until the staff asked us to leave. I asked her if she would like to meet for lunch the next day about two in the afternoon. She said she would love to. I went to my room and lay on the bed in a cold sweat. She had to be one of the most perfect ladies I had ever met, and damn, she had to be married. The next morning I called the office and had one of the staff bring my car from Frankfurt to Amsterdam. I met the car at the airport and gave the driver a plane ticket back to Frankfurt. I had completed my meetings in the morning before going to the airport but did not check out of the hotel. Somehow I knew something was right. I called my secretary and told her I would be taking a week holiday but I would be checking in regularly.

I was already in the restaurant when she arrived. I stood up to greet her and gave her a light kiss on the cheek. She did not do the North American thing by recoiling. She looked radiant and was very well dressed, more European than North American. She told me she had been shopping that morning and did I like her new outfit. I told her it was beautiful but I left out the part how she made it look that way. I did not want to rush things.

We had a very pleasant lunch. I can't remember what we had but it must have been good. Our easy conversation went on endlessly, until the waiter asked us to leave because he had to shut down the restaurant so he could set up for dinner. I apologized and we left. I turned to her and said, "I don't know how to ask this, and feel free to say no, but since you are here for a holiday and you do not know Europe would you be interested in a guided tour? I have some time off from the office and would be delighted to show you around. Of course you will have your own room. I just wish for you to enjoy your holiday. A week is a long time to be alone for a holiday. I felt

I was rambling and when she turned away I felt sick. Turning back she said that she loved the idea, but separate rooms would be a must.

Our time together was the best time I had ever spent with anyone, ever, at any time. I will remember that time for the rest of my life. She told me of her life and I told her of mine. She told me that this trip with her husband was to be their last chance to save their marriage and he had fixed that situation real good. She told me that, even if she separated from her husband, he was the kind of person that would always be her best friend. I only hoped she was right. I told her about Lore and how I sometimes felt that there were three of us in the bedroom. She looked surprised and said that was one of the main problems with her husband. He had once known a girl he was going to marry but she was killed in a car crash many years before and he had never been able to let her go.

The separate rooms lasted two nights. We headed south from Amsterdam and along the Rhine Valley. We visited many little towns, vineyards and some castles. We stayed in small hotels and some pensions. We sampled as many local foods and wines as were available. The weather cooperated and we had bright sunny days and warm, clear nights. Nothing could have been better.

She was perfect for me in every way. I had never even been close to anyone like this before. I now knew what Lore had meant when she had told me about Will.

The one week stretched into two and a half. I was truly in love for the first time in my life. We had to return to Amsterdam so she could make her plane flight home. Our parting was difficult but she insisted that she would need to be alone with Will as she knew that he would be waiting for her at the hotel.

I left to drive back to Frankfurt with a very heavy heart. I kept seeing her disappearing from my life. Two days later I got a call at home and she told me she had moved out and mentioned that Will was probably stuck in Amsterdam trying to get home.

I tried not to laugh, while crying at the same time.

The telephone bills were very high from both sides of the Atlantic for the next two months. Work suffered, as I was a total mess. I was even worse when the time came for her to meet with Will to give him the divorce papers. I was afraid that he would give her a hard time and delay the time when we could be together. She had told me that she trusted him and said he would not object to give her her freedom. I could not believe anyone could be that considerate. I then remembered how Lore and I had separated.

I flew to Toronto and Judy and I flew back to Frankfurt together. She had a one-way plane ticket. I had never been so happy in my whole life. We were quietly married six months later, as soon as the divorce was final. Apparently Will was still her best friend and let her go the easiest way possible. I was impressed.

I went to head office shortly after we came back from Canada and upon seeing Lore, I told her I had met my version of Will and thanked her for her good wishes.

We had a lovely daughter, Liv, very quickly after getting married. Apparently we were not as careful as we had thought when we were together on our little holiday. Eighteen months later our son, Gerhard, was born. Mother and Father were very impressed. A boy heir for Father and a little girl for Mother to spoil.

We had good results from our agents in North America and one of the projects was the supply of some specialized equipment for a chemical plant in Canada. The process chemicals were new to us although the actual process resembled a number of other ones we had done. We were not worried about the equipment working but wanted the project to go smoothly. We were hoping for a good referral that we could use on a number of other projects that we were putting in quotations for. The client had a number of questions that needed to be answered and they volunteered to send an engineer to our plant for meetings. We gladly accepted because a good relationship with a good engineering company in North America would be to our benefit. The trip coincided with our company's fiftieth anniversary so I felt it would be best to invite him to join us. The meetings were scheduled and invitations printed. All we had to do was to wait for him to come the following week.

The engineer had arrived, apparently a day early, and went exploring on his own. Our people had met him at the airport and told me a little about him. He was average build, well dressed, spoke good German by North American standards and wanted to just sightsee by himself. I felt he had probably never been in Frankfurt before so I hoped he had fun by himself and not gotten into too much trouble.

On Monday morning he arrived on our doorstep, bright and cheerful with a stack of drawings and specifications. When I saw the paper he had brought with him I became concerned that the meetings would never be over.

The part that disturbed me was that he was so familiar, sort of like I had been around him for years.

He did not need any of those drawings as he had it all in his head. The meetings went very well with very little changes required on our equipment. Some of the changes he had suggested were later incorporated into our standard equipment because they would raise the throughput of the equipment by twenty-five percent with no extra cost to our manufacturing group. I was so impressed I jokingly offered him a job. He looked at me real hard and started to laugh. I couldn't figure out why. He reached into his pocket and pulled out an old battered business card and said, "Your company name struck a cord in my memory. You may not know that I am not a saver of things but sometimes some things are worth saving. When I decided to come over here, I remembered a card that I had gotten from a German soldier a few years ago. Actually quite a few years ago. Your name is the same as the one on this card. You couldn't be this person, could you? And by the way, I don't do bridges anymore."

I laughed and told him that the job offer still stood.

Chapter 15
Hanna, at the Train Station in 1945

I thought it was the worst day of my life. I did not realize it but that day was yet to come. I stood in the doorway of the train, waving back to Will as the train pulled out. He was standing in the rain looking as dejected as I felt. The only difference between us was my clothes were dry. My face was covered with tears, making it as wet as Will's, only I could not tell if it was the rain or tears on his face.

I went to my compartment and spent the rest of the trip back to Vienna alternating between staring out of the window and staring at the ring Will had given me. The train traveled in the rain and blackness all night to get to Vienna. Father was at the station to meet me. I got very little sleep during the trip.

Father took me home and gave me some warning that Mother was not in good condition. I was shocked how she had deteriorated during the time I had been away. Father let me sit with her a while and then took me downstairs to the den and proceeded to tell me how sick she really was. The doctors had told him she had cancer. Nobody had known about it until she had gotten very sick and by that time she was given only six weeks to live. I broke down in tears. What was happening to my world?

During the next few days Father was very close to me. He stayed home from the office to be with Mother and me. In one of our talks, he looked carefully at me and asked, "Who is he?" I asked him what he meant. He smiled and quietly told me that there was something different about me, maybe I even seemed somewhat more grown up. I looked at him, smiled, and told him about Will. I told him about my time with Will, how we met and how wonderful he was, that he was in the Canadian Engineers, and as much about his background as I knew. He smiled again and told me he had had several conversations with Ingrid. She had provided some information about Will and certainly she approved of him.

I was quite relieved to have Father on my side. This meant most of my battle was won. I showed him my ring and told him about Will's proposal to me. He was quite surprised and asked me if I really knew what I was doing. I told him how much we were in love, how we had spent so much time with each other and I could see our whole life together. He was quite concerned about where we would live. He was pleased he was an engineer, meaning I was keeping with the family tradition.

I received a letter from Will telling me about his new posting. I cherished that letter and put it on my desk with the three pictures I had of Will. The fourth picture I had was Will and I together. I kept it in a small leather case in my purse.

Mother died two weeks later. It was so depressing to be beside her and watch her slowly slip away from us. I felt totally lost without her. We were never that close as I had always been much closer to my father, but I still missed her terribly.

Two weeks after Mother died I got a packet of letters from Will in the mail. I was overjoyed until I realized there was two covering letters, one from a friend of Will's expressing his regrets and one a copy of what had been sent to Will's family in Canada.

He had been killed by a mortar while he was working on a bridge.

Today really was the worst day of my life.

My whole future had just collapsed. Father found me crying in my room and sat down beside me. He thought I was crying about Mother until I passed him the two letters telling about Will's death. He hugged me and told me no one should have this much sorrow in two weeks, let alone a lifetime. He stayed with me for a long time and took me down to the living room, where we just sat and cried together for the rest of the evening.

I now discovered another small problem. Every morning when I got up I felt ill to my stomach. I initially thought that it was stress caused by the death of Mother and Will. I went to a doctor to get something to settle my stomach and he gave me some news that I did not want to hear.

I was pregnant. Whoops!

When I returned home I decided that I might as well tell Father sooner rather than later.

Father was not pleased to say the least.

Father escorted me into the library and sat me down on a chair in front of him. He wanted to know what really happened and I told him about our weeks in the mountains. He was totally furious but I reminded him of my birth date and their wedding anniversary date. He laughed at me and told me to mind my own business. He gave me a wink and we both chuckled. He then became very serious and told me that two things had just happened. The first, there had been a wedding in secret, not just an engagement, and the second was, he had approved of the marriage but it had been kept quiet because of my mother's illness. We went out later that day to a jeweler he knew, who would be discreet, and he bought for me a simple gold wedding band. Next we were off to a man in the most disreputable part of town, who produced a wedding certificate. I never asked how he knew about a jeweler who would be discreet or about the documentation creator. He then made arrangements for both a marriage and death announcement in the newspaper. He told me that I had to tell my friends myself but to stick to our story, to the letter. I promised I would and until after I married Dieter I did just that.

The day after I got home and found how sick Mother was, Gisele and Aunt Ingrid came to Vienna to be with us. Ingrid decided to stay for a while before she headed back home. I believe they were with us for at least two months before they went back home. I had to tell Gisele about my pregnancy and she chastised me for not being more careful. I told her we had been careful but obviously not careful enough. I never told her about our total abandonment of anything resembling birth control. We were simply so oblivious to reality that we never even thought of the possible consequences of our love. If we had, we would not have cared. Anyway, I made Gisele promise to tell anyone who asked that Will and I had gotten married and she had stood for me. She agreed because being a widow was far better for the family than being an unwed mother. The death of a soldier husband was a very common occurrence in those days.

I went back to school to finish my commerce degree but had to take time off for the birth of the baby. Father arranged for tutors to ensure my studies were not missed. You should have seen Father's face when he found out that the baby turned out to be twins. I wasn't sure whether he was pleased or horrified but I was still in shock. After they were born he loved them and enjoyed spending many hours playing with them. The twins were named Wilhelm and Stefi. Wilhelm looked just like Will and everybody said Stefi looked like me. I was very happy with them. They filled my life with love and the will to go on. They gave me the permanent link to Will, whom I still cherished. I used to sit and become so very sad when I realized that Will had never met his children and they had never met their father. As they grew older I told them about Will and how wonderful he was.

I think the twins gave me an excuse not to get into any relationships with other men. I had no interest anyway and they kept Father from pushing the situation for a suitable suitor. I was a widow and that was acceptable.

Can anyone explain how a man who had been so staid and proper to his own children can make a complete fool of himself when his grandchildren are around? That is what happened to Father. He was so delighted with them. I believed he transferred all his love that he had for Mother to them.

I finished my degree and went to work in Father's engineering firm. We hired a nanny to look after the twins as I felt they needed someone with them all the time in their own home and I was in the office as long as Father was.

The twins grew fast and Father had suggested that we take them to Vienna from our estate to celebrate their second birthday. We went to Aunt Ingrid's home in Vienna and had a lovely party with lots of presents for the twins. They were barely old enough to figure out what a birthday was but that did not stop them from enjoying their presents—or, more accurately, the paper the presents were wrapped in.

Aunt Ingrid had moved back to Vienna as her husband, Gerhard, had finally returned from South Africa. Gerhard had been gone for seven years and had been able to see that Germany could not win a war against the whole world in the long haul. He had made a number of friends who were British and then with their help was able to convert most of his investments into gold, which he was able to hide. He brought it home and converted it back into new investments. Aunt Ingrid and Uncle Gerhard became quite comfortable financially. He spent a substantial amount of money on renovations to their small estate and also purchased a small home in a better area of Vienna. They now split their time between the estate and the new home in Vienna. Their new home was within a block of our old home, which had been destroyed by a fire. The electrical wiring had been faulty and luckily enough we had already purchased and moved to our new home in the country and had the old one for sale. We then sold the land on which the old house had stood to a development company. They had indicated to us that they wanted the property for a future development and would sit on it for a couple of years.

We had a wonderful evening. Gisele was there with her new husband. He was a lawyer with a large law firm. She had finally settled down from her wild days and had become a very sedate housewife. She was even talking about starting a family. I thought maybe the twins had been an influence in that decision.

We had put the twins to bed in one of the bedrooms and since it was very late Aunt Ingrid convinced us to stay overnight and not go back home until the morning. That evening I had been quite upset because I had left my purse at home. Father could not understand why that was a problem. He was a man and couldn't possibly understand the importance of a purse to a woman. The real reason was one of the pictures of Will was in it and I always looked at it before I went to sleep. Without the picture I did not sleep well that night.

We arrived home late the next morning to find the police waiting for us. We could not understand why they were there, that is until we were informed of the disaster that had occurred.

Our maid had been in a fight with the gardener. He had insisted that she go into town to pick up some gardening supplies. She was somewhat lazy and objected. They had a bit of a scrap and she had relented but not easily. Instead of taking the estate truck she had taken my car. She was a very headstrong girl and we were thinking that we might have to let her go. She had stomped out in her impetuous manner, jumped in my car and roared down the drive and out onto the road. The car had not made the corner at the bottom of the drive and burst into flames after it rolled over. We had left the nanny for the twins at home for a rest and she was able to confirm the various stories. The police could not understand why my purse was on the road open, with the contents scattered. Obviously I had left my purse on the front seat of my car. They wanted me to confirm that everything that had been in my purse was still there. I went over everything but was shocked to find that the only thing that was disturbed was the picture of Will and me together which had been torn in half with my half gone.

Nobody could help me figure out what happened. The police told us that their investigation of the area around the accident had shown them a car had stopped. Footprints told them that two men had gotten out and a scuffle had occurred and the car had left in a hurry. The police had no witnesses and had to assume the only two witnesses panicked after they arrived and left. The tire prints were that of the most common tire that was manufactured in Europe.

I was very upset, as another tie to Will had vanished with the picture being destroyed.

As time marched on the twins made sure that any spare time I had was occupied. As they grew Wilhelm began to look more and more like his father and Stefi looked more like me.

I had started out in Father's engineering firm as an assistant in the accounting department and later moved into the engineering area as a specification writer. I had a stint in the personnel department, where there were several difficult times when we had to reduce staff. I made myself a promise that I would do everything possible to ensure that we had no more layoffs. Several years later I moved back into the financial part of the organization and worked hard to make sure we quoted the projects realistically and collected our money in a timely fashion.

Father was impressed with how my work had progressed and

asked me if I would like to become vice-president. Who could turn down a promotion like that, so I happily told him, "Yes!" I still lived at home and with a substantial salary, not being used, I purchased back some of the outstanding shares that had been sold to get the company going. I managed to buy back all but twenty-five percent of the shares in the company. Father and I now controlled seventy-five percent of the company, of which I held thirty percent and Father held forty-five percent.

Father decided to step down as the president and just sit as the chairman of the board of directors. I took the job as the president. A few of our senior staff were quite upset but I dealt with them quickly and as firmly as necessary. I had a good track record and soon put down any dissention with actions.

The company flourished. Father and I acquired a lot of money and still kept our staff happy with higher than average salaries.

Chapter 16
Hanna's Life Continues

I went to Father to explain an idea that I had developed. If the company was to continue to grow more without becoming so large that we would be vulnerable to market fluctuations we needed to branch out into other engineering fields. He inquired as to how we would do this, what areas would we branch into and where would we find the appropriate people. I told him we should get into automation because we would then be able to present a complete package to our clients when they constructed a process plant or manufacturing facility. I told him that we should purchase a company that already existed and had an excellent track record. He looked at me, smiled and asked what company had I found that would meet this requirement. I told him of a company located in Frankfurt that would meet our requirements. I showed him their advertising material along with a list of projects they had worked on during the past ten years. They had an excellent reputation that had been upheld by all of their clients who had been contacted. I also mentioned that the president/owner was an elderly gentleman who held most of the shares and had just recovered from a heart attack. His son was running the business and from the information received it was apparent that he was doing an excellent job. I had calculated what I felt the company would be worth to us and what we should be able to buy it for. Father was clearly in agreement with my idea and suggested it would be a beneficial thing to maintain the son as an employee/manager on contract for five years to ease the transitions. He also told me he would speak to the board but felt it was a good acquisition for us.

The board, after much discussion and a lot of questions, approved the recommendation and we got our lawyers and accountants to do some more investigations to figure out what was a realistic purchase price. We wanted the company but intended on purchasing it for as little as possible. Why should we give away money if we did not have to? We did not want to insult the firm because that would only lead to problems down the road. The price that was calculated was quite close to what I had thought and we also created a number at which we would walk away.

Our law firm sent in one of their lawyers with our offer. After several sessions of negotiations we agreed at a price close to what we originally planned on paying. We got the son as a manager for five years. The main change to our original offer was that part of the purchase price was shares in our company.

We found out later that Dieter, the son, welcomed our offer for two reasons. The first one was to get his father out of the office and into retirement. Secondly, when Dieter found out he owned almost half the company and since his father took his part in cash and the share portion of the purchase settlement went to Dieter, he suddenly became quite rich.

Dieter was a good manager with a good head for business. With our financial backing he was able to accept larger contracts without worrying about financing the project. Dieter developed his division into an ever stronger automation engineering group. We became one of the best in Europe. The business that he developed matched perfectly with the rest of our engineering divisions and we became very successful building complete automated factories. Dieter's division also developed a number of patented processes. As a business unit, Dieter's was the most profitable in the organization. He was paid a good salary and converted as much as he could into shares, enabling him to increase his share ownership in our firm substantially.

Dieter's presence was required on a regular basis at head office. Sometimes he helped with quotations or attended project meetings, while other times he was needed for general business or financial reasons. Dieter and I spent considerable time together in meetings and from time to time would attend social functions together. The rumor mill was busy, but with no juice the rumors quickly faded.

Father, I guess, was just being a father and would regularly inquire about me getting married again. He did not feel it was proper for me to not have a husband, and more importantly, the twins not to have a father figure. I was not interested because in my heart there was still Will. From time to time Father would tell me to let go and get on with my life. I was always angry with him for that suggestion and I told him so. He once said he would take matters into his own hands. I told him that he had better not try.

Father was still active in the company as the chairman of the board of directors, and still held the majority of shares in the company. He had considerable pull around the office.

One day I was extremely busy in my office when I got a telephone call from him asking me to come to his office immediately. I was upset because of the timing as I had a lot to do that day. I walked into his office and Dieter was standing there looking somewhat upset.

He actually looked very embarrassed.

My father had a sly look on his face, sort of like a kid who had just raided the cookie jar and the dog got blamed. He looked at both of us, laughed at me, and then said, "I am proposing for you two, as you are both too stupid to see how a relationship would be good for both of you." In unison we said that we were not in love. He laughed and said, "You foolish children, love has nothing to do with it. It is the company that counts." He then told us he was arranging an engagement announcement at the next company function so we had better get our arrangements in order. We both stammered a list of useless words. He waved us off like two children and sent us back to our offices.

We did exactly as Father told us.

Father went shopping in Vienna and surprised us with a new home, completely furnished. I think he pulled in some old favors and got good prices on the contents of the house. The furniture was not quite what I liked but I had no time to go shopping, so we just moved in. Dieter seemed happy enough but was away a lot because he had to find a replacement for himself in Frankfurt. He had a lot of help from the personnel department and in spite of his misgivings and several arguments, he had finally accepted their recommendation.

The twins enjoyed Dieter and he seemed to be very comfortable with them. At first he was a little distant, probably because he had no experience with children of any age. After a few months, he warmed up to them and they to him. Our weekends gave us time to be together as a family. We did many activities together, such as hiking, skiing and even a few sports matches. We also took holidays in Switzerland for skiing and Italy for the beaches. To the outside world, we were a cozy little family. On the inside, I think I was the problem, because I still missed Will, especially when we were having fun. I knew I was not being realistic but that was simply how I felt. I somehow believed in my heart that Will would appear one day.

The automation division in Frankfurt was still doing well after Dieter moved to Vienna, although not as good as it should have been. We had conducted an audit and discovered some irregularities with which the new manager had been involved. Dieter had been right about not hiring him. The now red-faced personnel department had insisted that he was the best person for the job. Dieter's feelings had been correct. After firing the manager, Dieter now had to spend a lot of time in Frankfurt to get the automation division back up to speed and assure our clients of its solidarity.

Initially Dieter would go to Frankfurt on Monday and return on Friday evening. As he straightened out the mess and began doing more projects, he would spend the odd weekend there working. This pattern got to the point where he was home only one weekend a month.

Dieter came home one Saturday and told me that because he was spending so much time in Frankfurt he was going to get an apartment near the Frankfurt office. I agreed that it would be better than a hotel room. After a few months of this, I felt the whole situation was anything but fair to Dieter. I called him and asked him to come home that weekend and he said he would.

He arrived in Vienna Friday evening and came directly home. I was sitting in the library waiting for him with a glass of wine. I knew it was one of his favorites. He accepted the glass and we clinked a toast. I asked him to sit down and told him there was something that I wished to discuss.

I did not know how to start as I felt very awkward about what I was about to tell him and how he would react to it.

I started by telling him that I considered him to be my best friend and I really wished for us to remain that way. He thanked me and said, "We will always be best friends, no matter what morsel you may have waiting for me." I choked and then took a few moments to collect my composure before I continued. I asked him to listen to what I had to say before making any comments. I told him he was my best friend and I felt that I was being unfair to him. We were married on paper only. He really lived in Frankfurt and not Vienna. I said that in my mind I lived with Will and I could never see letting him go. I told him that Will had been a Canadian and had been in the Engineers. We had never actually married although he had proposed and I had accepted. I showed him Will's signet ring that he had given me as an engagement ring. I then thought about Will, clenched it in my hand and started to cry. After clearing my voice, I told him that Father had created the story of the wedding as it made my family situation much more acceptable to Vienna society. He asked me if I had ever gotten proof of Will's death. I told him that one of Will's friends had written to me. The letter told me of his death and had enclosed a copy of the letter that was being sent to his family along with all of the letters that Will had written to me. I told him that had been the worst day of my life. I then showed him a picture of Will. He looked at it and told me that there was no doubt that Wilhelm was his son.

I grabbed some more resolve, gulped, and continued to tell him that I wished to release him from any obligations to me so that he could continue his life without me and maybe marry if he found his version of Will. Dieter was somewhat shook up but he agreed that we should separate. He said he had come to believe we should have stayed friends rather than getting married.

Our agreement was easy to work out as both of us had more than enough income and investments. Money was not an issue. We agreed to remain best friends, which we did. Dieter moved the rest of his things to Frankfurt. The twins missed him but welcomed him when he did see them.

The company was somewhat shook up when we separated but the

rumor mill quickly settled down when it became very clear that we were still quite in control, did not have any disagreements in any meetings and still remained the best of friends.

I understood his world and he understood mine.

Chapter 17
Hanna's Life After Dieter

Dieter's division continued to expand quicker than the rest of the company and Dieter continued to convert all of his profit sharing into shares. He slowly increased his share value to fifteen percent of the company. I also knew he had substantial investment, elsewhere.

A couple of years after our separation I needed to call Dieter about a question that had come up on a project. I was told by his secretary that he was in Amsterdam on business and had called for a driver to take his car there. He then had called later and told her he was taking two weeks off but would be checking in regularly to deal with any problems that might come up. I put the phone down and stared at it thinking that was quite out of character for him and there could only be a "she" to create such a change. I continued to stare at the telephone, thinking about Dieter and myself. I then turned to the picture of the twins on the desk and thought that Dieter was better to them than I had been to him. I hoped that this was as true a girl for him as their father had been for me. I then turned to the window, stared out for a long while, turned back to the picture and whispered to it that I wished they both would be as lucky as I had been to have found true love, as short as it had been.

My wanderings were soon interrupted by one of the project leaders bursting in with some pressing problem.

Back to the current reality.

Just over three weeks later Dieter was back for some meetings. I left a message for him to come to see me.

After his meetings, he came in and stood in front of my desk with a rather silly grin on his face. I looked him over and said, "As your best friend, I think you have something to discuss with me." I added that this was not the place for such discussions and suggested that we had better go to lunch.

He stared at me for a moment, then turned, smiled and said, "Yes, you are right and I now know what you meant when you told me about Will." I smiled and told him I was extremely happy for him.

Lunch took four hours.

He told me all about her, how they had met, about getting his car there, and about the two best and happiest weeks of his life. I jokingly said, "Thanks, I thought we had a monopoly on wedded bliss." We had a good laugh over that one. He then confessed about the slight problem of her being married and added that she had said her marriage was not in very good condition. I chuckled and commented to him that they all say that. Dieter was a little indignant and explained about her husband missing their two weeks of holidays. He told me about the situation with her husband and about his previous love being the biggest problem in their marriage. I smiled and said, "Sounds like us, doesn't it." Dieter caught the drift and casually suggested that maybe her husband was Will. I got upset but tried not to show it, and told him not to talk such nonsense. We both became quiet for a while. I was thinking about Will and Dieter was thinking about his chances with his new lady. At the end of our lunch I wished him luck and said I had a feeling that everything would work out in the end as he really did deserve true happiness.

Little did I know how right the prophecies would turn out.

Dieter was tied up with some projects that were close to shipping but were a little behind schedule. He was unable to make it to head office for any meetings for the next two months. I called him to set up some time, during his next trip, to discuss a strategy for a project we were thinking of quoting. His secretary told me he had gone to Canada for a short trip and would be back in two days. I thanked her and said I would call back later. I hung up the phone and again stared at it for a few minutes. Many thoughts went through my mind. This could be either very good or very bad. The more I thought, the more confusing it became. Either Dieter had gone to bring his new love back to her new home or to try to convince her to come to be with him or just a visit because they missed each other too much. I hoped it was the first because the visit was asking for a broken heart and the convincing could end up either way, with the status quo being the odds that she would likely take. I sincerely hoped she was coming back with him. His secretary had told me he would be back to work on Tuesday. I called that morning, early, because I could not wait any longer to find out what happened. I felt like a schoolgirl calling her best friend to find out how the hot date went. When he answered his phone all he heard was my voice asking him how successful his business trip had been. He paused for a moment and told me that Judy was now in Frankfurt with him. We both cheered on the phone. I told him his presence would be required in Vienna at his earliest convenience, asked him to bring Judy and told him that we really did need to discuss work items when he came. I was never so happy for someone else as I was at that moment.

Judy was an extremely nice person. She was kind to everyone and worked hard to learn German so she could fit in with Dieter's family. I became very close to her as we seemed to have a lot in common. She endeared herself with Dieter's parents when they were told that she was pregnant. I joked with Dieter about the fact that it was obvious that they saw more than scenery on their two-week holiday. He was a little embarrassed but very happy. Judy did not seem to be concerned that she was no longer working as a chemist, except for maybe mixing baby formula. Their baby girl was born. Dieter was a little over the top about being a real father. They called her Liv. Gerhard, their son, was born about a year and a half later. Judy sure knew how to win the hearts of her in-laws. Deliver a daughter for Grandmother and a son for Grandfather.

Father was always quite concerned for me. I believe he could not understand how I could go through life without a proper man to look after me. I tried to tell him, many times, that I was doing quite well by myself and did not hesitate to point out that the twins were well balanced, well loved and excelling at anything they did. The twins were ahead in school and would be entering university a year before they should. The only thing that shook up Father was they had both decided that they did not want to go into engineering. Wilhelm was planning on law and Stefi was planning on an art degree. Both had shown themselves to be strong in their chosen fields. I could see that Wilhelm would eventually head for politics and Stefi had already won some prizes for photography and writing. I was very proud of them and told them so. I only wished Will had been there to share their growing up years.

Father came into my office one afternoon and told me that he had been looking at some old records and had discovered that the company was almost fifty years old. He told me that the company should have a dinner in honor of this milestone. He thought that we should invite our active clients and maybe even some who had been clients in the past and could be again in the future. We bantered back and forth for a while and came to an agreement that it could prove to be very beneficial and a lot of fun for us and the staff would get to meet some of the clients they had worked for, spoken to but never met. I failed to tell Father it would occupy him for several months and keep him out of the day-to-day operations of the company.

Father liked to do things right and I knew it would be an expensive affair but I also knew it would be money well spent.

Little did I know how well spent!

Chapter 18
Will Goes to Vienna

I had not been in Europe since the disastrous holiday with Judy, so I was looking forward to the formal function that Dieter's company was hosting. I remembered my times during the war and how I had enjoyed many of the European ways of doing things. I thought of all the good times with all of the wonderful girls and especially my time with Hanna, as short as it had been. I thought it was remarkable that such a short time with a person could lead to a lifetime of love.

I rearranged my flight to Vienna so it left early the next morning. I wanted to spend some time there to have a look around and enjoy some of the history of the city. I had spent very little time in the city when I was last there, about fifteen—or was it twenty?—years ago, right after the war. That was when I had gone to find Hanna, as my true love, and found her in the burning automobile.

I checked into the hotel where Dieter had arranged for me to stay. I then changed into comfortable shoes and good old-fashioned blue jeans, grabbed my camera and went touring. I had a wonderful day and even tried out a dessert or two in some of the coffee houses. The concept of the coffee house with good coffee had just arrived in North America. I had welcomed it with open arms but knew the coffee was not as good as in Europe. I felt all would even out with time.

Late that afternoon, I returned to the hotel and passed through the lobby. The concierge informed me that I had a message. I picked it up and went to my room. It was from Dieter, asking if everything was in order and suggesting that I join him for a drink at the bar. I changed into something more appropriate for an early-evening drink in the bar of a very good hotel. Blue jeans were all right to go sightseeing, but not for evening drinks.

I took the elevator down to the main lobby and inquired where the bar was located. I then took the stairs up one flight to the mezzanine level and located the bar.

I went in and saw Dieter sitting by himself at a table near the wall. The bar was a very pleasant comfortable place. The décor was proper old European, much like a men's club. It was paneled with a dark wood; the lighting was dim and supplied by small glass chandeliers. There was a musician quietly playing a piano over in a corner. He was supplying only background music to the several low conversations among other patrons in the bar. The bar was slightly smoky but not objectionably, mostly from pipes or cigars. I sat down with Dieter in the chair he indicated as available for me. He asked what I would like to drink. I requested a scotch on the rocks. The waiter inquired what brand and I simply asked for a good single malt. Dieter smiled and then requested the waiter to bring the best of his single malts. The waiter hid a little smile and left knowing he had two businessmen with an expense account.

We discussed the usual work-related stuff, as businessmen do, such as projects, staff, staff headaches, banks, and on and on.

I was sitting with my back towards the door of the bar. I noticed Dieter look towards the door and saw his face light up. I heard footsteps and started turning to see who was coming and heard a very familiar voice say, "Will, what are you doing here?" I quickly finished turning, stood up, grabbed Judy and gave her a big hug. I kissed her politely as good friends do, held her at arm's length and told her how wonderful she looked. We both turned towards Dieter, who sat with a drink in midair and a shocked look frozen on his face. I then realized who the German engineer was. Judy laughed and said, "Husband Number One, I believe you have already met Husband Number Two, and by the way I love both of you, only differently." Judy and I sat down with Dieter and we all started to talk at once. The strangest thing happened. Our conversation moved comfortably and freely, as if we had been close friends for a great many years. We covered topics that included wine, food, their children, early days, war years and of course work. As we talked, time flew by and Judy said that she was hungry. Dieter suggested we go to a restaurant near the hotel, which we did. The restaurant was elegant and the wine list was superb. The meal was wonderful and we talked until the wine got to us and the restaurant staff reluctantly suggested we leave. I think they just really wanted to go home. In our conversation Dieter mentioned that I would get to meet the president of the engineering company at the party the following evening. He told me that Lore was his first wife but they were still best of friends. He told me a little about Lore's father, who had founded the company and was now the chairman of the board of directors. Apparently, the planning for this affair had been done by him. This project had been left to his whims as a means to get him away from interfering with the day to day operations of the company. The company structure was much different now because of the growth in the business and some of the department heads were getting quite upset with what they considered his meddling in the operation of their groups. Dieter mentioned that Judy had met Lore when she first came to Germany and over the years they had become good friends. They had not seen each other for at least a year because of either work or family commitments. Judy told me a little about Lore's twins but said that she had not seen them for a while. She had heard they were doing very well in school. Judy looked carefully at me and said, "You know, the boy, Wilhelm, looks a lot like you but any similarity will probably diminish as he grows older. After all, who would want to look as ugly as you do?" I turned and feinting a dejected person, told her thanks for the compliment.

We all got back to the hotel in one piece. I was certainly happy I was not trying to drive a car. Upon entering the lobby, we looked at the bar, shook our heads, "no," and took the elevator to our appropriate floors and went to bed. Sleep came quickly as it does when you have had too much to drink but not so much that you get the spins. Morning arrived, bright through the window, and my head hurt. Damn it, I wished I had closed the drapes. I staggered to the bathroom, took a couple of aspirins, closed the drapes, dropped back into bed, pulled the covers over me and got another hour of sleep while the pills worked on my head. When I woke the second time I was in much better shape. I got up, shaved, showered, dressed and went down to the dining room for breakfast. I could only handle coffee and for a while I sat with a book, not exactly reading very much, until Dieter showed up. He did not look in very good condition either. I decided to order breakfast and tough it through. I was not going to let these Europeans beat out a Canadian when it came to drinking stamina. Breakfast was a simple sweet roll with butter and preserves. Dieter smiled and asked if I could not handle the meat and cheese breakfast. I laughed and told him it was too early for a high fat meal. He chuckled at me and told me I should not be the lecturing one about healthy foods after seeing what I had consumed the night before. At that point I felt that I should be prudent, dropped the subject, and asked how Judy was. He said she was going to be a while before she would be able to come down. We chatted some more about work and went back to our rooms. I grabbed my camera and jacket and went out to see more of the city. I visited some museums, art galleries and castles, doing the tourist thing. I got a little overzealous with the camera and I ended up taking several rolls of film.

Tonight was the big gala. I thought gala was the best way to describe "the little get-together" that I was going to attend. The affair was formal. All of the men were to wear tuxedos and all of the women, according to Judy, were coming in long gowns. This was going to be a big splash with lots of peacocks wandering around. The tuxedo that I had picked was classic but understated. I had decided to purchase it rather than rent. Either way was expensive but if I purchased it I would be able to use it later. After all, one would never know when it could come in handy; weddings, funerals or maybe even a birthday. The suit set me back a good chunk of change. The tailor Dieter had recommended in Frankfurt had to rush to get it finished. I believed that if Dieter had not purchased a lot of suits from this tailor over the years, I would not have gotten such good service. He had done an excellent job on the suit and it was quite complimentary to me. I had invited Dieter and Judy to stop by my room for a glass of wine before we went down. The affair was being held in the ballroom of the hotel, which was convenient for us. I wished to go with Judy and Dieter as they were the only people I would know there. After introductions, I would be on my own for a while. We all had business to tend to and I already had a few names of potential clients I wished to meet. Dieter had a lot of guests he had to make sure he greeted and had a brief talk with. My German had picked up over the last week so I felt I could be understood. Dieter and Judy arrived right on time. Judy looked very elegant in her dress. It was a long, light green fitted gown that complimented her figure. Judy had kept her slim, athletic shape even after having two children. She had told me she was still active in a number of sports such as tennis, skiing, swimming and running and it showed. Dieter had a tuxedo that was very classy. It looked great on him. I only hoped I looked as well turned out as they both did. Even though I was going with them, I felt a little lost without a partner. Judy suggested that she would have a glass of white wine, jokingly saying it was too early in the evening for red wine stains. I complied. Dieter and I stuck to our red wine. We finished our glass of wine, picked up our jackets and invitations, and went out the door and down to the ballroom.

Chapter 19
Hanna Going to the Party

Father had been very occupied with his plans for our little company's fifty-year celebration. He had been so busy that the little celebration was now a grand affair with three hundred guests, black tie and an expensive meal at a very good hotel in downtown Vienna. Dieter had a number of guests he had added to our original list. Most of them were from large German companies but he had added an engineer from a small Canadian firm. Dieter was supplying some equipment to them for a Canadian facility they were working on. I could not comprehend why he would bring someone who would be of little future use and would not fit in very well with an all-European crowd. It would be highly unlikely he spoke any German so he would more than likely feel uncomfortable. I was already having arguments with the accountants on our ability to write off the expenses of this affair. I guessed that I should leave some things to Dieter's discretion; after all, his division was the most profitable in the company. So I chose not to question the additional meal. He must be doing something right.

I had planned to buy a new dress for the affair but I had been so busy at work that there had been no time even to go looking. In the late afternoon I started looking through my closet to see what I had not worn for a while, at least long enough that some of the wives at the affair would not remember it from previous functions.

Stefi came in as I was searching. She was coming tonight, as was

Wilhelm. Neither of the twins were very excited as they could only see it as a bunch of antiques prancing around, drinking too much and making fools of themselves.

Stefi and I were on speaking terms from time to time, although lately she had been friendlier. I hoped she was growing out of her teenage attitude and perhaps I would no longer be the stupid, backward, outdated mother. She was a teenager and had developed a mind of her own and it was unfortunately as strong as mine. I would look at her from time to time and realize that she was growing up and was not giving me any more problems than I had given my mother. I decided to put up with some of her outbursts and lay down the law on the rest. It was good to be able to pick your battles. Wilhelm had been much easier than Stefi although the two did synchronize their stories.

Tonight, in spite of her unwillingness to go, Stefi was in good humor. She sat and watched me search through the closet looking for a dress, taking out some and putting them back. She could see that I was getting nowhere. She got up, walked over to the closet, sifted through the dresses and pulled out a white one. Stefi looked at it and told me she had never seen me wear it. I stared at the dress and realized it was the dress that I had worn when I went out with Will on our first date. I quietly told Stefi that it was the dress from the first date with her father. She laughed saying that she would bet that I couldn't fit into it now. I smiled and decided to take her up on her bet. I grabbed the dress and put it on. It still fit but was a little too snug. Stefi looked at me and told me that I looked great but thought the dress would suit her better. She asked why didn't I wear another white dress and if she wore the one I had on, we would look just like twins. I smiled and told her it would be fun. We both got dressed and admired ourselves in the mirror. Stefi laughed and said that we would knock them dead. I looked again at myself in the mirror and told Stefi that something was missing. She looked at me inquisitively, laughed, dove into my drawers and pulled out a white shawl. I was shocked and told her I could never wear it because her father had given it to me and I had promised him that I not wear it until we were together again. Stefi noticed a slight tear in my eye and told me that she believed her father would have wanted me to wear the shawl from time to time and to think of him when I did. I sat on the bed and after a few moments collected my emotions and told her that she was probably right. I put the shawl over my shoulders and we went on to finish dressing Stefi. The white dress looked amazing on Stefi and to complete her outfit I gave her a set of my pearls to wear for the evening. She looked great but it was a shame that there was nobody for her to impress.

Father was staying with us that evening so he would not have to return to his estate after the party. He was waiting for us in the study when we came down. He let out a low whistle and I feigned disgust while Stefi gave him a big hug. We planned to arrive somewhat after the first group of guests. Father believed that the host should let the guests get comfortable and get their pleasantries over with before being subjected to the required praise that they felt they had to give to the host.

We arrived at the hotel and the concierge was waiting to escort us to the ballroom. On the way there, Father jokingly mentioned that we would probably get the royal treatment when we arrived because the concierge knew who was going to pay the bill and, more importantly, who would be supplying his tip. He was right. The concierge was literally gushing over us. I think I heard more adjectives for beautiful than I ever thought possible. When we arrived at the door of the ballroom Stefi looked at me and asked if that guy was for real. I laughed and said, "Anything for a tip."

Wilhelm shook his head and added, "What a dork."

We entered the ballroom and the conversation generated noise level in the room slowly diminished as the guests realized that we had arrived. They all turned to the four of us. I looked around and did a quick scan to determine whom I would need to greet first and whom I would make a point of spending a little more time with. Father was doing the same. Stefi and Wilhelm were checking out if there was anyone of their age there and where the nearest exit might be. I spotted Dieter over near the bar standing with Judy. I would see them as soon as it was possible. I had not seen Judy for a year or so because of work and travel constraints. I noticed them talking and stop just as they acknowledged my glance. They smiled and gave a little nod. I wondered where the Canadian was. He was not with them so I assumed that he was probably out trying to find an axe to cut down a column, thinking it might be a tree. Father and I then walked down the steps with Wilhelm and Stefi following. We received a pleasant murmur. I guess Stefi was right, we were knocking them dead.

Father and I started our circulation, greeting all of our guests. We greeted each guest with his partner, made the usual small talk and continued on. I mentally planned the return circulation to pick up the especially important guests.

Chapter 20
Will at the Party

Dieter, Judy and I arrived at the ballroom behind a number of the guests. Dieter and I went to the bar to get drinks for all of us. As we walked back to Judy with the drinks, Dieter did the usual greetings as well as introducing me to those on our route. When we arrived back, Judy was having a conversation with a client of Dieter's. It was obvious she was not comfortable with him being as close as he was. I stayed with Judy and Dieter interjected and moved off with the client who had been bothering Judy and introduced him to another client of theirs. Dieter then had to circulate and greet the guests he had invited and who were here without their wives. Dieter and Judy would later circulate together to greet the guests who had come with their wives. Dieter returned and I excused myself and went to find the men's room.

As I returned I noticed the room was quieter than before. On the other side of the room I could see a party of four, one being an older gentleman, one being a blonde with shorter hair, another blonde much younger and a young fellow circulating among the crowd. They had their backs to me so I surmised it must be the owner of the company and his party. I wasn't sure how they would receive me as an outsider. I spotted Dieter and Judy standing over near a group of men beside a table so I walked over to them. Judy smiled when she saw me coming and when I arrived she told me that Lore, her twins and her father had arrived. She laughingly told me Lore's father liked to be the center of attention.

The room was very crowded so it took some time for the party to work their way over to us. I was talking to Dieter and Judy and had been jostled so my back was towards the approaching party. They were talking to a small group next to us when Dieter motioned for me to turn around. I slowly turned not wanting to bump into anyone, especially with a drink in my hand, and came face to face with a girl who looked exactly like Hanna. She was just as beautiful as Hanna had been when she walked to meet me on our first date, complete with the same white dress. She was slightly younger than Hanna had been. Judy let out a stifled scream when she saw me standing beside the young man. I stared at the girl and she stared right back with a look of puzzled recognition in her eyes. I was so shocked that I was numb and my glass just slipped through my fingers and hit the floor with a deafening crash. The blond lady with the older gentleman turned to see what the noise was. She saw me and just stared. I stood frozen and stared back. We just looked at each other for what seemed to be forever while the rest of the people drifted away, not unlike what had happened many years before. I could see a small tear forming in her eyes and she broke the spell with a tiny whisper saying, "Will?" I choked back the largest lump my throat had ever had and my eyes slowly traveled down to her hand where they riveted on my signet ring on her hand. I quickly looked up and said, "Hanna."

She answered with a tiny "Yes." She stepped towards me as I did towards her and we met in the middle, both in tears and in each other's arms. When she was in my arms I knew it was Hanna. The old feelings came back stronger than they had ever been. My heart felt like it was going to burst. We just stood there in each other's arms for a long time. Dieter later said that we just hugged and held each other for ten minutes. The rest of the people at the party started to buzz with excitement trying to figure out what this performance was all about. Dieter and Judy were the first to figure out what had happened. Dieter turned to the crowd and told them that two people had just returned from the dead. He then turned to the twins and told them that they could meet their father as soon as their mother would let him go. Stefi started to cry and Wilhelm just stood there, silent in shock. Judy went over to the bar and got a number of napkins and brought them to us. Hanna and I parted but only far enough so that

I could stand with my arm around her. She quietly called Wilhelm and Stefi over and introduced me saying, "This is your father."

Hanna's father just stood there quietly, trying to sort out what was happening. He had a happy expression on his face when he realized who I was. He came over to me, shook my hand and then quietly told Hanna that he would look after things until she felt able to continue. Dieter and Judy grabbed Hanna and me and the twins and quickly escorted us into a room adjacent to the ballroom. Hanna and I sat down together on a sofa and held each other as tightly as we could, shaking like leaves in a storm. Dieter took the twins aside and told them to let us be for a short time as we had about twenty years of pent-up love to let out. He told the twins of our twists of fate, that Judy had been married to me and he had been married to Hanna. It had been like Dieter and Judy had been there to make sure we were available for each other when the time came. Both Hanna and I were unable to get into what had happened as all we could do was hold each other. She was still as beautiful as she had been many years before. I did manage to tell her that my offer of marriage was still on the table and she told me her acceptance still held.

I stood up, holding her hand, and asked if she would like me to accompany her on her rounds. Her father might need some help. She was not going to let go of me until Judy dragged her into the ladies' room to fix her makeup. I told her I would not be going anywhere without her.

I watched her go with Judy and I turned around and walked over to the twins. They were both apprehensive but I put my arms around both of them and for the first time gave them both a big hug. Stefi started to cry and Wilhelm was stiff, with an I-don't-know-what-to-make-of-all-of-this look on his face.

Stefi whispered out loud to me, "Mother kept her promise after all."

I stepped back and smiled and said, "I bet we stole the show from your grandfather." This broke the tension and they both laughed. Stefi left for the ladies' room and as I watched her go I wondered what the promise had been. Wilhelm stood with Dieter and me, still looking quite lost. Dieter turned to Wilhelm and said, "Believe it or not but I knew your father before your mother did and I did not realize the connections." Wilhelm shuffled his feet and stood quietly. Hanna, Judy and Stefi came out of the ladies' room. Hanna was absolutely beautiful but as you can guess, I was biased.

The six of us walked out into the ballroom with Hanna on my arm. We must have been radiant as everyone in the ballroom met us with applause. We spent the rest of the evening meeting and talking with people. Hanna was glued to my arm. The head table had to be rearranged so I could sit beside Hanna. Her father ran around that evening with a glint in his eye. Hanna said that he was happier than he had been in a long time and he was generally a happy person. I never got to discuss anything with the people I had on my list but I did not care.

Later that evening when the celebration was over I went back to Hanna's home with her, Stefi, Wilhelm and her father. Hanna and Stefi went upstairs to change. Her father looked at me, questions in his eyes. I walked over to him, smiled, and said, "There will be no sleep tonight as we have so much to tell each other. What happened, what went wrong and where we all went." He smiled knowingly, shook my hand, and went upstairs to bed, a very happy old gentleman.

I went into the lower bathroom and changed into more comfortable clothes. Hanna came down and we went into the den, snuggled up against each other on the couch, and started to tell each other our stories of how we got to where we were today.

Chapter 21

Hanna Arrives at the Party

On the drive over to the hotel, Father and I decided to change our method of circulation through the crowd. Our new idea was that we would circulate as a group of four. We wanted to include the twins so they would not feel too left out and try to make a run for the nearest exit. We knew that they were not exactly happy to be there. Wilhelm was very unhappy as he had to wear a tuxedo similar to what Father was wearing. Wilhelm, not so lovingly, had referred to it as his monkey suit.

We slowly worked our way through the crowd greeting each individual or couple as we came to them. We had identified several guests who required slightly more time than others. In spite of his objections it was clear Wilhelm knew what was expected of him and he greeted each guest with a kind comment. Stefi just went along with a sweet smile and a warm hello. We worked our way over towards Dieter and Judy, who were talking to a guest who had his back to us. I assumed it could not be the Canadian engineer because he was not wearing a lumberjack shirt and work boots. As we approached Dieter and Judy, Dieter noticed us and motioned to the man to whom he was talking that we had arrived. I heard Judy give a stifled scream. The person to whom they were talking turned and stared at Stefi and Wilhelm. I heard a crash and I then turned to face him. There was something frighteningly familiar about their friend.

I stared at him.

I glanced at Wilhelm.

I went into shock.

It could not be!

He was dead!

Did I not have papers that showed it?

I had to ask!

I choked on the single word! I could hardly get it out! My mouth had become instantly parched. He looked as shocked as I felt!.

I yelled out as loud as I could.

It came out as a whisper, "Will?"

Silence!

He stared!

He said nothing for what felt like an eternity.

His lips then formed a very quiet "Hanna?"

I knew that I had been right and my emotions got the better of me as I started to cry. I choked a "Yes" that was barely audible.

I stepped towards him and we met halfway, both in tears, and flew into each other's arms. When he wrapped his arms around me I melted like I had when we first met so many years ago. My heart felt like it was going to explode. I just stood with his arms around me for a long time. I wanted to never stop feeling his body against mine, giving me an energy and warmth that had long been missing.

Dieter later said that we just cried and held each other for ten minutes. Father later told me that the rest of the people at the party started to buzz with excitement, trying to figure out what the commotion was all about. He wasn't any help to them in supplying an explanation. Dieter and Judy were the first to figure out what had happened. Dieter turned to the crowd and announced that two people had just returned from the war now more alive than dead. He then turned to the twins and told them that they would be able to meet their father as soon as I would let him go. Stefi started to cry and Wilhelm just stood there totally silent and in shock, scraping one foot on the floor. Judy got a number of napkins and brought them to us. Will and I separated but not too far. I wanted to stand close enough that his arm would still be around me. I got my emotions under control enough to call Wilhelm and Stefi over and quietly introduced them to their father.

Father was standing nearby trying to sort out what was going on. He looked very pleased when he realized who Will was. He came over to us, shook Will's hand and quietly told me that he would look after things until I felt I was able to continue. Dieter and Judy grabbed the four of us and quickly moved us into some sort of meeting room beside the ballroom. Will and I had no strength left so we sat down on a sofa and he held me tightly. I wrapped my arms around him to get him as close to me as I could. I was never going to let him out of my sight again. Will whispered that his marriage offer was still on the table and I told him my acceptance had not been withdrawn. I smiled and told him that he would not need to ask my father for permission.

When we had recovered some composure and strength Will stood up, not letting go of my hand, and asked if he could accompany me on my rounds to greet the guests. I did not want to let go of Will but Judy dragged me into the ladies' room to repair my tear-damaged makeup. Will's smile told me that he would not be going anywhere without me. Stefi came in a couple of minutes later while we were in the restroom. She was very excited and told me that I had kept my promise after all. I had no idea what she meant and had to ask her what she was talking about. She reminded me about the promise I had told her about, not to wear my shawl unless Will was with me. I choked back another tear, fixed my makeup again, and we all headed back to my future.

We walked out into the ballroom with Will beside me. I latched my arm through his and I was definitely not going to let go. I felt happier than I had been since our two weeks at the mountain hotel. Dieter had gone back out into the ballroom to give a preliminary explanation of what had happened and who Will was. We were met with applause when we entered the ballroom. I felt like the beaming bride. We spent the rest of the evening meeting and talking with people. The staff of the hotel rearranged the head table so that I could sit beside Will. We went through the introductions of the head table and the usual round of speeches. Will got up and made a short speech about us, briefly telling the guests that the war could no longer claim us as casualties. Most of the people in the ballroom had been affected in some way by the war so they responded with a

119

cheer. Father was bouncing around the ballroom like a kid with a new toy. I think he realized that he finally was going to marry me off for good. I was glad when the party was over. It had rapidly become a distraction from spending time with Will. I asked Will to come back to our home. There was no way I was going to let him stay at the hotel by himself and me at home alone. When we got home, Stefi and I went upstairs and changed. Father came to my room, knocked on the door, kissed me good night and went down the hall to his room, looking tired but very happy.

When I came downstairs Will had changed into much more comfortable clothing. He met me with an embrace, a loving long kiss, and led me to the couch in the den. We sat down together, I snuggled up to him, fought back tears of happiness and we started to get caught up. I started by asking him what he thought of the fact that he was a father of twins.

He smiled and said, "That is for tomorrow, tonight is for only us. We have so much to share with each other and to discover what really happened."

We talked into the early hours of the morning until we fell asleep on the couch in each other's arms.

Chapter 22
Will's Story Continues

The next few days went all too fast. I rearranged my flight back to Canada to give me an additional week in Vienna. Hanna told the managers at her company she would not be in the office because she was taking a holiday. She told them she would be available for any problems but they had better be big problems. Hanna's father spent some time with us but spent most of his time in the office covering for Hanna. I informed my office that I would be spending extra time in Vienna with my future wife. That brought some silence on the telephone and probably some buzzing in the office. I also explained to our project supervisor what had transpired in the meetings in Frankfurt and how to continue with the design. I gave him the phone number at Hanna's home so he could call me if it was necessary and reminded him about the time change.

With all of our work under control we now set about to rediscover who we really had become and for me to learn about my family.

I told her about the mortar on the bridge, how the identification tags had become mixed up and my subsequent medical condition and transfer back home. She told me about her mother, their move to the country and the maid who had destroyed her car. She then added that the strangest part of the maid incident was the missing half picture. I told her that her story sounded all too strange and asked her to show me the picture. She got it out of her purse and passed it over to me. I then told her that I could answer the mystery of the missing half picture. I reached into my wallet and pulled out the half picture and matched it to her half. I laughed and said, "I guess this confirms I was really there looking for you."

Stefi and Wilhelm came down a little later in the morning. They had remained upstairs for a while, almost like they were afraid to believe I was really there and each had wanted the other with them for support. I told them I wasn't sure how good a father I would be because I had no experience but I would work very hard to make sure that everything worked well for all of us. I also told them that their mother had told me how wonderful they had been to her as they grew up. Stefi laughed and told me that her mother had been totally impossible to get along with for the past year or so and hoped I would be able to put up with her. I had several friends who had teenage daughters so I had seen firsthand how the conflicts between mothers and daughters progressed. I laughed and said it would not be a problem as I could probably help her mother become smart again in the next year or so. They both wanted to know where we would live. Would it be in Vienna or would it be in Canada? Hanna and I had not gotten as far as that part. It was my responsibility to answer that question so I told them that they would definitely remain in school in Vienna because it would be too hard to change schools at this time. I think they were a little disappointed as at that time North America was definitely more active with the flower children than was Vienna.

Hanna and I looked at each other with a realization how difficult the next period would be. We knew that we faced a lot of previous commitments made with both family and work. We both had heavy responsibilities as principals of companies, although Hanna's was a much larger organization than mine. I smiled at her and told her that I would be able to wrap up my work commitments and move to Vienna although it would take some time to get everything arranged. I wanted her to accompany me to Canada on my return, to be with me and to meet my family. She was very responsive to this idea and felt her father could handle her work responsibilities for a short period of time. I told the twins, if they would like we could take some holidays to see North America. It would be great for them to meet their other grandparents. They looked at me, at each other and back to me. They had never given it a seconds thought that they had another set of grandparents. They both thought it would be great to be able to travel back and forth to Canada over the years.

We talked as a family for the whole day. I asked the twins about their school and their friends. Wilhelm remembered that there was a ski trip planned at Christmas time and asked if I would be able to go. I informed them Judy had already invited me a week ago. They looked shocked that I knew Judy well enough to be invited on the ski trip. They wanted to know why I called their mother Hanna and not Lore, as most of her friends did. I told them that had been the way that Gisele had introduced us. They both looked in wonderment and asked in unison, "You know Aunt Gisele?" I chuckled and shared with them how I had first met their mother. Hanna had mentioned that Gisele now lived in Vienna. I suggested what fun it would be to invite her over for a dinner without telling her that I was there. That would give her a bit of a surprise. The twins agreed it was a great idea. I presumed that Gisele had changed a little as we had because I had not seen her since 1944. Our conversations went on and on. The twins wanted to know about life in Canada. Did everyone have a dogsled, how long did the snow last and a mixing of other questions, all standard to me as I had answered all of them before in South America, Mexico, USA and South Africa. I always came prepared for these questions so I went to my briefcase and pulled out a small photo album, which had typical pictures of Canada in summer and winter, including the cities. I think they were somewhat disappointed in how urbanized it looked until they saw the wilderness photos.

Hanna called Gisele and asked her to come to dinner that evening. She told her it was very urgent and she had an important surprise for her. Gisele sensed some intrigue in the dinner request and said she would cancel whatever she had on that evening and come over. She pushed Hanna to tell her what was so important but Hanna simply refused, telling her that she would just have to wait.

We dedicated the rest of the day to the twins. We all wanted to get to know each other as I had missed their entire life up to the present.

The most frightening comment I heard that day was the statement near the end when Wilhelm said, almost in passing, "You know, I think I know you better, as my father, than most of my friends know their fathers, who have been with them all of their lives. Their fathers are away or at work so much that they hardly ever see or talk to them, not even on the weekends." I tried to rationalize that one by thinking that I would have been different if Hanna and I had not become dead to each other just after we had met. In my heart I wasn't so sure that I would have been any different. I then made a promise to myself that it would not happen to us. I looked carefully at Wilhelm and told him, "If that ever starts to happen please let me know and I will change right away."

Gisele and her husband came to dinner that night. They had chosen to leave their children at home because they both had exams the next day in school. She walked into the house with a big question written all over her face and the rest of it on the tip of her tongue. She could hardly contain herself and worked very hard to get by the front-door hellos before blurting out, "What is so urgent? What is the surprise? I have been going crazy all day trying to figure out what it could be. I called around and no one seems to know. You aren't pregnant, are you?"

I walked up behind her and said, "Not this time." She stopped, vaguely recognizing the voice, turned and looked at me. Her hand covered her mouth as I stepped up and put my arm around Hanna and said, "Hi, Gisele, what's special today?" in English. I had remembered the greeting I had used at the coffee shop when she had been practicing her English.

All she could say was "My God," over and over again. Her husband looked at her trying to figure out what had happened, turning to us to get some help in understanding what was going on. We were of no help. She then followed by saying, "You're dead," repeated several times. She reached over, touched me, put her arms around me and started to cry. She leaned back and said, "I want the whole story now."

We all laughed and I said, "Not with your coat on and not without a drink. Something stronger than coffee this time."

She answered with one word, "Scotch," followed by "straight." Her husband looked totally lost and a little concerned about the drink. I watered it down quite a bit. It was going to be a long

124

evening. Stefi and Wilhelm settled right in as they realized, with their cousins at home, they would be able to listen to the adult conversations.

We talked before dinner, during dinner, and after dinner, all without taking time for a break. We had lots of laughs including what Judy's reactions had been when I got stuck in Mexico. I insisted Gisele tell me all about her life. Over the next few years I was able to find out just how wild Gisele had been before she settled down. That night she tried to let me believe her life had been quite boring. I didn't believe her. Everybody had their chance to tell a story. We also solved some of the problems of the world.

The evening finally broke up and as Gisele left she grabbed me and told me not to die again or she would come after me herself. I assured her I was here to stay.

The week went by quite quickly and I soon realized I had to go back home. My office had called many times and our client was getting quite upset because I was still in Europe and not at home solving all of their problems. I didn't give a damn about their problems but I had made a commitment. Hanna had gone into the office for a couple of afternoons to deal with some of their concerns but she left the twins to guard me so I wouldn't get away again. The twins showed me around Vienna and even introduced me to some of their friends as their father. I had problems getting used to my new position as a father, accepting it as gracefully as I could. It was my turn to blush.

Hanna and I decided that she would accompany me when I went home. She made the necessary work arrangements and her father volunteered to stay in Vienna with the twins. They were somewhat upset with us because they were not able to come with us to Canada as they were still in school. We promised to take them on the next trip to Canada, assuring them both that there would be many opportunities for them to visit Canada for many years to come.

We flew back to Canada via Frankfurt on a Saturday. We had a three-hour stopover in Frankfurt, so Dieter and Judy met us at the airport. They were glad to see us as a couple and Judy reminded me of the ski trip during the Christmas break. Dieter was carrying a very large roll of drawings for the project which, somehow, I had forgotten was the original reason for this trip. He handed them to me and told me all the new changes had been incorporated. He said the upgrades alone would have justified the extra week in Europe. He then handed me an envelope with all of the customs papers for the drawings. As we all hugged each other good-bye, Judy and Dieter reminded us not to forget to return. We settled into our seats and snuggled up close to each other. We had a glass of wine each and lots of water. We did not eat or drink anything else. The flight was uneventful and when we arrived in Toronto we separated to go through Customs and Immigration. We did not let each other get out of sight. Hanna just told them she was visiting some friends but I required a little more time because of the drawings. We took a taxi to my home. I don't think Hanna was surprised in what she found. My place was suffering a little from too long under the control of a bachelor. The place was clean because the cleaning lady had been twice since I had left for Europe but that was about all you could say for it. We planned on getting some sleep but we were both too excited. I called my parents to tell them I was back from Europe and would be down to see them tomorrow. I told Mother I had seen Judy and she was doing quite fine. I also told her I had a surprise for her. She assumed I had picked up a small present for her.

In a way I had.

Three of them to be exact, two to be presented at a later date.

Hanna and I went out for dinner and then we took some time to see the sights of the city. She was pleased with how vibrant the city looked and how clean it was. I could not resist a dig at her and told her I hoped our igloos seemed comfortable enough. My ribs hurt for an hour. We went to bed happy but very tired. Hanna was in my arms once again and we were alone.

The next morning we took my car and drove down to my parents' farm. It was located about a hundred miles from my home and Hanna was quite surprised when she figured out in kilometers how far we went. We discussed how the visit would go and we agreed that I would be the one to tell them about their new grandchildren, the twins. I told her this short drive was nothing in a country as big as Canada. The massive space in the country amazed her.

We drove into my parents' farm and Hanna looked around and

told me it looked much like I had described it years before. My mother met us at the door. Father was still out in the barn.

Standing on the front porch, Mother looked at us and knew there was something very permanent about our relationship. She looked very hard at Hanna, knowing she had seen her somewhere before. Her expression told me she could not remember where.

I smiled and said, "Mother, I would like you to meet Hanna, your daughter in-law to be." Mother didn't say a word, she just stared with her mouth slightly open. Hanna told her that she was pleased to meet her, using her accented English. Mother's face brightened up, remembering all that I had told her about Hanna, and she said, "Will was right when he said that he would find you someday. After he came back from Vienna I tried to get him to give up on you."

I added, "By trying to marry me off to every unmarried girl in the county." She hushed me, grabbed us and hustled us into the kitchen, made us sit down and poured us each an ice tea. She then looked at me and told me to go and get my father. I did as I was told. I told Father about finding Hanna at the party but did not mention the twins. Hanna and Mother were still talking when we returned to the kitchen. We all sat down together and I then told my parents that they were grandparents to twins.

Father looked carefully at us and said, "You really work fast, don't you. You only went to Europe two weeks ago."

I laughed and said, "They are eighteen years old and you will get to meet them as soon as we can arrange it." They both looked at us with a little question and lots of shock on their faces. Hanna reached into her purse and brought out a picture of the four of us. All they could say was, "Oh my God."

Mother then jumped up and gave us both a big hug. We all just stood there saying nothing until Mother broke the silence with two words—"The wedding?"

I laughed and said, "Not yet but we must have had one of the longest engagements on record and you will certainly be there."

We talked for most of the day. I went to the barn to help Father do the evening chores and Hanna helped Mother get dinner ready. I suspected that Hanna got to do little more than sit and watch.

Mother and Father were quite interested in the fact that Judy had married Dieter, who had been married to Hanna. I believe she was dying to call Judy's mother to tell her all of the news. As we were leaving, Hanna gave the picture of the four of us to Mother. Mother was so happy she was almost in tears. Father did his usual quiet, almost blank, expression. I knew that after we had left Father would let out his emotions in private with Mother. The next morning Mother would be melting the telephone lines to all of her friends and especially to her sisters.

On the way back home that evening Hanna told me she thought my parents were wonderful and made her feel so welcome. Her only wish was that we would not talk so fast because her English was a bit rusty.

The next day I went into the office with my roll of drawings and got back to work. We had a series of meetings and then headed out to the client's office with our new drawings and a lot of good news for them. Hanna stayed at the house and got caught up on her sleep. I came home that evening, all happy to see her. She was as happy to see me and met me with an embrace and a good-evening kiss. I had called her earlier in the afternoon about going out to dinner and she told me that would be a great idea as everything in the refrigerator looked like a science experiment.

We decided to go to a small French restaurant downtown. It had always been a favorite of mine, the food was great and I loved the atmosphere. The restaurant was so small that the bread baskets were hung from the ceiling by ropes that you raised and lowered. We chatted for a few minutes and then I started to tell Hanna about a problem that I had encountered that day on one of my projects. I stopped short. She looked at me and asked if there was something wrong. I explained how I felt that Judy and I had drifted apart because all we ever talked about was work. We had never really discussed anything to do with us and I was not going to let that happen again. I hoped that from now on our conversations would center on us and our family and the work chatter must be secondary. I also added that we had a lot of years to catch up and I fully intended to do just that. Hanna was quiet for a second, obviously thinking about what I had said and how to respond to my little outburst. She then said that she thought that what I had said was an excellent idea but wondered how we could do that as we were both principals of our companies and our life to date had been controlled by our work. I thought for a moment and suggested that we could either sell out our portions of our companies or become silent partners. We would have more than enough money to invest elsewhere and have an excellent lifestyle for as long as we were around. I leaned across the table and kissed her and told her that I intended to be around with her for a long, long time. I thought for a moment and said that I would speak to my lawyer tomorrow about the wording of my partnership agreement and to the accountants about the worth of the company. Hanna smiled and quietly added that she thought she knew someone who might be interested in buying into her company. Dieter had been acquiring shares in her company since they had bought out his company a number of years ago. She also knew he had substantial investments outside of her company. Hanna felt he might be interested in purchasing enough shares from her so that he would have a controlling interest. That would allow her to step down but still have a very good income. I became somewhat embarrassed as I knew her company was worth far more than mine and stammered, "I did not mean that you should quit. I wasn't suggesting that you should support me."

She laughed at me and countered with "I do not want to hear about your old-fashioned ideas. Fate has put us in this position." She felt that we obviously were meant to get ourselves financially stable before we re-met. We might have otherwise ended up drifting apart like Dieter and her and as Judy and I did. We both felt that we now had the time to devote to each other and we only had a short time with the twins before they made their own lives. Hanna told me that she used to worry how she would feel when the twins left but now that we were together, she knew that her life would be full forever. I was concerned because both of us had very busy careers and to abruptly stop our current fast-paced work schedules when we were both just over forty would not be simple or easy. Hanna agreed that we could not just walk away from our companies on a moment's notice but we would need to arrange an orderly transition. It would take some time. She could already see the division heads lining up to grab her position. She felt that Dieter would make a better replacement than any of them. She also felt that my partners would be getting a little upset with the amount of time that I was not in the office, and suggested that we must find a way for them to think that my departure was their idea. I then thought that we would still need something to keep us occupied and what could be better than a project for both of us to focus on. Neither one of us would do very well living the life of the idle rich. I told Hanna this and she agreed but felt that our new project could wait as we needed to focus all our energy to free ourselves from our companies at this time.

The next part of our lives would be a whirlwind of wedding plans, the wedding and the freeing up of our future for other endeavors.

Chapter 23
Freeing Ourselves

Hanna and I were together for every moment, awake or asleep, except for the odd meeting.

My partners were getting very upset.

My mind was not really on work although they were very pleased with how my project with the chemical plant was progressing and the client was now starting to hint about an additional project at a new site, only "slightly different." In the engineering design world "slightly different" usually means that the only thing the same is the name of the company that owns the plant. The schedule for the new project tentatively called for the design criteria meetings to occur at the same time that Hanna and I had planned our wedding. I used this as an excuse to hand the new project over to one of the other partners. He was concerned about continuity of the design knowledge from the existing project. It took some time for me to convince him that he was more than capable of handling the project. My partners were livid when they heard I was going back to Vienna with Hanna. I was not going to let her get out of my sight and she was doing the same. All we both wanted was simply to be together.

Hanna was using an empty office to handle some problems at her office. The long-distance calls also irritated one of my other partners. He was the "major in minors" type of guy, always running around trying to nickel and dime everything to death.

Hanna and I were both quietly sowing the seeds of discontentment.

When the partners discovered I was really going back to Vienna on the following weekend they were furious.

131

Did I not have projects underway?

Who was going to look after them?

I really don't think that I convinced them that the projects were in good condition. I had picked the various group leaders for the projects because I knew they were the best. The projects did not need me, except as a figurehead. I told everybody I would be back in two weeks.

I had a copy of our partnership agreement with me when we flew back to Vienna. I had been the one to set up our partnership but I wanted to study it in detail to determine what I needed to do when I returned. I also brought with me a copy of the last five year-ends and our current financial status.

Hanna and I boarded the plane, sticking close together. We got to our seats and settled down for the long flight back to Vienna.

We arrived in Vienna mid morning and this time we cleared customs together. The official looked at us closely before taking our passports and asked if we were married. I smiled and answered, "Not Yet." He stamped our passports, hardly even glancing at them, and wished us congratulations.

As we walked away, I turned to Hanna and asked if it was that obvious. She laughed and answered, "I guess it must be so, but do we care?"

We arrived home. I called it home now because it felt like that to me. My family, new as they were to me, were there. Hanna's father had gone to the office but the twins were still at home. They had not gone to school that day because they knew we were coming home. Each had a thousand questions and they asked all of them simultaneously and at high speed. My German was still less than perfect, so I laughed and then asked them to slow down. Hanna took over and told them how she loved Toronto, how my home looked and jokingly told them of the bachelor disaster it had been. She also told them all about my parents and how wonderful they had been to her. They were fascinated about having and meeting their new grandparents. Stefi was totally intrigued that she had a grandmother now and wanted to hear all about her. Hanna and I promised them that we would take them with us on the next trip, probably in three weeks.

I figured that if I stretched my return to Canada from two weeks into three, my partners would become even more upset as they realized that I no longer was a productive member of their team and would soon start to figure out a way to buy me out.

Hanna looked at me and said, "I thought you said we would be going to Canada in two weeks."

I winked at her and said, "Yes, but Wilhelm and Stefi will need the extra time to make sure their schoolwork is caught up and preferably be ahead because we will probably be there for two weeks." The twins objected but Hanna agreed with me and tried to put an end to their objections.

Stefi jumped in with a tirade on Hanna as to how could she possibly know that her schoolwork would require extra time and we should go as planned in two weeks.

I had to step in and strongly advised that three weeks would be our timing and we would not tolerate a needless outburst. Stefi spun around and stomped off leaving behind the comment, "You're just like all of them."

I turned to Hanna, who looked embarrassed, and said, "I guess this officially makes me a father." Hanna and Wilhelm looked at me and then they both burst out laughing. I suspect Stefi did not appreciate our laughing as she did not show up for lunch. Hanna went to her office and I accompanied her. Wilhelm went off to school.

At dinner that evening Stefi acted as if nothing had ever happened.

Hanna arranged for Dieter to come to Vienna to discuss business and he brought Judy with him. Judy and I had a great visit while Hanna broke the news to Dieter about our tentative plan to sell him the controlling interest in the company. He was quite excited, as that had been a dream that he always had, but he believed it would never happen. Dieter told us he would require time to liquidate most of his investments. Hanna and I had a number of discussions on the procedure for selling the company and one of my suggestions was for Hanna to arrange a share swap for some of Dieters better investments. This worked well for Hanna as she now had an income separate from the company.

Now it came to our biggest concern. It was in the form of Hanna's father. We were very bothered as to how he would respond to our idea about Hanna leaving the company. I was worried that he would blame me for putting her up to it.

Hanna's father had dropped around to our home in Vienna and told us he would be in the country if we needed him and could we come out for the afternoon and dinner on Saturday.

Hanna packed an overnight bag and I questioned her as to why it was needed as we were only going for the day. She laughed and told me that the afternoon and dinner invitation really meant we would not get to leave before Sunday afternoon if we were lucky. Stefi and Wilhelm had parties they had already planned to attend so we arranged for the cook to stay at the house until they got home. The day was clear and warm and as we drove out to the estate we discussed various scenarios and how we would approach Hanna's father on our plans. We arrived and we were escorted by Hanna's father to the garden at the back of the house.

The house was quite large and the gardens quite extensive. We got the grand tour of the gardens including getting to meet the newest additions to the flowerbeds. Hanna abandoned us and I got the total tour of the grounds, the house and the outbuildings, one of which used to be the stables. I was quite impressed.

The house consisted of a center hall plan with four large rooms and two smaller ones on the main floor. The four larger rooms consisted of a living room, parlor, dining room and one big bedroom. The two smaller rooms were a kitchen and an office/library. The upper floor was accessed by a large staircase going up from the front hall. Upstairs there were two large bedrooms, three smaller bedrooms and two bathrooms. The furniture was comfortable and dated but did not have the too heavy or too dark look. To my eyes it looked very expensive, but tasteful. The attic had separate servants' quarters and a storage area. The storage area was full of one hundred and fifty years of family collections. There was access to the wine cellar off the dining room. I was very interested in the collection of wines I spotted there. Hanna's father told me that some of the wines were there when he purchased the house about twenty years ago.

I emerged from the tour intact but still having a great fear about dealing with someone who so much enjoyed his connections with the past. How would he feel about selling the company that he started and was his baby?

Hanna met us on the deck at the back of the house with three glasses of chilled white wine and a warm smile.

God, I love this girl.

The deck overlooked the gardens and the countryside, which spread below us like a manicured green carpet. It was hard to believe that such a peaceful setting, not too many years before, had been the site of a war. Hanna passed each of us our wineglass, smiled and said, "I must go and see what the cook has put together for dinner and I will unpack our bags." I knew that I was being left to the mercy of her father.

Hanna's father, whom I was now instructed to refer to as Father, sat down in the chair next to me and turned to me and said, "Now I have your undivided attention, I would like to get to know you. It seems like you might be here to stay this time." I laughed and told him that I would be able to answer most of his questions and I intended on staying around forever.

He asked to hear my version of how we met and what had happened that made us both believe that we were dead. He seemed happy that the stories matched with what he knew from Hanna.

He asked what my plans were regarding where we would live. He was pleased that we were planning to live in Europe and not moving the twins to Canada. I believe he was afraid that we would all move to Canada and leave him alone. He asked about my work and my company in Canada. He was interested in how I was going to handle the buyout with my partners. I told him I had brought our financial statements from the last five years, a copy of our work in progress, a summary of our bank statements and a copy of our partnership agreement. I mentioned I was going through them to formulate a plan of action. He seemed impressed with my planning. He then inquired about what I thought about his company.

Here it comes. I could sense that he was now digging for information regarding Hanna's and my plans.

I told him I was very impressed with the quality of work that I had seen from his company, although most of what I had seen had come from Dieter's division. I said that I believed that the quality would extend throughout the rest of the company.

Never hurts to butter up your father-in-law to be!

He turned away and, looking into his wineglass, wistfully spoke quietly into it and said, "I have worked very hard for many years to provide for my family; successfully, I may add. Hanna joined the firm and was my pride and joy as she stepped up the corporate ladder. I stayed on long after I should have to make sure she had the support that she needed. I know that from time to time, my presence was resented by some of the managers but I do really take joy in driving them nuts. Keeps them on their toes." He chuckled with the last statement and then became serious again and turned to me asking, "What do you and Hanna believe is the right direction for you to take?"

I was now on the hot seat and there was nowhere to go. I sat quietly for a short time looking at the peaceful valley, and waiting for some kind of divine intervention to help me with my answer.

It never came.

I then turned to him and spoke quietly saying, "Hanna and I have looked at many options and as you know sitting on an airplane gives you plenty of time for discussions. We have many things to consider. The twins have their own plans, Stefi is planning on an artistic career and Wilhelm is considering law. I would not be a good manager in a European engineering firm any more than you would be a good manager in a Canadian engineering firm. The philosophies are too different." I paused for a moment staring at my wineglass to collect my thoughts. Hanna's father let the silence stand and waited for me to continue.

I complied and followed with, "Hanna and I have a lot of lost time to make up and we wish to be with each other as much as possible. We also believe that we are too young and too work oriented to ever lead the life of the idle rich. Not that we have the funds in sufficient quantity to be the idle rich." Hanna's father chuckled at the last statement but did not take his eyes off of me. He was not going to let me off the hook. I then took a sip of the wine and continued, "Hanna and I have given some consideration to getting involved in some kind of business where we would both be together every day, all day." I turned and then asked what he thought he would do in our position trying to throw the conversation into his court.

He smiled and said, "I am not in your position, but you have no requirement to create an engineering company that your children could eventually take over because they both seem to be taking an alternate direction in their lives. If you had a business that fit with the career choices of the twins, I would suggest that it would be advantageous to build it up until you no longer wished to run it. For now, your next step would be to sell out your portions of your companies and invest the money wisely so your legacy to your children would be in a form that was useful to them at the end of your life."

I did not know how to respond to that statement but decided to pursue his line of thought as it might lead indirectly to what Hanna and I planned to do.

I then started again and told him that Hanna believed that for her to remain in her present position would require much more of her time than she was willing to dedicate and that as she would prefer to spend the time with the twins and myself she was giving some thought to resigning

He looked somewhat concerned and countered with, "Who would you believe could step in and become the president of the company?"

I smiled and said, "Dieter would be more than capable."

He gave me a sly grin and said, "When were you two going to let me in on all of your plans?"

I realized at this point that he had a very good idea what we had in mind and was playing with us.

My only concern was whether he agreed with what we had in mind.

I then asked him if he would care for more wine. He smiled and told me he had more than sufficient and as I had hardly touched mine, I should not require any more.

So much for that escape route. I guessed I had better continue with our conservation. He was not going to be sidetracked.

At this point I decided that the direct approach was probably the best route.

I then started again by saying that Hanna and I believed the best route for us was to sell a number of shares to Dieter, so that he would have sufficient interest in the company that a promotion to president could not be challenged. I told him that Hanna and I knew that we would need to maintain a reasonable income so we could continue a lifestyle similar to what we were used to. He was quite surprised when I told him that we had talked with Dieter and believed that a cash purchase of some shares and a share swap with some of Dieter's other investments would be best. It would give us an income without any problems with capital gains tax. I suggested that it might take some time before my partners could come up with the cash to buy me out but that was a problem for me to solve. Hanna's father interjected at this point by saying that any problem of mine was now a problem for Hanna. I realized what he had meant so I apologized and started to continue.

We were interrupted by Hanna, who came to tell us dinner would be ready in fifteen minutes and wondered if we would like to freshen up ourselves for dinner. I welcomed the interruption as it gave me time to formulate my next response. It also gave me some time to talk to Hanna and get her feedback on what had transpired. We could then formulate a plan on how we would respond to her father's prodding.

Hanna and I went up to our room and I explained how our conversation had progressed. She did not seem overly alarmed on how far the conversation had gone without her. We then discussed our approach and felt that we should both be there during the next discussion as she knew how direct her father could be. We decided that we would work together during dinner to break the entire news of our plans to him and hoped he would react favorably. We did not want a family feud of any kind.

Dinner was wonderful. It consisted of wild boar, rice pilaf, vegetables, multigrain rolls and breads, wines and light conversation. Hanna's father did not let us get even close to what we wanted to discuss.

We retired to the library and he closed the door behind us.

We were now both on the hot seat.

He smiled and told us there were too many people in the dining room for family discussions. I failed to see how one cook could destroy all of the family plans but this was his home and he was head of it.

The three of us sat down and he served us a glass of armagnac. He considered it much better than cognac because he believed it was much smoother. I agreed.

He started by looking into his glass and saying, "This drink is like a life. Much work has gone into its creation. Time has been used to let it mature into a thing of beauty and as life is, its beauty must be sampled in the proper place and context for its true self to come forward."

Hanna and I both knew this was not the time for interjection. We sat quietly, waiting for him to continue.

Continue he did, and promptly put us in our place as his children.

Smiling he then stated, "I believe what you two are planning is a good idea. The company has grown far beyond what I ever envisioned. It has become an impersonal monolith. The company in the past had a heart. I used to know everyone by name and had at the least some knowledge of their families. Now I barely know the division managers. The company is no longer me. I am going to resign as the chairman of the board of directors, which means the company must purchase all of the shares that I own. The shares will become available for the managers and staff to purchase. I have some ideas for more extensive gardens and I need some extra funds for those and another project."

He paused and we knew that we should not interrupt. We knew things were going our way and did not want to disturb the situation. We both looked at each other, wondering what the project was.

A few minutes of silence and he continued, "Will has indicated that you might wish to retire from your position as president. In consideration of the arrival of Will and your wish to catch up on lost family time, I think that would be an excellent idea. Will has also indicated that you two would like to find a business where you could both be involved together. I might have found a solution. I am not as much of a dotting old fool as you believe."

We tried to rebuke that statement but he hushed us like two children and continued, "You both have knowledge of good food, wines and entertainment. You both are very good with people. Hanna, you are excellent with Europeans and have very good management skills. Will, you understand the requirements of the North American clients and how to manage their whims."

Hanna and I looked at each other. We were at a total loss where this conversation was headed. The only option we had was to let him continue, so we did just that.

He followed by saying, "I have done some research and found out that a certain establishment, which by the way was the site of the deed which resulted in the greatest grandchildren ever conceived, might be available. The building will need some upgrading as little has been done for thirty years. With that upgrading and some good promotion it could become reasonably profitable. I may add that the establishment is in Austria not Germany as both of you thought. The only part I dislike is it is a long way from Vienna.

Hanna and I looked at each other, questioning each other with our eyes. How did he find out where the old hotel was? We were not even sure of the name or location of it ourselves.

He saw our surprise and laughed saying, "I bet you can't figure out how I knew the name of the hotel that you two young rascals went to. Hanna's mother and I went to it before we were married. I recognized the hotel from your pictures that were taken when you were there. Hanna, you were the result of that escape from my parents and your mother's parents."

It was Hanna's turn to be shocked and mine to chuckle. Hanna glared at me when she heard my chuckle. I quickly assumed a smug look but she could still see the amusement on my face.

Hanna and I both felt it was now our turn to get involved with this conversation so we both jumped in.

I told him that he had a better memory than I did. I asked if he really felt that Hanna and I would make good hotel keepers.

Hanna added that the hotel clients could not be worse or more demanding than some of the engineering clients she had dealt with. I added that she was probably quite right. Hanna's father then told us that after I arrived on the scene—taking the glory away from his party, by the way—he realized that things would not continue as they had been.

The telephone rang interrupting our conversation.

It was Wilhelm telling us that Stefi was in the hospital. She had been in car accident with several of her friends. He said she was all right but they wanted to keep her in overnight for observation.

Chapter 24
All's Well
That Ends Well

Hanna was a mess worrying about how Stefi was doing. We grabbed all of our stuff, including Father, and headed back to Vienna. Wilhelm told us that everything was under control but Hanna, her father and I wanted to know firsthand and the only way was to go there ourselves.

On the way to the hospital Hanna recovered her composure somewhat and asked me if I still thought being a father was the best. First there was Stefi's outburst and now a medical emergency. I smiled, hugged her close and said, "The learning curve is steeper than I thought."

Hanna smiled and said, "You should have been here during the early years with childhood colds, falls, scrapes, fights at school and all of the trials and tribulations of growing up."

I wistfully looked out the window and sighed. I only wished I had been there.

We arrived at the hospital. Stefi was bruised but basically uninjured. The doctors wanted to be sure there were no internal injuries before letting her go home.

Wilhelm was there with his girlfriend, about whom we had only heard rumors but nobody had actually met her.

The accident had occurred at a dance where someone had gotten upset and left in a huff. The driver had been drinking and roared out of the parking lot just as Stefi and her girl friends drove in.

Head on.

Stefi was in the backseat and went over the seat into the front seat. Her injuries were to her chest and stomach as she hit the back of the front seat.

Seeing Stefi in good spirits relaxed Hanna and the rest of us substantially, so we diverted our attention to Wilhelm's girlfriend. She was initially awkward having to meet The Mother and soon warmed up to all of us. She was much more interested in meeting the new father, having heard all about me. I guess I passed the inspection as I got lots of smiles. Hanna's father sat quietly near Stefi's hospital bed, looking relieved but very tired.

We talked to the doctor, who assured us that Stefi was doing just fine but he could not release her until the next morning because there was no staff to do the release documents which would let her leave the hospital. We had a big discussion and decided we would go back out to Father's home and Wilhelm would bring Stefi out in the morning. He looked at us and at his girlfriend with a big question on his face. Hanna smiled and told him he should bring his girlfriend out also. He beamed at that suggestion.

We drove the hour back out into the country to Father's estate. When we got there Hanna's father suggested our discussion would be best continued in the morning before the twins got there. He was very tired what with the dinner discussions and our Stefi emergency.

Hanna and I retired to our room, unpacked our bag again and headed to bed.

She snuggled up to me and I whispered into her ear, "Did you ever think that we are not setting a very good example for our kids?"

Hanna lifted up and looked at me and asked, "What do you mean by that?"

I smiled and said, "Don't you think the fact that their parents are not married sends a wrong message to them? I think we should get some real wedding plans started as soon as possible."

Hanna gave me a big kiss and said, "As far as I am concerned we are married but you are right, we should make it official. I think the best place would be here. Father would not need to travel. There are lots of bedrooms for guests, eight if we count the attic rooms. Most of the rooms would require some updating but the cost would not too high. There is an excellent caterer in town and our cook would love to have the chance to oversee everything."

Hanna then turned over onto her stomach, leaning on her elbows, and looked at me. She continued, "How many guests would there be? There would be your parents and your sister and her husband. How many others from your side?"

I laughed and said, "We will need a list. Actually three lists. One for guests who will come, one for guests who might come and one for guests who won't come."

Hanna got up, found a pencil and a pad of paper and we started to make our lists. The final list was actually quite short with only about thirty-five people on the three lists. We wanted to keep it small and manageable. The list with the won't-come people contained mostly friends of mine who we thought would not be able or want to spend the money for the trip but I wanted them to know that they were welcome.

The next morning we met Father in the summer dining room. He was quite cheerful but suggested that late nights were no longer a good thing for him. We told him about the wedding plans that we had made the night before. He agreed that we should get married as soon as possible as after all with the way we were acting there might be an incident like the last time we were together. We assured him there would not be.

He thought that having the wedding at the estate would be the best but he would require some time to get the old castle livened up. He said there would probably be some guests that he would like to add to the list. We laughed and told him that we did not need the list expanded to three hundred and fifty.

Over breakfast we changed the subject to the company business and we told him we would be taking the twins to Canada to meet their other grandparents and the rest of my family. He wanted to know when and we told him in about two weeks.

Late that morning Stefi, Wilhelm and his girlfriend arrived, Wilhelm having driven them from Vienna. We did the family hugs and tears thing and then Wilhelm disappeared with the current love of his life in tow to give her a tour of the place.

Stefi sat with us, a little worse for wear but acting as her old self.

She told us again what happened and we suggested that it was the luck of the draw being in the wrong place at the wrong time. We assured her that she was not in any trouble and we would not give any lecture, other than for her to remember what too many drinks can do.

We shared our wedding plans with her and showed her the guest list. I had purposely left her name off and you should have seen her face when she discovered it. She was quite indignant. I laughed and told her that she could be either a bridesmaid or the flower girl. She quickly chose the bridesmaid telling us she was much too old to be the flower girl. Hanna was planning on asking Judy to be the maid of honor and I was hopeful that Dieter could be the best man.

Hanna's father suggested that Stefi go and find out what Wilhelm and his girlfriend were doing. Off she went, leaving us to further our discussions.

Hanna's father took the opportunity to share with us what he had been up to during the past few weeks while we were in Canada and during the time after we had returned.

He had checked out the old hotel and gone to see it. He had come to an agreement of sale with the current owner, who wished to retire, and had made him an offer subject to our approval. He planned on using some of the funds from the sale of his shares to make a substantial down payment for us on the hotel. He told us that it would be our wedding present. This was the project that he had mentioned earlier. He felt that the sale of the house in Vienna where Hanna now lived would provide enough funds to renovate the hotel and upgrade all of the facilities. All he wanted was twelve bottles of the best wines from the wine cellar. He then told us he had already picked out the bottles.

Hanna and I were very excited and I was somewhat embarrassed by his generosity. I had been brought up with North American standards, where a couple was expected to make it on their own.

He told me firmly that in Europe if a father could get his children started off he was just doing his job as a parent. He then added that he would be more than comfortable with what was left.

I stammered my thanks for his generosity.

Life was certainly becoming much different that I had ever

expected when I came to Europe to solve some engineering problems.

Wilhelm and his girlfriend went back to Vienna and Stefi stayed with us for a couple of days while we finalized the details of our wedding plans.

We went to talk to the caterer and plan the meals.

Neither one of us was very active in the church so we met with a non-denominational minister, who agreed to marry us.

The caterer helped us arrange for a marquis tent on the back lawn. We both wanted to write our own vows and the minister encouraged it.

Father contacted a painting contractor who was to paint the trim on the outside of the house and all of the walls on the inside.

We went to an upscale linen store and purchased new linens for all of the bedrooms and bathrooms. Most of the mattresses needed to be replaced so they were added to the purchase. We then arranged for everything to be delivered after the painting was completed.

We had picked a date for our wedding that suited as many people as possible, including the contractors doing the painting who would be finished, and the paint would have time to be thoroughly dry. The date had been set eight weeks away. This gave us time to go to Canada to settle some of my business affairs that I needed to finalize and for Wilhelm and Stefi to meet my family.

That was a whirlwind two weeks. The invitations had to be printed and mailed. We mailed the Europe invitations from Vienna and we planned to mail the Canadian ones in Canada.

We then arranged the tickets for the four of us to fly to Toronto and began to pack our things. Hanna suggested that I take along a spare suitcase so I could bring more of my things back from Canada. Wilhelm and Stefi were very excited and had consulted me on what to wear. They did not want to look strange. They wanted to look North American. I ensured them that blue jeans were the standard.

The four of us took a taxi to the airport and settled in for the long flight to Toronto. Hanna and I sat together, as close as we could. We talked about our plans, the hotel, her father's generosity and how the twins and my parents would react to each other. We also mulled over the strategy that I would use to convince my partners to buy my shares. Everything seemed to be falling nicely into place.

Chapter 25
First Family Visit to Canada

We arrived in Toronto after an uneventful flight with only one stopover in London. Hanna and Stefi had persuaded us to spend one night in London. They were only interested in one thing—shopping. Wilhelm and I did the usual tourist things, seeing the Tower of London, London Bridge and what ever else that happened to meet our fancy. Hanna and Stefi did a little damage in Harrods and were beaming as they showed us their loot.

In Toronto we took a cab to my home. Stefi and Wilhelm looked around at it and casually mentioned that it was nice but certainly smaller than their home in Vienna. I don't think they were too impressed. I reminded them that only one person lived in the house and he was never there.

As we all agreed to wait until the weekend to visit my parents, we did the downtown tour as well as a quick look at the suburbs. The twins were surprised at the distances as we traveled from place to place and the space of the area and the size of Lake Ontario located on the south side of Toronto. Hanna had been experiencing the same surprises during her first trip so she was able to play the expert.

The next morning we left the twins at my place and went to the office for the morning. My partners met us in my office and were very displeased that I was a week late coming home. They were very upset to say the least, and made some suggestions about my lack of dedication to the company. They were also making noises about some new projects that had come in that I would need to manage. Our subsequent conversations upset them further when they realized that I was really moving to Vienna. One of the partners made the comment that he felt it was time for me to leave the firm.

Finally they were thinking my way!

I turned to him and told him that it might be a good plan for me to follow his lead but I could not just leave the company. I did own a substantial portion of the company and my shares would have to be purchased by the other partners or by new partners. I then told them that I knew what the value of the firm would be and how much the shares that I owned were worth.

All of the partners sat in shock as I turned and went out into the office to see how the chemical plant project was progressing.

It was on schedule and the hours used to date were well below what we had estimated.

I checked on Hanna and she was working on some documents that she had brought with her. She looked at me and said, "I'll be happy when this part is all over."

We went home at noon and took the twins out to lunch. After lunch we dropped them off on the main shopping corridor downtown and went back to the office.

My partners had used the intervening time to have nonstop discussions on what to do about me. I was the first of the partners to leave the firm because all of us were fairly young and not within normal retirement age.

They called me into the boardroom but I waited several minutes before I did go in to meet with them. They asked how I came to the figure for the value of my shares. I explained how the valuation was determined using the work in progress, a value for goodwill, money in the bank, and several other factors. They were shocked how high the figure was and they made many comments on how would they ever come up with the money. I explained how it could be a combination of money from them and additional funds derived from new associates and partners that they could bring in from existing employees. Their faces showed silent shock. I suggested to them that this day had been coming for a long time and if it hadn't been me it would be one of them. I then explained that in order for the firm to continue to grow new blood was needed and ownership was one of the best ways to create devoted employees, who would work hard to build their equity in the company. I showed them how the bank would give a loan to purchase the shares using our cash on hand and their personal notes as collateral. This, I explained, would give them time to determine whom they wanted as new associates and partners and I would no longer appear as a salary-drawing, non-productive employee.

I thanked them all, placed a copy of the information on the table and left the boardroom with a large internal smile and a straight face. I met Hanna and we went to pick up the twins downtown.

The twins were at a small restaurant, where I had told them we would meet them. The owner was George, an old friend of mine. He was quite startled when Wilhelm had walked in because he looked so much like me. He had asked Wilhelm his name and when he replied, with his German accent, George became totally bewildered and quickly returned to the back of the restaurant to contemplate what he had seen.

Hanna and I walked in, spotted the twins, walked over and sat down with them. As we inquired how their shopping day had been, George recognized my voice and hurried from the back of the restaurant. He greeted me warmly and then looked at Hanna, then me, then the twins and realized we were a family and started to stutter something. I laughed at his difficulties and decided to put him at rest and said, "I didn't know I had a family either until a month ago." We all had a drink and a light snack and headed home. Me with my prize, Hanna, and the twins with their prize purchases. Toronto did not have the selections in their shops that Vienna had but it had the brand names that the twins had only heard about so they were extremely pleased. When they got home they would have different things than any of their friends and that to them was very, very important.

We ate our dinner at home that evening and talked about the day and what we wanted to do during the next few days. I told them of a restaurant in Toronto called Vesuvius that had received recognition several years running as the best pizza in Toronto. They were both quite intrigued by the concept of ordering a custom-made pizza and

149

having it delivered to our home. We all agreed we would have to order in pizza the next night for dinner. I told them that I thought it was truly the best pizza I had ever had. They fully agreed after filling their faces with several slices each the next evening.

The twins were intrigued by the television shows. I was bored as usual with them. Hanna had no interest either.

The next two days were a repeat of the first with endless meetings with the partners, accountants, and lawyers. On Thursday afternoon I told them I would not be in on Friday. That produced another round of comments, all of which I ignored.

Friday morning we all drove to my parents' home and again I heard the observations how different Canada was from their home. All the time they were truly intrigued by the wide open spaces and the distances between everything.

We arrived, again Mother meeting us at the door and Father somewhere out in the backfields. Mother was very excited to meet her new grandchildren and had made more food than would be required to feed an army for a week. Stefi was so excited to meet her grandmother that she had started to babble and started to drop into German when she spoke. I had to keep reminding her to speak in English. Wilhelm was just as excited and unsuccessfully tried to hide it. Hanna and I were quite amused with his performance. I left Stefi and Hanna with my mother so they could get to know each other and Wilhelm and I took the truck and drove out to the fields to locate Father. Wilhelm was quite excited to ride in the truck and was amazed again with all of the open space around us. We found Father in one of the backfields, all dusty but smiling as he recognized me when we drove up. We got out and walked over to him. His face showed shock when he looked at Wilhelm and realized that he finally had a real grandson. He kept saying over and over how he could not believe how much we looked alike.

The rest of the afternoon and the following two days were taken by a family getting to know itself. Wilhelm and I helped Father to do the chores around the farm. Wilhelm was totally intrigued by the cattle and other livestock that were part of a standard southern Ontario farm. He had been born and raised in Vienna and his only country excursions had been to Hanna's father's estate. Stefi and

Hanna spent most of their time with my mother in and around the house. The farm home was furnished comfortably but certainly not expensively. Stefi seemed to enjoy the lack of formality. The three girls all went into town to check out the shopping. The shopping was very limited compared to Toronto, although Stefi managed to find some more labels that she had heard about that were not available in Vienna. Meals were the usual farm style—plain home cooking and lots of it.

Mother was in her element. She had a young male with a huge appetite to feed again.

My parents were really excited to hear about our wedding plans. They were both very pleased when they opened their invitation and found the two plane tickets for them to fly to Vienna for the wedding.

Monday morning we drove back to Toronto. Hanna stayed with the twins and I went to the office. My partners were practically standing at the door waiting for me. They had been working all weekend trying to sort out the buyout. My lawyer joined us after lunch. The meetings and discussions went on all that afternoon, through the next morning and into the following afternoon before we had a tentative agreement.

I had elevated my selling price because I knew they would try to beat me down. I had a minimum value that I was willing to accept before I dug in my heels. On Friday morning we met to finalize the details of the agreement and by noon the lawyers left to have the final documents completed. It had been a tough week. On Friday evening we celebrated with the partners and their wives. I believed some of the other wives made note on what had transpired and were making plans for their future.

On Saturday morning we all got up early, packed our bags and headed north in the car. I was so happy to spend the day giving Hanna, Wilhelm and Stefi a scenic tour to my favorite place, Georgian Bay, and to Silverthorne Lodge, where I had rented a cottage for the following week. The cottage was just off the beach and the food in the dining room was superb. The water was warm and safe for swimming. Stefi was quite taken by the son of the family in the next cottage. He was clearly smitten with her. Her bikini did nothing to slow down his hormones. Watching the situation develop over the week was quite amusing except for the fact that she was my daughter. I was getting close to tying her to her bed until she was twenty-five. Hanna was much more rational. He was from near my parents' home and was quite disappointed when he found out she was from Vienna. The week could not have been better.

Hanna and I got to relax and spend time with each other.

Stefi found her first love and Wilhelm had a great time with some other boys in the area mostly kicking a ball around the beach and swimming. They once did get into a few bottles of beer. None of them were in good shape the next morning but no harm had been done.

We drove back to Toronto and met my parents at my house. They had come to see us off. We all hugged each other good-bye but were glad that we would be seeing each other in a few weeks. It had been a wonderful visit and the twins had really enjoyed spending time with their new grandparents.

Father and Mother asked the twins if they would like to come for a longer visit later in the summer emphasizing the point 'without their parents.' I chuckled and Hanna looked surprised when they both replied with a yes at the same time.

Later during the flight home Hanna discussed the twins' trip and laughed when I said, "I don't think they realize what they are getting themselves into, two city kids for two weeks on a farm."

Hanna smiled and said, "I think Stefi has alternate ideas. Do you remember the boy in the next cabin? He lives only twenty miles from your parents."

I quickly turned to her and feigning horror said, "Now you tell me."

The trip home was uneventful. Hanna's father met us at the airport and drove us home. He went back to his country estate and we caught up on the jetlag.

Chapter 26
The Wedding Plans

Now that we were at home it was time to get serious about our wedding plans. We also needed to make a trip to check out our new hotel and get the renovations started. Hanna and I knew that there was a lot of work to be done and a lot of decisions to be made on how the renovations were to be approached. I knew from previous field experience that any renovations done on old buildings would be a lot more complicated than most people initially think. A building as old as the hotel would have many secrets hidden behind its walls. Some of these secrets would probably require major structural work to repair.

We flew to the airport nearest to the hotel, rented a car and drove up to the hotel. The drive was spectacular and Hanna and I talked on the way, commenting on how neither one of us remembered coming this way before. I thought a large part of the reason would be the small detail of about twenty-some years since we had been there. Of course there was the other factor that we had eyes only for each other when we were last here.

When we arrived we both recognized the hotel although someone had unsuccessfully tried to do some modernization on the front entrance. We were happy to see that the red doorknobs were still there and that they were as big as we remembered. The modernizations had been messed up badly. We had requested that the previous owner be there for a handover meeting. He was hesitant to meet us, obviously because he had tried to pull a few fast moves on us. We knew that he had already tried to increase his profit by moving some equipment out of the hotel and selling it. He had been caught by our real-estate agent, who called the police. We actually were pleased to have the stuff gone as now there was no need to dispose of it. We also knew he had falsified his reservation records to show that the hotel was much more successful than it really was. The hotel had already been closed so the renovations could be started as soon as we finalized the contractors. We suspected the deposits had not been sent back for the canceled reservations but rather pocketed by the previous owner. That was a detail which was hopefully not our problem.

The planned opening was estimated to be in six to eight months.

The previous owner had the same first name as his grandfather, Hans. Old Hans had been the innkeeper when Hanna and I stayed there. Hans showed us around telling us some of the history of the various rooms. He showed us the lower areas including the wine cellar. He laughed when he told us how Hanna's father had requested an inventory of the wine and how he had personally supervised the taking of the inventory. Hanna's father had then selected twelve bottles and asked that they be set aside for him. Hans showed us the kitchen and the area where he had lived.

The kitchen was going to require some serious renovations, which of course translated into serious money. The refrigeration systems, to put it mildly, were very limited. The whole area was very poorly laid out. The cook had an excellent reputation so we felt he would be kept on and hoped he could help organize the kitchen for better workflow.

Hans was very flippant about many of the things that he showed us. He tried to rush us past areas that needed repair or in areas where a repair had been done in a very haphazard manner. I had to tell him that we were only after information and he already had his money so he need not worry about the deal falling through. I felt very uneasy about Hans. He gave me the impression that he could not be trusted, sort of like the stereotype of the greased-back-haired used car salesman.

Something bothered me about the basement, especially the wine cellar area. I quietly asked Hanna to get rid of Hans by doing an upstairs tour. She looked at me with a question in her eyes. I smiled and told her that I would tell her later, after Hans had left. She smiled and complied. Hans and Hanna went upstairs and I excused myself saying I wished to look outside. I walked around the outside of the building, making mental notes of the walls and foundations. They were both of stone and showed no differences except where you would expect it. I then went down into the basement and paced off the various areas making some notes in my book. I checked the wine cellar and again paced it off and noted the dimensions. Something did not add up. I then made a sketch of the area and determined that there was an area missing along one end of the lower area adjacent to the wine cellar. I then went up to the main floor and paced it off and determined that one wall must be about eight feet thick. I returned to the basement and checked the wine cellar. One wall seemed a slightly different stone construction than the rest of the basement. That wall had a lot of wine racks so it had been hard to check. I heard Hans and Hanna coming down so I quickly grabbed several bottles, put them on the bench, and pretended to be looking at them.

Hanna laughed when they came in saying, "I'm not surprised to find you snooping out the wine but I think Father beat you to it."

I laughed and said, "You never know."

She looked at me, realizing that I might know something she did not. We escorted Hans to his car, thanking him for the tour and asked him if he could help us with some questions later. He smiled and said he would be more than pleased to be of assistance at any time in the future. We both knew that Hans would not be available anymore as we suspected Hans was about to disappear from our part of the country. I was very pleased that he would be out of our hair. Something in the back of my mind told me that I had discovered something good.

I rushed Hanna back into the hotel and laid out my rough sketches on the table. I explained the differences between the basement layout and the outside of the building. Hanna looked at me and asked what could be in the missing area. I took her down to the wine cellar and showed her the differences in the stone that made up the walls. Three walls were the same structure as the rest of the basement while one, the one that was hard to see because of the wine racks, was different but not by much. It seemed to be of a younger construction. We then went upstairs and went to the wall that I estimated to be about eight feet thick. It was on the outside of a sitting room that, according to Hans, had at one time been the smoking and brandy room when the hotel had been in better times. The old bookshelves now were used for junk storage. I very carefully checked all of the woodwork surrounding the old shelving and noticed that the carpet on the floor was worn more in front of one of the cabinets. Hanna was looking at me like I was slightly deranged. I smiled and asked, "Did you ever see any of the old castle movies where there was always a secret passage to the dungeon? I think we might have one here someplace."

She laughed and said, "Oh, Will, this is not Hollywood, you know."

I laughed with her but continued with my search. I found an interesting joint in the woodwork and looking around saw nothing which could be used as a pry bar, so rushed to the kitchen and returned with two very sturdy knives.

Hanna laughed again at me with the comment, "I do not think you will need those to protect us from the monsters hidden behind that wall." Her laugh quickly changed to a look of interest when I inserted one of the knives in the crack and the cabinet moved. I got the larger knife into the crack and the cabinet moved outwards. I then got my hands on the edge of the cabinet and swung it open revealing an opening, which led to two stairs, one going down and one going up. Both of the stairs were very dusty, obviously not used for many years. I went back to the kitchen and got a flashlight. We both stepped carefully into the passage, and shining the light around, found an electrical light switch. I turned it on and the lights still worked.

Hanna tugged my sleeve and said with a chuckle, "Let's go down to the dungeon and count the bodies in chains and check out to see if any of the torture equipment still works."

I laughed and said, "Who's in Hollywood now?"

We went down the stairs, hanging on to each other like two kids in a haunted house. After passing through a small doorway we found ourselves in the other half of the wine cellar. There were two cots near the entrance, probably used by someone hiding from the Nazis during the war. The real find was rows and rows of cases of wine stacked tight along the walls several cases deep. I went over, dusted off some of the cases and checked the labels and vintage dates. The youngest that I saw was 1934 and the oldest was 1920. I gently picked up one bottle and holding it in my hand looked at Hanna and said, "The old Mr. Hans blocked up this area so the Germans could not get at his best wines. Do you realize the value of the wine in this cellar? If we sold this wine the renovations would be free."

Hanna's eyes riveted on the wine bottle. She came over and took it from my hands. Holding it up to the light she commented, "Do you realize what we could charge for a room if we have a wine list that includes what is here in this room? There must be twenty thousand bottles here." I looked over at the wall and quickly counted at least fifty wooden cases of Chateau LaTour 1920. They were stacked eight high. I was in shock. I did a quick inventory making notes in my book. The list contained some 1926 Chateau Haut-Briot, 1929 Chateau Cheval Blanc, 1934 Chateau Margaux and also some 1927 Cockburn and Taylor Ports. There were many other wines of less stature. I turned to Hanna and with a low whistle said, "The value of this wine is greater than the value of the hotel with the renovations completed. Young Hans never knew about this room or none of these wines would be here now. I'll bet he would be really furious if he ever found out about the wines that we see here and he missed selling them. I think we had better get a good lock on this room."

We then followed the stairs back up to the main floor and continued upwards to see where the other stairs went. The stairs went past all of the other floors and right up to the attic of the hotel. There we found a large quantity of furniture stored, mostly under dust covers. Hanna went over it checking some of the markings underneath and laughed under her breath. I inquired what was so funny.

She turned to me, with eyes sparkling, and added to our wonder by saying, "Old Hans did the same with all of the good furniture as he did with the good wine. He hid it from the Nazis. He must have replaced it with cheap stuff when the war started and either never got around to putting it back in service after the war or died before he could. If you remember, Grandfather Hans was very old when we were here in 1944. Young Hans probably never knew that this stuff ever existed. The only other person who might have known that this furniture was here would have been Old Hans's son, who was probably killed in the war. We will truly be able to return this old hotel to its original splendor."

I told Hanna we had better get the passage closed up before any workmen decided to investigate. I then suggested we would need to get a vault-type door on the wine cellar as soon as possible, but until then we should hire a security company. We planned to renovate the attic and make it an apartment for Hanna and me. We agreed that we would move the furniture into storage elsewhere and then get new upholstery for it and that the wine must not be moved because if we did we may ruin it.

The following week we had the furniture removed and placed in storage but not before we had a stonemason block up the wine cellar. He did not see what was in the wine cellar. We had told him the area was access to an old water storage tank and the floors were unsafe. Since the doorway at the bottom of the stairs leading into the cellar looked very small and grimy, I think he thought that my story was plausible. Two weeks later the furniture was sent for refinishing and new upholstery. The owner of the refinishing company was astonished at the furniture, saying they had not seen anything like it for many years. He was amazed to get so many pieces in such good condition. The furniture was comprised of all of the bedroom pieces including beds, chairs, side tables and mirrors as well as the dining room pieces including the tables and chairs, mirrors, pictures and sideboards. All of the pieces from the old smoking room were there including sofas, chairs, tables, mirrors, pictures, and a large stack of books. We even found some carpets rolled up. Old Hans had really cleared out all of the good pieces. Later on we located a lot of dishes, glasses and stemware stored in another part of the attic along with a box containing five spare red doorknobs. I could hardly believe that the attic stayed at the top of the building with the weight of the goodies that were stored up there.

We called Hanna's father the next evening to see if everything was still in order. He suggested that we come back to Vienna to straighten out some business items and see if we agreed on some ideas he had for our wedding. We asked him if he could give us the titles of three or four of the best wines that he could think of. He did, but wanted to know why we wanted to know. My only answer was, "We will tell you later."

We organized a local general contractor to oversee the project and left a couple days later with a bottle of the best wine for Hanna's father carefully wrapped in our carry-on luggage. We arrived in Vienna late at night and took a taxi home. The twins met us at the door with a million stories about their week at home.

Chapter 27

Will and Hanna Are Still Freeing Up Their Futures

The next morning Hanna went off to the office to deal with some of the issues that had come up and I called my old company to see what was happening with my buyout. I got the usual sob stories and I had to threaten my to-be-ex-partners with legal and media reprisals so they would get their lawyers moving again on the paperwork for the buyout. I was promised that the legal papers would be available later that week. I was not going to fly back until my lawyer had the papers in his hot little hands. I made a second call to my lawyer to bring him up to date on the conversation and gently suggested that he get off his butt and get his part of the paperwork finished. My frustration was building, as all I wanted was to get this whole thing over with so that we could all move on with our lives.

Hanna came home after lunch and we decided that we would spend the next couple of days finalizing the thousand little details around the wedding. We worked together all afternoon and got the guest list finished for the place cards and napkins and took it to the printer's. The rest of the printing had already been completed.

Hanna's father dropped in mid-week for a visit and to see what we were up to. I presented to him the bottle of wine that had come from the hidden cellar. His face lit up when he read the label of the wine. His only comment was, "Where did you get this bottle? The last thing I heard about this wine was that one of the very last bottles was sold at Christie's. This is amazing!" Hanna and I both laughed and told him there were at least two more cases and we owned them.

I then asked him if he could remember what the wine list had been when he was last at the hotel. He smiled and told us he vaguely remembered it was quite good with some special bottles that he could not afford. We then told him about the hidden wine cellar. He laughed telling us that old Hans must have been a sly old devil and laughed even harder when he realized how very upset that young Hans would be if he ever found out about the wine. The value of the wine at auction would be as much as the value of the hotel. He then said he would like to save this special bottle that we had just given him for the toast at our wedding.

I made several trips back to Canada to finalize my affairs.

The buyout by my partners was stalling because the partners were all dragging their feet. My lawyer was doing his best and was confident that the sale would go through but we wanted the price to stay as it was and not to be renegotiated because of an artificially low value created by the partners. I was getting very upset and decided to bury my frustrations with a good meal. The best place to go where I knew I would get a sympathetic ear was George's restaurant. I went in and sat down. George came from his perch at the till and sat with me. He had all sorts of questions about Hanna, the twins and life in general. I then told him about my problems with my partners. His face darkened with thought and then a glint appeared in his eyes.

I sensed that I had told my problem to the right person.

He told me all my partners really needed was just a little incentive. I was afraid of what he might be up to. He assured me that no one would get hurt, just a little shook up and he said it would cost me big.

I inquired "How much?"

George said, "How many?"

"Five."

"2500 cash."

Our negotiations were over and done one with in less than thirty seconds.

All George needed was a time when all five partners would be at their homes at the same time. I was getting more concerned as the conversation continued. I thought about this and told George that they would all be home Friday evening because there was a meeting scheduled early Saturday morning at the office that I would be attending with them. George smiled and said, "I open at 11:30 tomorrow morning, be here with the cash, all twenties."

With trepidation, I complied with the request the next morning. George accepted the money graciously. To clear my mind I went to talk with my real-estate agent.

I never heard until a number of years later what actually happened but when I went to the meeting on Saturday there were five ashen-faced partners who were telling their lawyers to shut up as they quickly signed all of the necessary papers to buy my shares of the company.

What happened was quite interesting. George had a sort of relative, who had some sort of relatives who were not as upstanding citizens as they could be. The relatives all arrived at their designated house at the same time, right around dinnertime. Wearing black outfits with a black facemask they kicked in the front door of each house, started up a chainsaw, which made a deafening racket in the house, and cut the living room chesterfield and coffee table in half and left. Each partner and his family just stood in shock as their telephone rang. Each partner had answered the phone and heard a voice say, "Stop screwing around and do what will be best for everyone in the end." Then a *click*!

I thanked them, picked up my paperwork and bid them good-bye and left with my lawyer. When we got to our cars in the parking lot he grabbed my arm and asked, "What the hell happened in there? Did you do something you should not have done?

I smiled and replied, "I did nothing at all. I guess their values of fair play must have come to the surface."

He shook his head and said, "Someone is bullshitting me but it's probably better that I know nothing more."

I then asked him to transfer the money from the sale of the company to Austria as we previously discussed.

I went back to see George with a five-hundred-dollar bonus for the cousins. I suspect it never got past George. I never asked.

My next couple of trips to Canada were not as stressful although I was busy finalizing the sale of my house, furniture and car. I had to do my rounds of good-byes. The whole thing was time consuming and very trying, especially some of the good-byes to my old friends. They all said they would come to visit us in Vienna but we all knew that, for most of them, it would never happen.

When I was not in Canada I spent most of my time at the hotel supervising the renovations. The old cook and I got along perfectly, especially when he found out that he was able to set up the kitchen as he wished. I did lend a little direction to him because we had some physical limitations but I was able to let him think everything was his idea. I kept a close watch on the integrity of the wine cellar as it was important that no one discover it and steal the wines. We definitively could not take the chance on anyone helping themselves.

Hanna and I were always together when I was in Europe and when I went to Canada she was able to accompany me on several of the trips. The twins came to Canada at the beginning of the summer and we took them to my parents for their summer holiday without us. They spent three weeks with their new grandparents, not without some trials and tribulations for my father and mother. Stefi, true to her hormones, contacted the boy she had met earlier and they spent a lot of time together. She even convinced my mother that it was all right that she go away with him and his parents for a long weekend. Mother obviously forgot how wild my sister had been at her age. I guessed time had tempered her memory. My sister had married a guy she met at a western dance. Although he was quite nice he would never become anything. He had avoided the draft by some technicality that he had never told to us or his family. My father was quite upset with him to the point of being ashamed that he was even related. My sister still thought he was great, so what could I say? Hanna had organized tickets so they could come to the wedding. There was no way they could afford to fly there themselves. I knew that they would also expect the rich brother to pick up the tab while they were in Europe. My big fear had been that they would plan an extended stay and expect us to be their tour guides for all of Europe. Hanna said she would look after that problem. She must have, because the airline tickets they got were only for one week and non-refundable. We had a number of things to look after at the hotel so we could not fly back to Canada to accompany the twins on their flight home. I called my parents and asked them to drive the twins to the airport for the flight home. Wilhelm and Stefi rather liked the fact that they were to make the trip alone and would have to fend for themselves, as the adults they thought they were. Stefi's boyfriend accompanied them to the airport as well as a girl whom Wilhelm had met who lived just down the road from my parents.

Just what we needed, two long-distance romances.

The twins got home in one piece with a thousand stories to tell. Most of the stories that Wilhelm told were about my father and they were a repeat of my times past. I had the heart to listen with interest and not interrupt Wilhelm as he told some of the tales. Stefi could do nothing but tell us the amazing attributes of John, the love of her life. Wilhelm was a little quieter about Susan from down the road, but it was not hard to tell he was quite smitten. Later that evening Hanna and I joked that it would be perfect if John and Susan discovered each other on the way back home, after they dropped Stefi and Wilhelm off at the airport. Judging from the letters that arrived on a regular basis, starting the following week, that did not happen. The twins were already lobbying for their respective flames to come to our wedding. I really did not want to pay for two more tickets to the wedding. I only said, "We will see if it is possible." One evening Hanna told me that she did not think it would be good for Stefi to get involved with someone from North America as there could be too many complications. I laughed at her and said, "Thanks for the compliment." She stammered and tried to talk her way out of that one. I hugged her and told her that us Canadians were not really such a bad bunch. She started to cry in my arms and I just held her tight and gave her a few little kisses. She recovered after a time and again tried to worm her way out of that one. I changed the subject to the hotel by wondering out loud how the refinishing of the furniture was progressing. She was pleased I had let her off the hook.

The rest of the summer was occupied with a whirlwind of details for both the hotel and the wedding. We had a few more surprises at the hotel although none compared to the wine cellar and no more complications than could be expected with the planning of any wedding.

I did pay for the two flames to come over to Vienna for the wedding and the twins were thrilled.

Chapter 28

Hanna Tells About the Wedding

Will and I must have driven each other crazy the last week before the wedding. We had guests coming in from Vienna, Germany and Canada. We had initially put most of the Canadians on the might-come and will-not-come lists and they ended up on the guess-what,- I'm-coming' list. We had to arrange extra accommodation in a hotel in the village near Father's estate. Wilhelm got a full-time job as the airport driver. Stefi got the job as the greeter and where-to-put-your-stuff girl. Father was the warm host who flitted from guest to guest making sure all was in order. Everyone got settled into their appropriate accommodations with as little fuss as possible. We tried to keep the English-only-speaking guests with someone who spoke English and German and we made sure the hotel always had staff available who spoke some English.

The wedding was in my mind absolutely wonderful. My lifelong dream had finally come true. I wore a long, white, simple, straight gown of soft silk with a fine lace top, low cut underneath, and white shoes. I had worked hard in the previous weeks and any excess weight had been disposed of so it fit very well without too many bumps in the wrong places. I bet Will that I was not a gram heavier than I was back in 1945. Will chuckled at me and asked if I really knew what I had weighed back then. I told him of course I did but we both knew that was a lie. Back then weight was never a problem. I could eat and drink whatever I wanted and I always stayed thin. Now

I had to work at it a bit harder. I wanted to do the blushing bride routine and so I did not let Will see me the day of the wedding. In spite of his protests, he spent the night before the wedding in a room at a friend of my father's. He was quite indignant but went along with my whims for the sake of tradition. Judy, Gisele, and Stefi accompanied me as maid of honor and bridesmaids. Dieter was Will's best man and Wilhelm and Tom, a friend of Will's from Canada, were our ushers. Father spent his time running in circles and fussing over everything.

The wedding went on without a hitch. When Father walked me down the aisle, Will was waiting for me with the silliest grin I have ever seen on a man. I believe I was not much better. The photographer took many pictures inside the main house, in the garden and in the carriage that was usually stored down by the stables. He had it brought to the front of the main entrance. I thought it was a bit silly but I was proven quite wrong when the picture proofs were delivered to us a few days later.

The wedding was in mid afternoon followed by the photographer, who made sure the wedding party missed most of the afternoon refreshments. He took his time running around rearranging everything for that perfect shot. He certainly was a pain but he was very good.

The reception and dinner were held in a giant tent that we had installed in the yard behind the house. The location overlooked the valley and with the bright warm sunshine the setting was perfect. The guests filed in to the tent and found their respective seats. Will and I, with the rest of the wedding party in tow, took our place at the head table. I was almost as happy as the day that Will and I had found each other at the company reception. The usual toasts followed, spoken in German and English, and then Father got up and announced that he wished to propose a special toast to us and he would be using a special wine for that toast. He unveiled the bottle on a unique stand designed so he could pour without mixing the sediment. He told everyone the vintage. There was a gasp from a number of people at the wedding when they heard it was a Chateau LaTour 1920. They were amazed that he would actually open the bottle, as it was so rare. Will and I smiled because we knew that we

166

still had at least twenty cases left. Father did not even know that little tidbit.

The wine was wonderful and it was worth every penny that the guests thought it cost. The other twenty or so cases were about to make us very rich. Only a few actually tried the wine as the word traveled around the tables as to the value and a lot of our guests just said they felt it would be better if those who appreciated fine vintage wines tried it because it would be lost on them.

Will and I had talked to Father and we all felt the wedding would be a good place to begin a little promotion for the new hotel. Later during the reception, when Will and I were circulating, a number of people asked where that bottle of wine had come from. We answered that we had given it to Father, it was one of many from our wine cellar, and we were planning on opening a few of the select wines each per month at our new hotel. All those who had interest in wines asked the same question—what other wines did we have? Will answered simply by saying there were many other wines just as good, some not as well known but equally as good. They would be able to see our wine list when we had it ready. They all wanted to know when the hotel was going to open. We got their business cards and told them we would send them the schedules and the wine list when they became available.

Even though we were living together and had two older teenagers, everyone was doing their best to get rid of us like it was always done, with a young newly married couple. They did not want us around to spoil their party.

Will and I got changed into our going away outfits and we were chased out of "their party." We left and went to a small hotel, two towns away. Will had found the hotel when he was driving around getting goodies for the wedding. It had a small spa attached and we spent the following morning having a variety of treatments in the spa. Initially Will was a bit apprehensive about the spa idea but he did enjoy our treatments, especially the massage.

I will get him schooled into some of the European ways before I am finished.

His Canadian way of making love does not need to improve.

We got back to my father's home later in the afternoon. Many of the guests had come to the estate and we had a great time visiting with everyone. Eventually everyone started to drift away to catch flights and trains to get home. Again Wilhelm was kept busy being the taxi driver. I inquired how everything went after we left. Wilhelm all of a sudden looked very guilty and so did his girlfriend as they kept looking at each other. We definitely suspected that they had spent the night together. I knew that I had better tell Will to have a talk with him. I only hoped it was not too late. After all, Will and I knew what could happen.

At dinnertime the only guests left were Dieter, Judy and Wilhelm's and Stefi's current flames. The Canadian group was dead on their feet because of the time differences and had all gone back to the hotel. Dieter was planning to go to the Vienna office on Monday morning and Judy was going to the home of her in-laws to pick up their children and then fly home. Dieter would follow that evening and they would meet at home. The two young beaus had flights back to Canada early Tuesday morning. We had to keep our eyes on these four young people for two more nights. Then we could relax. Will and I would then go back to our hotel and have a sort of honeymoon while the place was being renovated around us.

Chapter 29
Will Tells About the Hotel

Hanna and I arrived back at our hotel on Wednesday afternoon. We had bought a car for use at the hotel because it was cheaper than renting a car every time we went there. There were no real problems with the renovations and the wine cellar was still intact. The contractor had the usual string of problems that needed to be solved and questions to be answered.

The interior paneling had been stripped of the many layers of paint. The last layer was the original varnish. We had the painters re-varnish the wood in a slightly lighter color, more to the modern palate. This also gave a much brighter look to the interior of the hotel. We made a trip to the company doing the upholstery and Hanna chose the fabric style and color. The only stipulation I made was that the material must be tough and very stain resistant. She chose a medium-blue corduroy with a slight mottled background pattern. I was concerned about the durability but Hanna and the upholsterers both assured me it was the best choice. I agreed and when the first chair was completed as a sample, it was amazing.

Ha, wonderful, one more thing to stroke off our lists.

We spent the rest of the week at the hotel looking after the many things that were happening at the same time. Room renovations, plumbing, electrical, telephone wiring and the telephone exchange, heating and air-conditioning, kitchen stoves, room layouts, curtains, drapes, linen and a myriad of other goodies. I never ceased to wonder at all the things that were needed to make a hotel, even as small as ours, run efficiently.

We flew back to Vienna on Friday, arriving during the evening. We grabbed a light meal, having avoided the airline cuisine. We then drove home to our family. Everything seemed in order until we went through our mail and discovered that we were paying to keep the telephone cables across the Atlantic in continuous operation. It seemed that both Wilhelm and Stefi had been maintaining good contact with their respective loves on the other side of the Atlantic. We told them that this had better stop. Stefi did her usual "You don't understand what life is about" performance. Wilhelm was somewhat better but he definitely let us know we were ruining his life by restricting his calls. We told them we would have to go back to work to pay for their calls. I then had a brilliant idea and suggested that it might be more beneficial if they both got part-time jobs in order to pay for the calls or maybe they should sharpen up their writing skills. They both stomped upstairs to their respective rooms. Hanna and I just looked at each other, shrugged, gave each other a hug and went upstairs to bed.

The next morning I went downstairs early, got the newspaper and opened it to the job want ad section. I placed it right in front of where the twins sat. Hopefully this would send a big hint.

They did not find it amusing.

The twins left for school and Hanna and I had a quiet morning at home. I called the telephone company and had a block put on all outgoing overseas calls. We knew we would be on the twins' shit list but we had to maintain some control over them.

That afternoon we were home when the twins arrived from school. Everything was just perfect and we had a wonderful evening with them. They let us know what was happening in school, nothing special, just the standard stuff. Stefi went up to her room to change. Wilhelm waited for her to go upstairs and then told us he was worried about Stefi because she seemed to be ill every morning but did recover quite quickly. Hanna and I looked at each other with a look that said, *Oh shit.*

Hanna immediately said, "I think I had better go up to see what is happening with Stefi."

Wilhelm looked at me with a big question on his face. I sat down and asked him if he had ever heard about a woman having morning sickness. He then looked really shocked and said, "I have but I never thought that it would be possible for anyone I knew to have it happen to them." I quietly told Wilhelm that it could happen to anyone, all you have to do is have sex. I added that it could have even happened to him at the time of our wedding. He looked embarrassed as he asked how we knew. I smiled and told him that he had looked so guilty after the wedding it was not hard to figure out what had transpired between him and his girlfriend. I then figured it was time for the sex safety talk. He looked a little disgusted with me when I asked if he had used condoms. He indignantly replied that he definitely had. I felt somewhat better that there was less of a chance that we were going to get a telephone call from Canada informing us of the impending birth of the heir to the family fortune. I also explained that condoms were not foolproof and they had been known to break.

Hanna came down looking somewhat upset. Wilhelm used the opportunity to disappear. Hanna told me she had a long talk with Stefi and emphasized how her life could be drastically changed with a baby at this time in her life. Stefi reminded her that Wilhelm and she had come out not too bad. Hanna told her that we had been engaged before we went on our holiday. It was a little white lie but the only person to dispute it was me and I was certainly not going to do that. Hanna also told her that wartime was a very different time. Stefi told her that she had heard that line many times before.

The following morning Hanna got in touch with her doctor and set up an appointment for Stefi that afternoon. Stefi was not happy to go see a doctor, accompanied by her mother. What was she, a child?' Tongue in cheek, Hanna reminded her that it seemed that she had not acted as a responsible adult. Wilhelm went off to school and Stefi stayed home under duress.

Hanna and Stefi went to see the doctor and I busied myself dealing with a number of items for the hotel that were best obtained in a larger center, such as Vienna. I also sat down and created some job descriptions for the new staff we were going to hire. I had always found it advantageous to have a description of duties for staff members as it eliminated a number of disputes between staff after they had been hired.

Hanna and Stefi arrived home late in the afternoon. They came through the front door with a number of bags from one of the better ladies' clothing stores in Vienna. They were both beaming. Whatever had happened was obviously not as serious or as permanent as we had believed earlier in the day. Stefi took her purchases upstairs to her room. Hanna motioned me to walk into the den. When we got there Hanna told me that the doctor had done pregnancy and blood tests right after they had got there and sent them to the lab. He then had given Stefi a thorough examination. The doctor was part of a private clinic, which had its own labs and had gotten the results of some of the blood tests as well as the pregnancy test before they left. Stefi had a bowel infection that, after a lengthy time without food, caused the stomach to become upset, hence the morning sickness. The pregnancy test was negative and we were all relieved. Hanna had to put up with Stefi reminding her about how she had overreacted. Hanna simply told her she had dodged a bullet and let it be a lesson. Stefi came down later and did not make any comments about her visit to the doctor. We also did not make any comments because we felt the lesson had been learned for both of the twins and felt it was best to let everything lie low for now.

We went out that evening as a family for a quiet dinner. During the evening Stefi and Wilhelm asked if they could come to see the hotel on the following weekend. Hanna started to say no because of the lack of sleeping rooms but I quickly said that there were no completed rooms for them to sleep in but we would be able to work something out. I thought it would be a great opportunity for the twins to check out the hotel and the surrounding area. Stefi and Wilhelm were quite pleased but not as pleased as I was. After all, I had just become a father and was not ready to become a grandfather just yet.

The rest of the week was somewhat saner. We dealt with a number of hotel-related issues, such as ordering equipment and supplies. We made our rounds of the kitchen appliance supply companies, the kitchen pots and pans companies and the janitorial equipment companies. We obtained catalogues and set up accounts with some of them. A few trips to the bank for letters of credit also filled our time.

Friday afternoon we all went to the airport and flew to the hotel, completing our trip in the car that we had left at the airport. The twins were amazed with the hotel and when we turned on all of the lights they stared in wonder.

Our plans for the hotel included a deck running full across the back, which overlooked the river and faced down the valley. We wanted it to look like it had always been there but needed the construction to be secure and modern. My intention was to make an insulated strong room out of the area below the deck so our wine would be in a secure location and, as important, at a constant temperature year round.

I had contacted a construction company and they were coming the next day to look at the job and give us a quotation.

We gave the twins a tour of the hotel. We showed them everything but the secret wine cellar. Not that we did not trust them but if they did not know about the wine they could not accidentally mention it in a conversation.

Wilhelm did pick up the fact of the missing area in the basement and I explained that there was an old water cistern attached to the basement. He was more observant than I thought he would have been. I had called earlier in the week and had the cook arrange to have two beds moved back into two rooms for the twins. The two rooms were close to the room in which we were staying in until the renovations to the attic were complete. We had decided to make the attic into our personal suite and leave many of the beams that held up the roof exposed. The end effect was to have a very personal warm hideaway for Hanna and me. We were planning to have two small bedrooms built in the other part of the attic for the twins to use when they stayed at the hotel but nothing was finished up there yet. We all retired for the night. Hanna and I lay in bed and recanted the week and the close calls we had encountered. She laughed at me as she enquired if I was still enjoying parenthood and married life. I told her nothing could be better because she was with me. She gave me a big hug and we went to sleep.

Morning came with a racket downstairs, as some earth moving equipment arrived at 7:00 a.m. The contractor coming to discuss the new deck had brought his equipment with him. I got up, grabbed two coffees and went out to greet him. I had brought a North American coffee-maker with me and it had a timer. Some of the Europeans would shake their heads at it but they never refused a cup. I had to bring a transformer to convert the voltage from 240 to 120 so it wouldn't blow up.

The contractor and I had a discussion as to what we wanted and I showed him the drawings I had made which described all of our requirements. The only thing we did not know was what we might find under the ground. We knew that no one had done any digging in the last fifty years. We discussed the requirements and agreed on a price. He felt we should go slowly to see what was hid without disrupting it too much.

The contractor started and the only thing we discovered was an old foundation that was probably from a stable that would have been at the rear of the building. We did find some old tools and a couple of swords from the 1600s or 1700s. We decided that they would be hung somewhere near the bar as a keepsake.

Everybody was interested in how big and deep the hole was for just a rear deck. By Saturday afternoon the hole was completed and the contractor was gone. He was coming back on Monday to set up the footings for the walls and everything would be formed and poured that week.

The twins had fun and were happy to explore the various nooks and crannies of the hotel with boundless energy. They were fascinated by the hidden stairway when I showed them. Wilhelm was even more intrigued with the stairs that went down to a stone wall. I explained again the cistern and he looked at me with a look that said, *"You're bullshitting me."* I still did not confess what was really behind the wall.

The twins left in the car to explore the surrounding area and came back in time for dinner. They would not take the chance that they would have to pay for their own meals.

We all enjoyed a well-prepared dinner with lots of conservation and afterwards went into the lounge and sat in front of a roaring fire. We were very pleased that we had kept the cook on staff. He was an excellent chef and enjoyed showing off his skills especially as our instructions for him were to develop several new menus using only the best ingredients. He was in heaven. The fire burned long into the evening, as there was no shortage of wood to burn because of all the renovations going on. Wilhelm used the opportunity to ask us directly what was going on with the alleged water cistern. He said that he felt there was more behind the walls than we were telling him. He told us he was hurt because he had a feeling we did not trust him. Hanna and I looked at each other and we gave each other a very slight nod.

I looked at him and said, "The reason that we have dodged around that subject is because it is not a cistern. It in fact is a second wine cellar and the wine in there is worth at least twice what this hotel is worth. We are keeping a close guard on it because we do not want its existence to get out and the wine to disappear. That wine is the key to the success for this hotel. People will pay a fortune to have that wine with their meal and we intend to capitalize on that simple fact."

The look of comprehension on Wilhelm's face gave us his answer before he told us, "I will never say one word about that wine before the hotel opens. After the hotel opens I know a lot of kids at our school that have fathers with a lot of money and are very fussy about what wine they have with their meals. I will quietly spread the word as to what wines you have when the wine list is available."

Hanna and I smiled at each other. We both felt that we had handled this one correctly. Stefi just sat quietly and then said that she would not say a word until the hotel was open.

We talked with the twins about their school and how they were doing and what they intended to do when they graduated. Both had not changed their minds. Wilhelm was still looking at law and Stefi was interested in arts. Hanna then told me that Stefi had some good ideas about how to decorate some of the rooms. We listened to her ideas and they were truly very interesting. I asked her to make some sketches so the men working on the interior could understand what her thoughts were. She said she would make the sketches next week and would bring them back the following weekend if she could. We spent the rest of the evening chatting and played a couple of card games. I taught them a card game that I had played in Canada and they taught me a game that they played in Europe. We had a lot of fun together with many laughs.

On Sunday afternoon we drove the twins back to the airport and made sure they had keys for the car we had left at the airport in Vienna. I suspected the car would get a good workout all this week without Hanna and me being around. Hanna and I stopped at a small restaurant for an early dinner together with some quiet adult conversation. We then drove back to the hotel and to our surprise there was a dark gray van parked right in front of the hotel. I asked Hanna to stay in the car and walked slowly around to the back of the hotel. I could see a light on in the room where the secret passage to the basement was located. I hurried back to Hanna and told her to go down the road to the pub and call the police. I said that I suspected someone believed we had headed back to Vienna and it seemed their intentions were to help themselves to our wine as there was a light on in the old smoking room. She asked what I was going to do and of course told me not to do anything stupid and get hurt. I promised her I would not get hurt. She left and I went over to the van and found the door unlocked. I opened the engine hood and discovering that it was a gasoline engine, removed the coil wire from the distributor. I then went to the front door, took off my shoes, and got the keys that locked the door to the basement. I looked over at the fireplace, still filled with the cold ashes from last night, smiled to myself and picked up the ash pan and filled it with ashes. I walked quietly to the wine cellar entrance, looked down and immediately saw two guys talking as they pounded away at the stone wall that I had installed at the entrance to the wine cellar. I let out a bloodcurdling scream, pitched the ashes down the stairs, which then became a white cloud, slammed the door shut at the top of the stairs and turned out the lights. I then placed a couple of planks that were at least two inches by eight inches across the door and nailed them solid to the door frame, screaming as I did it. Next I jammed two more planks against them. The other ends were jammed against the stairs that went up to the attic. I then went outside, stopping at the front door to put on my work boots and walked around to the back, where there was some construction equipment. The backhoe had just what I was looking for—a chain. I grabbed it and went in through the front door and through to the back room, stomping hard on the floor as I slowly walked around, rattling the chain.

This was all quite fun, doing my version of a Hollywood episode.

I went slowly into the back room, stomping my feet, to the door at the top of the stairs where I could hear the guys pounding on the door. I shook the chain hard, rattling it on the landing in front of the door and let out another scream as loud as I could. The pounding stopped dead. I then flicked the lights on and off, screamed again just for effect, and quietly left. I took the chain around to the back, changed into my shoes, cleaned the dirt off of my hands and walked down to the road, where I could see Hanna and the police car coming. I told the policemen what I had done and they had a good laugh and got into the spirit of things. They suggested that we leave and let them handle the situation. Hanna and I drove down to the corner and we let the police have their fun.

Later that evening we talked to the police and they told us the remainder of the story.

When I had the wall built I had it built as a double wall with about a foot of space between the walls. The walls had been sprayed with a waterproofing liquid and I had filled the space with water. The last coat of the waterproofing material was a red color and it was obviously not quite dry when I added the water. It had stained the water red. The two potential wine thieves had just broken through the first wall and were staring at the red liquid oozing from the wall when I screamed at them, threw the dust, slammed the door and turned off the lights. The rest of my little act made them even more frightened. The police went into the hotel and told them they had been driving by and heard a scream and decided to investigate. They heard them banging on the door and removed the planks and let them out. Several enquiries and a tearful confession resulted in two very frightened guys in jail for the night. The police also told us that most petty crooks are very superstitious and they believed no one would attempt another robbery. They suggested that we let the workers see the stairwell and catch a glimpse of the red leaking wall. The word would get around like wildfire and no one would bother us. We agreed but felt we should have people living in the hotel all the time now. The police left and Hanna and I snuggled together in front of the fire and I told her all about my little ghost story. She had a really good laugh over it and inquired what Hollywood movie had been used for my antics. My answer was simply "Every ghost movie I have ever seen." We went to bed and we still continued to chuckle over the whole affair.

The next morning I contacted the old grounds keeper and asked him to come in to see us. He had told us that he wanted to retire but we had heard some rumors that he wished he hadn't. His wife had died a couple of years ago and he had told us that he wanted time to do a lot of fishing but was now finding there was just too much time on his hands to miss her. He was overjoyed to be asked to come back and when we asked him to live at the hotel and act as a night watchman he was even happier. I also arranged for a security company to come in and install some cameras and connect them to a monitor and recorder located in the caretaker's room. Hopefully this would ensure the security of the wine.

Work went on. The twins came to visit several more times. We made many trips to Vienna. Hanna's father came to visit regularly. The rooms were finished one at a time, all with Stefi's decorating ideas. The furniture was delivered and put in place as the rooms were finished. The refinishing and new material looked fabulous. The kitchen renovation was completed and the chef was starting to purchase the staples he needed. I was shocked at the amount of money we were putting out for the hotel startup. *C'est la vie!*

The rear deck was completed, with a stone face built to blend in with the hotel so it looked like it had always been there. We added a vault-type door leading into the old wine cellar, which opened into the new wine cellar. We carefully moved all of the good wine into the new wine cellar under the deck.

The wine was now secure.

Our suite in the old attic was complete and we moved up there. The space was great and we both were happy to have our own private world that was truly ours.

We then planned the grand reopening of the hotel and sent out limited invitations. The invitations included a copy of the menu for the evening and the wine list. We wished to start out with a big bang so we included one glass of the best of the best wine. The evening package included pickup at the airport, the evening meal with one glass of our special wine, breakfast and lunch the next day and transportation back to the airport. The price I won't say, because truly it was ridiculous. Our opening was sold out in two days, with many clients booking for the following weekend. The father of one of Wilhelm's friends attended the grand opening. I guess Wilhelm had really marketed the wine list as he said he would. I had contacted a renowned wine steward, who agreed to attend. He was quite skeptical about why I called him for the opening of such a small hotel. He was hesitant about committing himself until I told him what I wanted him to open. His only request for payment was a glass of the wine for himself. No problem!

The opening was an astounding success and we kept a number of the local taxis busy running back and forth to the airport. I had included the taxi ride as part of the total cost as we did not want to appear to be cutting corners in any way. The meal was superb and all of the guests seemed very impressed. The wine steward gave an incredible talk about the wine and the history that was involved with it. He was one of those lucky people who was doing for a living what he loved best. He was in love with his topic and his enthusiasm showed in every aspect of his presentation. We paid him an honorarium for his expertise and provided his transportation and accommodation. He was a very happy man.

On the Sunday after the opening he asked me where I had gotten the wine. I laughed and told him to come with me and took him downstairs to let him see for himself what we had. Before I opened the vault door to the wine cellar I made him promise that he was to tell no one about what he was about to see. He spent the whole time in the wine cellar looking at bottles saying, "My God, my God." He suddenly became very disturbed. Looking around he noticed that the wine cellar was new and wanted to know how much care had gone into moving the wine. I explained the procedure that we had gone through to ensure the sediment in the wine was not disturbed. He looked pleased. We went back upstairs to the lounge. He then gave me a list and told me whenever any one of these were opened he would gladly come to open the wine just for the privilege of being there and tasting the wine. I knew that we now had a friend who would generate a lot of very well-heeled clients who would be willing to pay anything just to be part of one of our tastings.

We were now well on our way to success. All we had to do was make the wine and any new replacements last until we no longer wanted to run the hotel.

The steward left by taxi for the airport.

I rushed back inside to see Hanna. She was busy working on the accounts and was smiling as she added up the columns. We had had a very successful grand opening. I told her about what had transpired with the wine steward and her smile grew even wider.

Our weekend specials grew in reputation and the chef worked very hard to produce some of the most unusual and exotic meals, each one designed around the wine of the evening. As the reputation grew so did the price. We were now charging three times what we did for our opening and the backlog of reservations continued. We also had developed a good business during the week with some business men who truly wanted to impress their clients.

Chapter 30
Will Continues with Life

During the next two years or so life was certainly good, in fact it was great. I had the most wonderful wife and we lived each day to the fullest. We were having a great time together running the hotel and had developed many new friends in the European moneyed circles. We found that most of the old rich had a quiet, comfortable reserve about them. They had nothing to prove, just the world, as they knew it, to continue. Dieter was able to attend a large number of our weekend specials. He was content just to be there and leave the best of the wines to be sampled by the real paying guests. Dieter and Judy stayed in one of our rooms in the attic that we had built for the twins. Dieter had made many very good business contacts during his stays at the hotel. We even cooperated to make sure that an appropriate guest was not left out when a particularly large engineering contract was being tendered.

The twins went off to university, Wilhelm went into law school and Stefi changed from an art degree to an interior design degree.

Stefi had developed quite a flair for interior design and her work at the hotel was incredible. The improvement from the first room to the last was so significant that she begged us to redo the first two rooms. We did and it was well worth the money. Every room was slightly different with coordinating colors, linens, drapes, carpets, paints and wallpapers.

Wilhelm and Stefi, much to our pleasure, drifted away from their loves in Canada. They still spent some time with my parents during the summer months and had their circle of summer friends in Canada but serious relationships did not develop. My parents would come to visit us for a short period of time in the early spring and in the fall but I suspect neither of them really enjoyed it because of the language barriers. Hanna and I traveled to Canada to see them when we could but the hotel kept us tied down. We did not mind it because we were tied down together.

Hanna and I had an active life. We kept fit by hiking and jogging in the summer, skiing in the winter and just a lot of running up and down the stairs every day. We ate the best foods, cooked in a very healthy manner. The chef made sure our portions were not too big. He had the philosophy that you must always have space for something later. Most of the time nothing was ever needed later. We did not believe in the American reasoning that if the portions were not enormous the food couldn't be good. Some of our clients from the US would say to us that they had been initially amazed by the small portions but never did feel hungry later.

All of our regular clients developed their personal preference for a specific room and some would not come unless their particular room was available for them. We even created a system of storage closets for our guests so they could leave their favorite hotel clothing at the hotel and would not need to bother with luggage when they returned. When a client left, all of his clothing would be cleaned, laundered, folded or hung in its appropriate closet, ready to be placed in the room when they returned. It became quite amusing to realize you would have a hotel full of the same people wearing the same outfits time after time. No one really noticed their attire because everyone was interested in the same thing—wine.

I was contacted by a number of the wineries when they realized that we had some of their vintage wines that they did not have. I was able to trade a case of a particularly good year for two hundred and fifty cases of younger wine but still very good vintages. We were now quite successfully bartering to extend the operating life of the hotel. The wineries never knew how many cases of the top vintages we had and we were not about to tell them.

Our chef was in his heaven. He had to create new and exciting dishes, based on the wine of the evening, using only the best ingredients, all for clients who appreciated his expertise. We served venison, wild boar, lamb, beef, chicken, pork, fish, bison, elk, bear and many other exotic meats and vegetables.

I was able to use some of the contacts I had made through my hunting friends in Canada to obtain the wild game from there. If there was sufficient time between major dinners we sometimes sent the chef on a buying trip to make sure he got exactly what he wanted. He usually took his wife and they got a paid vacation while grocery shopping. Not a bad deal for either of us. The reputation for food at the hotel rivaled the wine list and we had many visits from renowned chefs from all parts of Europe. We even had a visit from a well-respected chef from New York City. The cook got his title changed from Head Cook to Head Chef. He was quite amazed when he was asked to give talks at some of the better culinary schools. All this from "just a cook," as he described himself, who had learned his trade by just trying out new things on his own. He once came to us and told us he would never leave because no other place would ever give him the freedom that we did.

Hanna's father was a regular visitor but his age was starting to catch up with him. His proximity to Vienna allowed the twins to visit him on a regular basis and he was often more knowledgeable about the affairs of the twins than we were. Hanna and I both understood that parents are always the last to find out about what was really happening with their kids.

We got a call from him one Sunday evening asking if we would be at the hotel on the next Tuesday. We told him that we had nowhere else that we could go with the number of guests we had coming that week.

"Good, pick me up at the airport. I will be on the two o'clock flight."

Then he hung up. I put down the telephone and turning to Hanna explained what her father had said and asked if she had any idea what that was that all about.

She shook her head and said, "We will not find out until Tuesday after dinner. Obviously we are going to have a family meeting."

Hanna's father arrived and she picked him up at the airport as he expected. He greeted everyone at the hotel in his usual jovial manner. We had his bags put into a small room on the main floor so he would not have to climb up to our room in the attic. He made himself comfortable in the lounge and we went about our work. He had dinner with us and afterwards when the guests left he asked for the lounge door to be closed.

Time for the Family Meeting!

Father started off by telling us that the twins had been to visit for the weekend and he had made several observations. The first was based on the fact that Wilhelm's friend Helmut had accompanied the twins and it was more than obvious that he was much more interested in Stefi than being just a friend of Wilhelm. He smiled and told us that from the look of Stefi and Helmut, Helmut might just be that special someone for Stefi. He also added that he believed that Stefi did not yet even know that herself and felt that we should know about this budding romance, so that we would not be too surprised. He added, "But now for the real reason for my visit, which is Stefi. As she will be graduating this spring, she will obviously need a job. She is doing extremely well at what she does and after observing what she has done here, I am confident that she will be very successful. As a result, I have approached Dieter with the suggestion that the company should expand from just engineering to include an interior design group. Dieter listened very closely to my idea and concluded that this would be an excellent direction to move towards. He also agreed that Stefi would make a great first employee within this group and that they would add a draughtsman and a project coordinator when required."

Hanna and I looked at each other and inquired if Stefi knew anything about Father's latest plans. He replied, "Why would she need to know until the plans are finalized."

Hanna and I shook our heads and explained that young people today are very headstrong and Stefi might have some other ideas as to the direction she wanted her future to go. However, we agreed that we would meet with Stefi to see what plans she had in mind for herself and let him know the outcome. I knew that this would not be a pleasant conversation.

He then continued on and brought out papers that he asked Hanna to sign which made Hanna joint owner of his estate near Vienna and gave us copies of documents that showed he had converted a number of his investments to joint ownership, half with Wilhelm and half with Stefi. I looked at Hanna with the question *What is going on?* 'in my eyes. Her look mirrored mine.

I asked Hanna if she could get us a brandy. She got up, went over to the cabinet, and then announced that a better bottle of brandy might be in order and left to get it.

I looked at Hanna's father and noticed he looked more tired than usual and asked if everything was all right. He looked at me, with sadness in his eyes, and said, "I need to put my affairs in order because I have cancer and I have had it for a while. I did not want to burden you two with my health problems. I may have only six months and I want to leave everything as simplified as possible."

I leaned towards him and said, "I think you have several things in your favor, one being the fact that I waited twenty years to finally meet you and you are not going to get away from me that easy. The second, doctors have been known to be very wrong. The third is cancer would not have a chance with you because you are too ornery."

He gave me a tired smile and followed with "Thank you for your assurances but we will just have to wait and see. Please do not tell Hanna until I ask you to. I have a number of other things to look after during the next little while. I am so happy that you and Hanna managed to find each other. It has relieved my mind of a very heavy concern."

I promised him that I would not tell Hanna about his health and changed the subject to the hotel, just as we heard Hanna opening the door. She looked at me as she entered the room and I gently shrugged. Hanna's father saw the movement and smiled. Hanna asked what we had been talking about without her to keep us under control. I told her we were guessing what brandy she would be bringing. Hanna poured each of us a glass and we sipped it. He asked us to talk to Stefi about the position and asked us to come to his place in a couple of weeks for a few more surprises—all good, he added. We then all made small talk for the rest of the evening. Breakfast and lunch were both very pleasant and we drove him to the airport in the afternoon. He flew back to Vienna and then drove himself home.

We drove home to the hotel and talked about the strange family meeting. I mused over my promise to Hanna's father along with my commitment to Hanna as my life partner. We went to bed and, as we lay very close together, I told her about what her father had said and why I had waited until after he had left before I told her. Many tears later she thanked me for telling her and how much she appreciated me waiting to tell her until after her father had left. She knew her father could never trust anyone who had broken a promise and she also knew that she would never have been able to control her emotions when she saw him in the morning. She added it would be hard enough in two weeks when she went to see him. I was confident that I had made the right decision.

Chapter 31
Father Rearranges Life

One day rolled into the next and before we knew it two weeks had gone by. We flew to Vienna in the late morning and met the twins for lunch. Stefi brought the love of her life, Helmut. There was no question they were both totally enamored with each other. Wilhelm looked slightly disgusted with both of them and commented it was the last time he would ever introduce any of his friends to his sister. Hanna and I had a quiet chuckle over the entire situation. We inquired how everything was going at school. Stefi was at the head of her class and would be graduating in a couple of months. Wilhelm knew he had a few more years ahead of him before becoming a lawyer and the same went for his friend Helmut. We asked Stefi what job prospects she had. She looked slightly downhearted and said that she had none at present, but postings and interviews had not yet started. She said that she was not worried. We told her what her grandfather had proposed and surprisingly she did show some interest in it. She commented that it would be nice to not have to enter the job grabbing market and all of the hassles and pressures that went with it. I emphasized that she would be generally on her own and would have to acquire her own clients. This would not be a cakewalk. She would really have to hustle and if she did not perform and make money for the firm within a reasonable period of time, Dieter would be asking her to find a position elsewhere. This really got her I'll-show-you back up and she said she would talk to Dieter herself. Helmut looked hard at her and asked if she was sure. She replied, "Definitely." Hanna and I chuckled to ourselves. Helmut was finding out for the first time how headstrong she could be when she set her mind to something.

When we finished our lunch we all went our way for the afternoon. Hanna had a hair appointment, Helmut and the twins went back to school and I had a list as long as your arm of things that needed picking up, arranging for or disposing of.

Hanna and I were to meet at Dieter's office at the end of the day. We wanted to know what had really transpired between Hanna's father and Dieter.

As usual I got only half of the things on my list. When I arrived at Dieter's office, he greeted me warmly and we waited for Hanna.

Dieter knew why we were there and had a good laugh when we told him what we knew of the meeting with Hanna's father. He countered with "I knew you two would be around to find out what the old fart had been up to." He explained he had already given some thought to expanding the company into some other fields. He said that the expansion idea had germinated at one of our fancy get-togethers where one of our existing clients was talking to him about a new villa he was planning on building. Our client had said he was very disappointed in every one of the architectural firms to whom his wife and he had spoken. He had said that he felt that the firms had no real interest in listening to what he and his wife believed they wanted. They were only interested in pushing on them what they considered were their newest and greatest ideas. Dieter had then decided to call one of his old friends, who had started an executive placement agency and inquire if there were any younger architectural employees who had good potential and would relocate from their present position. There were almost none but they did tell him of an existing small firm, with a very good reputation, that was struggling because of lack of contacts. Dieter smiled and continued, "To make a long story short I bought the company and decided to retain their original name. I then introduced my frustrated client to them and they now have the order. However, they were lacking a good interior designer and your father, with his usual impeccable timing, showed up with the idea of Stefi doing interior design within our organization. The whole structure in my mind is perfect. I have seen what she did at the hotel and I am very impressed."

188

We then told Dieter about our talk with Stefi. He chuckled and then inquired when she would be graduating. Hanna told him in about six weeks. He thought for a moment and said, "Great, it would be better two weeks earlier but she has to finish her exams, so I'll have to wait."

We had a few more discussions about the new company, the engineering firm, wines and when Dieter and Judy could plan to come and visit us next.

Hanna and I left with a good feeling about Stefi's future.

We drove out to Hanna's father's estate. The drive was quite pleasant, as spring had broken, the sun was warm and the world was becoming green again.

Hanna finally brought up the subject of her father's health. I had been wondering how long it would be. I had felt she would be happier to think about it and then discuss it when she was ready. We talked about his cancer.

Was it a serious type of cancer?

Would he go into remission?

We arrived at the estate and drove up the driveway to the house. Hanna was having more and more difficulty in keeping her composure.

We knocked and went into the foyer.

Nobody was waiting for us.

We looked at each other with apprehension.

I felt so helpless as I had no real answers. All I could do was be a good friend.

I put my arm around her and we walked towards the study, where I assumed that Father would be. It was on the south side of the house and was by far the coziest of any of the rooms in the house. We opened the door and looked in. A day bed had been placed in there and Hanna's father lay on the bed.

He looked absolutely terrible.

I had not needed to have made my promise to him not to tell Hanna about his health. She looked at him with horror and started to cry as she rushed over to him, wrapping her arms around him, asking him what was wrong and admonishing him for not telling her. He hugged her as tight as he could and he told her about his health and that it wasn't as bad as it looked because he had just finished a round of chemotherapy and it always made him look so very sick.

He apologized for not asking us to come one week later, when he would be feeling much better.

He told us that he had gotten the rest of his affairs sorted out.

Hanna got furious with him and told him, "We don't want your affairs. We want you sorted out."

He looked at her feebly and continued, "It was by the grace of God and good luck that I survived the war. I was nearly taken by the Gestapo three times and managed to pull enough strings to keep out of prison. Luckily enough, the war ended before I ran out of strings. I know because of those experiences that I have been living on borrowed time ever since. Twenty-some years of borrowed time, nobody owes me anything anymore. When it's my time to go I will go in peace. My life's work is complete, you are emotionally and financially secure. Will here looked after the first, mind you, it took him a long time to get around to it, and I then looked after the second. I have two wonderful grandchildren, who have turned out to be the best grandchildren anyone could ever imagine. What else could anyone ask for?"

Hanna looked at him and asked, "What about great-grandchildren?"

He sat up as quickly as he could and asked, "Do you know something I don't know?"

She replied, "No, but after watching those two packages of boiling hormones I think an engagement is not too far in the future. And if they don't take precautions, you will get a great-grandbaby before you know it."

Hanna's observation of Stefi and her beau broke the ice and settled down everybody's emotions. Her father then told us that his cancer was not too aggressive and the doctors were telling him he should be free and clear in another month. Later that evening he gave us each a list containing all the bank accounts, investments, insurances, location of his will and deeds. The list also explained what investments were to go to whom. Hanna and I were astounded. We both knew her father was quite comfortable but in reality he was probably worth ten to fifteen times what we had ever considered possible. He watched our faces and had a real laugh at our expense as we read the documents.

We all toasted each other and he went to bed quite early. Hanna and I sat up watching the fire I had set in the fireplace in our bedroom and talked about the day. Sometimes the conversation was happy, sometimes it was sad. We went to sleep early knowing that morning would be just around the corner.

It was.

Hanna's father was up bright and early looking quite sprightly but we could see he was putting on a good show for our benefit. We decided to leave just after lunch to give him some time to rest in the afternoon. We knew he would not rest if we were there.

Hanna was quite upset as we drove back to Vienna and then to the airport. We flew back home to our hotel and did a quick tour with the staff to ensure that everything had gone well and then checked our schedules to see what new reservations had come in.

There was another busy weekend coming. It would be followed by a very busy week with two small conferences, which were really corporate meetings. I had a number of good connections in Canada and the US and was able to bring over some very good speakers. A lot of European companies were interested in expansion into North America and I was able to fly in speakers who could give them a flavor of what business in North America was really about. The Europeans could not believe there was any difference between Canada and the US and were quite surprised at the different philosophies. We had to explain to them that Canada and the US were as different in as many ways as England and Germany. If we were to include Quebec, the French part of Canada, the philosophies could differ as much as France and Germany.

The conferences were exceedingly valuable to us and the Americans particularly were astounded at the price that some of our clients paid for the lectures because it included our special wines. The Canadians and the New Yorkers seemed less surprised. We were actually quite surprised at the responses as good wine tasting had not yet gained popularity in Canada. However, it was apparently appreciated by the top executives because of the extent of their European travel.

Another six months passed by. Stefi called one evening and asked if Helmut could come to spend the weekend. I said it would be no problem and waited for her next question. Stefi was silent for a second and then tried several different tacks before she finally asked directly if it would be possible for us to get two tickets for them because Helmut was still in law school and after all he was a starving student. Stefi then added she was still a starving new worker. She claimed she was still trying to make ends meet on her starting salary. I told her they would be able to pick up their tickets at the airport.

I got off the telephone and told Hanna about the request. We looked at each other and broke into a smile. We somehow knew why they were coming for a visit and that for some strange reason Wilhelm was not invited. I thought for a moment and asked Hanna to come for a walk to the wine cellar to pick a special bottle for the occasion.

We chose one of the best of the newer wines, saving a really good wine for the wedding.

We went together to pick them up at the airport and drove them back to the hotel. We kept the conversation on the level of Stefi's new job and law school. I think we drove them to distraction because we did not seem to be at all interested in the real reason why they were here.

When we got back to the hotel, I went to check on how the new construction for the garage was coming along and Hanna disappeared into the office. We had told them to get settled into two of the rooms at the end of the hotel, as they would be empty tonight. They looked at each other with a look of *What do we do now and how do we get into one room tonight?* For the rest of the day Hanna and I made sure we were never out of earshot of either a staff person or workman. I think the lack of openings for them to tell us their news drove both of them crazy. Dinner came and went still with either a staff member or a guest always around. We could see the look of frustration on both of their faces.

I suggested that we could all go to the smoking lounge, where nobody smoked anymore. Everybody went on ahead and I got the wine that Hanna and I had chosen earlier along with four glasses and followed them. We all sat down.

I asked if there was any special reason that they had wanted to visit that particular weekend. Had Stefi gotten fired, for example?

Stefi and Helmut both blurted out at the same time, "We want to get married." Stefi almost started to cry and Helmut started to stammer something.

I looked at them and asked, "Why?"

Helmut regained his composure and they unanimously answered, "Because we love each other!"

I then questioned, "Do you like each other?" They both looked at me as if I had two heads but answered, "Most definitely."

I smiled and said, "You can love and hate a person at the same time but if you like someone they can become your best friend for life. If you like and love each other you will be together for the rest of your life."

Hanna asked if they were positive in this decision. They both answered, "Yes".

I got up to get the wine and the glasses and poured it very carefully. Helmut saw the label on the wine bottle and gulped. I was pleased to see his appreciation of a fine wine. He looked at me, smiled and said, "You knew all along, didn't you."

I laughed and followed with "Emotions are best kept with family and friends. Emotions in the workplace always need to be controlled to bring about the outcome you require. You both have been broadcasting your emotions so blatantly for the last few months that you were probably the last to realize the direction you were moving in." Helmut and Stefi looked at me in shock. Hanna smiled at me.

I proposed a toast to their long and happy marriage.

We had clinking of glasses all around, followed by hugs and tears. Helmut looked slightly uncomfortable with Stefi and her tears of joy and relief. I went over to him, put my arm around his shoulder, pointed my glass at the two crying females and said, "Get used to it, it's hereditary and it does not get better with age." I clinked his glass again and told him, "Congratulations, You could not do better." He smiled back and told me I was a bit of a rat. I clinked again and told him that he would have to get used to my warped sense of humor.

The rest of the evening went well with lots of discussion on their future plans. Stefi told us they had gone to see her grandfather to tell him of their plans. She said he didn't seem very surprised but he was very happy for them. He had insisted the wedding would be at his estate, just as Hanna's and mine had been. Both Helmut and Stefi were pleased with his offer. We then asked how he looked. Stefi told us that was something she wanted to talk with us about because he did not look very good at all.

We told her about the cancer and how his chemotherapy was helping him but we were concerned about the long-term outcome.

Stefi really wanted her grandfather to be part of their wedding so the next few months were a flurry of wedding plans. The wedding was to be in the spring so now it was our turn to run in circles.

Stefi worked on the invitation list and the wedding details with Hanna. I helped with the wedding plans as best I could.

We invited Helmut's parents to the hotel for a couple of our weekend functions before the wedding. Helmut's parents were wonderful people. His father was also a lawyer, who specialized in real estate and worked for a company that managed buildings and properties. Helmut's mother was a real jewel of a lady and Hanna and she got along wonderfully.

Helmut's father was able to meet some very influential people at the hotel. His discussions with some of the guests at the hotel showed an extensive knowledge of his industry. The meetings resulted in a good collection of business cards. He was also asked if he would be interested in joining a much larger management firm to head up their legal department. After several weeks of negotiations he made the change and apparently received a fifty-percent increase in salary. The owner of the company later told me he was the best lawyer they had ever had and furthermore the most honest. Hanna and I felt quite pleased with the knowledge that Stefi was marrying into a family of such integrity.

We spent a lot of time flying back and forth between the hotel and Vienna. Usually one of us needed to stay at the hotel to keep it running smoothly and our guests wanted to see at least one of us when they arrived.

My parents flew over for the wedding and stayed only for a week. It was spring planting season so my father was antsy to return home.

Hanna's father stood up well throughout the wedding although we could see him failing fast. The last of the females were married and he now could relax. The wedding came and went with no more complications than could be expected for any normal wedding.

Hanna's father died two months later.

We had the funeral at his estate.

We closed the hotel for a week and canceled all engagements for that week.

All of our clients understood and in fact many of them came to the funeral. Hanna and I were overwhelmed with the thoughtfulness of everyone.

We went back to the hotel. Stefi and Helmut went back to Vienna. She returned to work and he began his final year. Wilhelm also returned to his last year in law school.

The estate was settled according to Hanna's father's wishes. Stefi and Wilhelm were quite surprised in the size of their inheritance but could not figure out why they had to wait until they were twenty-five before getting it. I had no real answer other than that was how their grandfather wanted it done.

Hanna took several weeks before she finally realized she could not just telephone her father whenever she wanted. It was quite hard for her. She had always been very close to her father, particularly because he was the only male role model she had in her life for forty years.

I did my best to comfort her but time was the only real cure.

Chapter 32
Hanna Continues

Wilhelm graduated with excellent marks and started to work in a small law firm. He still did not have a special love in his life. Will and I were both quite concerned that he would take his inheritance from his grandfather and spend it on fast cars and parties.

He didn't. He bought an apartment in downtown Vienna not far from his office. Will and I had mixed feelings about his investment. We knew it was a good investment but we were apprehensive because it was quite expensive.

We visited him and discovered the place looked somewhat familiar because he had obtained nearly all of his furniture from his grandfather. We inquired how he had arranged that and he told us that his grandfather told him to take anything that he wanted. He had selected special pieces, including two complete bedroom suites from upstairs. The result was a rather old-fashioned-looking apartment but very aesthetically pleasing. I asked him how he figured out how to decorate it. He laughed and said, "Simple, I just invited Stefi over for dinner and she couldn't stand the way it was so she gave directions and Helmut and I rearranged the furniture about fifty times. The curtains, towels and all that stuff were also easy. She just took me to her wholesaler and said buy this and that and I did."

Will and I had a really good laugh over Wilhelm's description of his apartment decorating. Wilhelm had certainly grown up very quickly after he left university. As a curious mother I did a quick check around to see if I could find any evidence of any permanent girls. I did spot a selection of contact lens cleaners, a box full of tooth brushes, a selection of different toothpastes, all travel sized, plus two large thick soft terrycloth robes and a hair dryer. I was rather interested in his approach to negating any objections by a young lady when she was asked if she would like to stay over. He was still obviously playing the field.

Wilhelm invited us to stay for dinner and cooked a very good dinner. Wine and conversation followed afterwards and we learned he was doing well working for a medium-sized law firm and had already gotten a nice pay raise. He did emphasize that it was not very substantial. Will and I felt he had his life in order and we both knew that the love of his life would come along eventually.

The doorbell rang and he looked quite guilty, with his eyes darting all over the place. I knew this must be someone who was being kept silent from us, at least for the time being. Will was coming in from the kitchen and said that he would get it. Wilhelm said he would but Will was much closer so he got to the door first and opened it.

The young lady was dressed in the garb of the traveler. She was beautiful. With a surprised look on her face she said, in a very peculiar, almost British accent, "There is no doubt you are Wilhelm's father."

Will looked at her, sort of tilted his head and said, "Not English, mmn...normal R's so not Australian, you must be from New Zealand."

She laughed, a most infectious laugh, and said, "You're absolutely right."

Wilhelm had now come over to her and put his arm around her, gave her a kiss and introduced her as Leigh, his best friend and also his girlfriend.

I looked over at Will and he smiled and said, "Busted."

Wilhelm stepped out into the hall and got her backpack.

Not just an evening visit!

The evening's discussions with them brought out most of the story, at least the parts they were willing to share with us. They had met near the start of a weeklong trek in the Alps several weeks ago and had hit it off really well. He had talked her into coming to Vienna to visit him and she agreed but only after she went on to Italy to inform her travel companions, who had gone on ahead of her, of her change in plans. She had caught up with them and informed them she was going back to Vienna to see a friend whom she had met on the trek. She had told Wilhelm she would come to his place the following week but had shown up three days early.

It was poorly hidden that they had missed each other badly.

Will and I had planned on staying over at Wilhelm's apartment but thought we might no longer be real welcome. Wilhelm told us that he would not hear of anything but us staying. He set the stage of who would be where by carrying Leigh's pack into his bedroom. Our presence was not going to change anything he had in mind.

The evening was a lot of fun and Leigh had picked up enough German to not totally be out of the conversation when we drifted into it. We did try to speak English as much as possible.

She told us she was from the Christchurch area of the South Island and was doing her "OE" that a lot of New Zealanders do. She did have a certain poise that comes from a structured upbringing and I did like that part. She was not a wild creature that one might expect from a small country, so rural in nature, but what did I know about New Zealand?

Will seemed very interested in the tramping in New Zealand and she was doing a good job of making it more interesting for him. She excused herself and went off to the toilet, as she called it. When she returned she sat close to Wilhelm and said that the apartment was far nicer than he had led her to believe. She had been very unsure of the address because of the building but the taxi driver had assured her it was correct.

She turned to me and told me that Wilhelm had told her he was just a clerk in a law office but now she thought he might have a somewhat better position. I assured her that he was just a lawyer on the way up, although fast, and if he kept up his present pace he would be a partner within a few years. She poked him in the ribs and told him he was real bad for misleading her. He told her he wanted her to like him for himself and not his wallet. She assured him she was not that kind of girl.

It was getting late so Will and I made our excuses and went to bed. They stayed up for a short time probably to make sure Will and I were asleep. We weren't.

They were not dead silent and they certainly had missed each other.

Wilhelm left early in the morning for work and arranged for Leigh to meet him for lunch. Will and I chatted with Leigh before we left for the airport. We asked her about her family and she told us her father was a lawyer in Christchurch and she had two brothers older than she and one younger sister. She was happy to share some of her stories about life in New Zealand.

On our trip back to the hotel Will and I had a good long conversation about Leigh. Will felt that a lot of things had changed for Wilhelm and the relationship seemed to be very serious but only time would tell if it would progress to become a long-term relationship. He felt that it was a long way to New Zealand and it is a very beautiful country and Leigh may get homesick. She may miss her family and friends and want to go back home.

Everything was in order at the hotel when we returned home. We had another busy week but Will and I had decided to take regular time off for ourselves. We had both put on some weight, indulging in too much wine and good food and not enough exercise.

We had learned there were a number of great treks in our general neighborhood and were now doing them and keeping a good log and photo collection of each trek. I wanted to make a tramping guide for our guests but I will admit it was getting out of hand because the number of photos was excessive. Will would laugh at me and tell me that the guests would not need to go trekking as they could just follow the picture album and the text describing the route.

Life had become even better.

Chapter 33
Hotel and Family

We received an interesting call one bright, sunny morning. It was from a law firm representing, as they told us, a large exclusive European hotel chain. Hanna and I could not comprehend the combination of large and exclusive and chain. They had heard about our hotel and knew that we had purchased the adjacent property giving us the land on both sides of the river and up the valley in both directions from the hotel. We now had an area that was very private and would remain that way.

They asked us if we would allow them to come to visit us and have some discussions regarding the possibility of them purchasing the hotel. We told them we did have several vacancies but the trip would be expensive. They informed us that would not be a problem. We booked them in and shook our heads. Hanna and I looked at each other and asked each other if we would be interested in selling. We had never considered that possibility. I told her that they would never pay what we would ask for the hotel. Anyway, it was too far off the beaten path, too small and too old.

We were wrong!

When they arrived, we gave them a tour of the hotel and the grounds. We then retired to the smoking room, where they presented an offer which was at least twice what I thought we might accept. They didn't even blink when I doubled it but they insisted the wine cellar remain. We told them it would, with the exception of a few cases of selected wines.

They departed the next day leaving us a written offer good for six months for an incredible amount of money. They only asked that we not shop the offer until it expired. They were willing to pay us for an option but we assured them that was not required. They then added that they believed us because they had checked out our integrity with suppliers and other sources.

Hanna and I went to bed in shock.

We then started to talk ourselves into selling the hotel.

It is strange how things seem to work out. A few days after the lawyers left our chef came to us, most apologetic, telling us that he wished to retire. He said he would stay with us until we hired a new chef and then he could take some time with the new chef to familiarize him with the workings of the hotel. We told him how much we appreciated him for his many years of service and told him we would start the process of replacing him as soon as possible. I also suggested that he write down the best of his recipes. He laughed and told us that would be a tall order because there were so many and his organizational skills left a little to be desired.

Hanna wanted to know why I wanted all of the recipes because any new chef would have his own way of doing things. I told her that a published cookbook would give our cook an excellent retirement income. I also added we might just have to terminate him when the new cook was hired and pay a good severance. Both the cookbook and the severance package would give him an excellent nest egg as a thank you for his years of dedication. His skills certainly had been very good for the hotel as our clients always raved about the food. We could not remember one single complaint. We decided to just sit on everything for a month.

We had to go to Vienna for some meetings and took some time to visit both Stefi and Wilhelm. Stefi and Helmut had just bought a new house. Stefi had been pregnant and had called to tell us that she had miscarried the baby. Hanna was still very concerned about Stefi's health and had discussed it at great lengths with me. We had not been able to come to Vienna for the best part of a couple of months because of the commitments at the hotel, so we were both very excited to see Stefi. She had just found out she was expecting again and her doctors were very positive about this pregnancy. She was still working and doing very well. Helmut had graduated at the same time as Wilhelm and had started with a large law firm in Vienna. All independent reports that we received indicated he was also doing exceptionally well in his career. We were both happy with how things were turning out.

We visited Stefi and Helmut and they proudly gave us the tour of their new home. I was very pleased with everything we saw but quite interested to find another collection of Hanna's father's furniture. Hanna and I later both wondered where it had been stored during the last few years and how much of the furniture had actually been sold with the house.

Hanna told Stefi that we were going over to Wilhelm's apartment the following evening. She got a funny expression on her face. Hanna immediately sensed it and inquired what was going on. Stefi stammered for a few minutes and finally decided to inform us about the situation to lessen our shock. Wilhelm and Leigh were going to announce their engagement to us when we got there and they had not been as careful as they thought. We were going to be grandparents two months before Stefi's baby was due. Stefi added that they had been talking about getting married and Wilhelm had already asked her many times. The impending birth of the heir to his family fortune was the final thing that convinced her that life in Vienna would be great. They were planning to be married in New Zealand at her parents' home.

Late the next afternoon we went over to Wilhelm's. He was not home from the office yet but Leigh met us at the door. The clothing that she wore was a little baggy but very stylish and hid her figure. She had been trying to get a job but work permits had been unavailable, so she had spent time doing unofficial research for Wilhelm on a number of cases he had been working on. She had spent some time working for her father in New Zealand and was quite used to law terminology. Her research had really helped Wilhelm in his cases and certainly did not hurt his position within the firm.

We made the usual small talk over coffee. It was not hard to see that she was a bit nervous to be with us without Wilhelm there. We did our best to make her feel comfortable but nothing seemed to work.

Wilhelm arrived about an hour later and she looked very relieved when she heard him at the door.

We had a pleasant evening but we avoided any opportunity for them to tell us about what they wanted to tell us. It was not too hard to dominate the discussions and keep leading them on to other conversations. They were both getting quite nervous so I finally decided to break the ice by asking when they were planning to get married. After all, they were already acting like a married couple.

They quickly looked back and forth at each other before Wilhelm blurted out, "In two months, in New Zealand."

Hanna turned to Leigh and asked, "Why so fast, is somebody sick?"

Leigh looked very nervous, gathered her composure and said, "I am but only in the mornings." Hanna laughed, got up, and gave her a hug and welcomed her into the family. I jumped in with a hug and handshake with Wilhelm.

Wilhelm looked sternly at us and inquired how we had already known. I laughed and told him they might as well have hung a sign on the door because Leigh had always worn tight-fitting clothes, she was sporting a ring and she had avoided alcohol in her drink. He looked at us and shook his head in disgust. Parents!

Chapter 34

Wilhelm Sets the Stage for the Sale of the Hotel

Leigh and I had gotten together with Stefi and Helmut several evenings and as a group we felt it would be better if Will and Mother were much closer to Vienna. It was awkward to fly back and forth to the hotel and the four of us had noticed they seemed to be getting very tired. We all felt the charm of the hotel had started to wear thin. Leigh and I had discussed the situation around my parents several times since she had become pregnant and we both felt they needed a change. Stefi and Helmut felt the same. This particular evening I had news for our group. One of my clients had a lodge located in the foothills just outside Vienna. The lodge was less than a two-hour drive from either Stefi and Helmut or Leigh and me. It was perfect. Will and Mother would be close enough for the family to get together but not too close for us to get in to each other's hair. I described the lodge as best I could but suggested that we could go up the next weekend to check it out and could stay over on Saturday night if we wanted to. Everybody was quite excited and the girls immediately jumped on the what-clothes-will-I-bring bandwagon. Helmut just rolled his eyes at me.

I explained the lodge had been in the family of my client for quite a number of years, mostly used by his grandparents and subsequently his parents. They had decided upon the death of the parents that because no one had any desire to go there, they might as well sell it and use the funds for a villa on the Mediterranean.

The following weekend we all piled into my car and we headed for our weekend getaway.

The girls packed enough food and clothes for a month. We could barely fit everything into the trunk.

The drive was uneventful and became very pretty as we entered the foothills. We got lost a couple of times and were forced to ask directions. The gate to the driveway was well hidden from the road. Once we finally located it we drove in and up to the front door.

The building was fairly large and somewhat spread out. The surrounding grounds were treed with a small lawn around the main building. There was a large separate garage which contained two antique cars.

I wondered if they came with the lodge.

The lodge entrance had a roof over it, which probably had been used for a cover during the horse and buggy days.

I dug the key out of the bottom of my pocket, opened the front door and we all went inside. The main entrance was wood paneled as were, we later found out, a large number of the other walls in the house. The paneling was of a lighter color so the building did not have a dark and dismal look. It was actually quite light and airy.

We opened the curtains on the rear of the house and found they opened up onto a view down a valley which was beautiful and inspiring. The four of us just stood there staring. I turned to Leigh and thought out loud, "Why would anyone want to sell this place?"

The answer from Leigh was a question; "How could anyone?" Then silence and wonder.

Helmut broke the silence. "Let's all go exploring. The girls can go upstairs and Wilhelm and I will check out the cellars and other lower areas."

Away we all went and we rejoined each other an hour later in the lounge, where I had lit the fire that had been set in the fireplace. Stefi located some glasses and brandy. The girls stuck to fruit juice, which Leigh had packed in a cooler. We compared notes.

There were four bedrooms upstairs and room in the attic for more if you wanted. The lodge lacked nothing. Sheets, blankets, towels, silverware, cooking utensils, china and glassware were all there and of top quality. There was even a decent wine cellar with some interesting but not outstanding wines.

To me, the building looked in excellent condition but that evaluation would be up to Father. After all, that was his department.

We all chose our bedrooms, although nobody would sleep in the master bedroom. It was almost as if that room was already a special place for Mother and Will and none of us wanted to invade their privacy.

Morning came and everybody got up, showered and dressed. We went downstairs for a cholesterol bomb of a breakfast. Stefi and I had developed quite a liking for the Canadian breakfast, which was toast, coffee, fried eggs, and bacon. It had taken Father a while but he was able to teach a butcher to prepare what was known as Peameal Bacon in Canada. Leigh and Helmut had also come to like it as much as Stefi and I. However, we did save it for special occasions.

The girls cleaned up the dishes from breakfast and Helmut and I decided to check out the grounds.

There were several outbuildings, one of which was probably a gardener's cottage. There were three others; a garage, a storage building and a stable for no more than three horses. If there were more we would look later when the girls came out. The grounds had a nice large grassed area which badly needed a good trim.

Stefi suggested we all go for a walk on the trail that we could see led up the mountain from the river at the base of the lodge. We all agreed.

Helmut led and we all followed. I was concerned about the girls, especially with their balance not being the best because of the babies.

They assured me they would be all right.

They weren't.

About five hundred meters up the trail Stefi slipped and came down hard. She gave a scream, which was a cross between a pain and a curse. Helmut turned around and ran back to her. I yelled at Leigh to be careful.

Stefi was crying, the result of a twisted ankle and probably a bruised hip.

We were all very concerned about the baby.

Helmut and I half carried her back to the lodge. Helmut continued to ask her if she felt okay. Was the baby okay? Was she okay? How did she think the baby was?

Stefi finally told him to stop asking if the baby was okay. It was only a twisted ankle.

He did stop asking, but did not stop looking very, very concerned.

We got back to the lodge and Stefi lay on the couch in the lounge. We got a blanket to cover her. Leigh brought in a bag of ice and we put it on her ankle, hopefully to stop it from swelling too much. Leigh chased the guys out and checked out her hip. A large bruise was forming but according to Leigh it did not look serious. She did suggest we take her to a doctor when we got back to Vienna. Helmut decided to get another opinion. Finding the telephone worked he called the local village and located a doctor, who, believe it or not, still made house calls. He arrived one hour later when Helmut and I were checking out the cars in the garage.

The doctor bandaged her ankle to support it, gave her some pain pills and assured us the baby seemed to be fine.

Helmut and I walked with the doctor to his car, thanked him and paid him for his assistance. We asked him what he knew about the lodge and to whom could we talk who might know some of the history. He gave us several names and bid us a pleasant good-bye.

The rest of the afternoon was spent exploring and checking on Stefi.

Her troubles now became fair game for a joke. We were not above teasing and we accused her of shirking her duties as chief cook and bottle washer by playing sick.

We left the next day at noon and stopped in the local village to see what was available in shops and services. Not a lot but the basics were there and they had a good selection.

Back in Vienna, I dropped Stefi and Helmut off at their home and Leigh and I went home. It may have been the fresh air but Leigh and I were both quite tired that night and went to bed early. As we lay in each other's arms we talked about Stefi's fall and how we hoped the baby would be all right. Leigh insisted that women and babies were very tough creatures and it would take more than a little fall to cause any serious problems.

I think she was just trying to make me feel better.

Tomorrow would tell.

We both spent the night with an uneasy sleep. I gave up and got up at six, had my shower, kissed Leigh good-bye and headed for the office.

Coffee on the way was good enough for breakfast.

I called Helmut at his office when he should have been there. He wasn't.

Leigh called and told me Helmut had taken Stefi to her doctor. The doctor then sent them to the hospital for a checkup to confirm everything was fine.

Later I called Helmut. This time he answered and told me he was about to call me as he had just got off the telephone with Stefi and she had told him there was nothing to worry about. I told him Leigh and I would be over that evening with dinner and to make sure Stefi did not fuss.

I called Leigh and told her what I had arranged and that I would call for a pickup from a good caterer that we used at the office.

Leigh agreed and would be ready when I got home.

It was now noon and I had gotten zero work done.

About two in the afternoon Helmut called from the hospital. Stefi was back in emergency and was in much pain.

I called Leigh and she told me she would meet me at the hospital.

Three traffic jams and forty-five minutes later I arrived at the hospital. Leigh met me in the waiting room. She had just gotten there and had just figured out what room Stefi was in.

We rushed up and found Helmut there with her. She did not look very good and was crying.

She had miscarried the baby.

The doctor had told her that the fall had not caused the miscarriage. It was just one of those things that happens and there had been no after-effects which would hinder her future pregnancies. He then told her that if she wanted she would probably get pregnant again very soon.

Everybody looked somewhat relieved except for Leigh, who was now quite nervous as she looked down at herself. I took her in my arms and gave her a reassuring hug and suggested we go home.

That night was a very emotional time. Leigh was upset about

Stefi and kept saying she thought I might leave her if it wasn't for the baby. I had to keep reminding her it was me who wanted to marry her and she who kept saying no until she became pregnant. The rest of the evening and late into the night it progressed in the same way with very little sleep and a lot of upset and crying.

By morning she had settled down.

I called the office and told them I would be late.

I called Helmut and got him just before he was going to the hospital. He had talked to Stefi and she was being discharged at ten that morning.

I stayed with Leigh until she told me that she would be all right and I had better go to the office. I called her when I got there and several times during the day.

We picked up the delayed meal from the takeout and went over to Stefi and Helmut's that evening.

The meal was excellent but we stayed away from the subject of the day before. Stefi broke the silence by telling us that she would call Mother and Will the next morning. We all looked at each other realizing that none of us had thought to call them. Stefi added she was planning to go back to work on the following Monday, much to Helmut's displeasure.

I then decided to tell them about a corporate client my company had. Our client had used us a number of times when they did not want their internal lawyers to know what was under consideration. The corporation was in the hospitality industry and was shopping around for a small hotel with an excellent reputation that could be converted relatively easily into a very exclusive spa. I felt that Mother and Will's hotel would meet their requirements. They had indicated their budget and it was very generous. I asked the others if they thought that I should present Mother and Will's hotel as an option.

After much discussion we all agreed if the price was right it would be best for Mother and Will to sell the hotel and move closer to all of us

I told everybody I would speak to the partners tomorrow and, with a little research, hopefully an offer would be made.

Leigh and I went home.

That night was far more restful than the previous one.

Chapter 35
Wilhelm Continues

My week was very hectic. I got in touch with our clients who were shopping for the hotel. We forwarded to them a detailed description of the hotel with the land description including the parcel that had been purchased by Mother and Will the previous year. We included several pictures of the outside and of various rooms inside. I had handled that transaction so I had copies of all of the surveys. I also discussed a possible conflict of interest in this venture with one of the senior partners because of my relationship. He assured me there would be no conflict because the sale, if finalized, would be actually handled by their in-house lawyers. Our company would get the finder fee, which would be substantial. He was very pleased with the possibility of the hotel being purchased by our clients. He also asked me not to say anything to Mother and Will, as it might have a negative effect on the sale. I gave my word not to tell them until everything was completed.

That evening Leigh and I stopped by to visit Helmut and Stefi to update them on the sale of the hotel and to find out how Stefi was feeling.

Stefi was in much better spirits. She told us she had called Mother and Will about the miscarriage and both of them were ready to drop everything and jump on a plane to come to see her. She convinced them she was fine and not in any danger and in fact would be going back to work on Monday. That seemed to calm them down somewhat but Mother was still quite upset. Both Stefi and Helmut were pleased with the progress to date on the sale of the hotel.

It was several weeks before Mother and Will finally made it to Vienna and by this time Stefi was pregnant again.

I got home a little late the evening that Mother and Will were coming. Leigh had almost begged me to be there when they arrived and was upset with me when I called her to tell her I would be about a half an hour late. She wanted me to be with her when my parents came because we had not yet told them she was pregnant and we were getting married. Stefi's problems had kept us quiet.

Will kept directing the conversation towards subjects they wanted to talk about and every time I tried to find an opening either Mother or Will closed it. I was getting very nervous and Leigh wasn't much better.

Will suddenly changed the subject again, but this time he asked when we were getting married. Leigh looked at me and I at her.

I blurted out, "In two months in New Zealand."

Mother turned to Leigh and asked, "Why so fast, is somebody sick?"

Leigh looked over to me somewhat shaken and turning to my parents said, "I am but only in the mornings." Mother laughed, and got up and gave her a hug and welcomed her into the family.

The conversation between us became very animated and centered on the new members of the family. Mother wanted to know all about Leigh's family, and did they know about the baby? Leigh told her they knew nothing except she had met a wonderful young man in Vienna. Mother wanted to know how we knew that the wedding would be in two months. Leigh had spoken to her grandmother, to whom she was very close, and some arrangements had already been started. Leigh was going to call her parents on the weekend and break the news to them. Mother and Will told us that they would make all of the arrangements at the hotel to ensure they would be able to attend. I was to book tickets so we could all travel together.

I took the opportunity to suggest to my parents that it would be best for them to move back to the Vienna area to be close to their new grandchildren. I jokingly reminded them that they were certainly getting up there in years.

That comment did not sit too well.

They then laughed and told us about an offer which had come

from a hospitality company. The offer to purchase the hotel was far above what they had thought the hotel might be worth. They also said they were considering the offer quite seriously but were not sure where they would move to.

Ah, the opportunity!

I told them about the lodge we had stayed at and if they were serious I could show it to them. My firm was handling the sale and we had the keys. There were no real-estate agents involved.

They were very interested.

Early the next morning I called one of the partners at home and explained what we were doing and asked if the keys were available. He sensed a good deal underway and offered to get the keys to my place within the hour and added that he would make sure all of my appointments were covered.

Money sure does talk.

The keys were there by 9:00 a.m. and we left to go up to see the lodge.

After several hours of exploration of the lodge, it was obvious Will and Mother were in love with it. I could not yet tell them of my involvement.

I was a little uncomfortable with the situation. Leigh tried to convince me that nothing would be different if they knew and a promise was a promise.

Mother and Will flew back to the hotel, excited about the lodge and ready to finalize the sale of the hotel.

To make a long story short, they sold the hotel for more than twice what they had ever thought its value to be.

They bought the lodge, moved most of their belongings into storage and arranged for some renovations to be done.

Will named their new home Silverthorne Lodge, after the first place where we had spent a holiday together as a family. It was a beautiful spot located on Georgian Bay, north of Toronto, and it had always held so many special memories for all of us. It was one of Mother and Will's favorite places and they had returned there over the years on several of their summer holidays in Canada.

Will brought with him several red doorknobs from the hotel. He installed one on each of the front doors. Now Silverthorne Lodge was really their home. To them, the red doorknobs were a symbol of their life, from where they started until where they were today.

I was offered a junior partnership with the firm, which I accepted, and we all headed off to New Zealand for the wedding.

Chapter 36
Wilhelm and Leigh's Wedding

Hanna and I flew to New Zealand with Wilhelm and Leigh. Stefi and Helmut were following in a couple of days. Wilhelm had some work to finalize and Stefi had a doctor's appointment. We stopped in Hong Kong, where we spent one layover day. Leigh would have preferred to continue as she was excited to see her parents but the tickets were less expensive to have a layover. The city was very fascinating but very expensive. We did a quick evening tour and went back to our hotel after a pleasant meal. We all retired early as the jet lag, a long flight and just sitting in an airplane wears one out. Our flight was to leave late the next evening. The time change was a killer to Leigh and Wilhelm. Hanna and I had traveled back and forth to Canada so many times in the last few years there seemed to be less of an effect on us.

We landed in Auckland and left one hour later for Christchurch. The flight basically followed the country southward. Following the flight down the country and checking the map I discovered we flew over Farewell Spit on the north end of the South Island. I was excited as it was on my long list of places to visit in New Zealand.

We landed in Christchurch, gathered our luggage, and walked out into the arrivals area. Leigh's family was waiting for us. There were many tears of welcome and a shocked expression when her parents got a good look at her.

They did not know they were becoming grandparents.

Hanna and I finally got introduced when the commotion settled down

Leigh's father was a lawyer with one of the larger law firms and their house reflected his status. Their home was big by New Zealand standards and beautifully furnished. There was not a lot of "stuff," which is normal in most European homes and even more so in North American homes. Hanna and I were shown a bedroom on the second floor, where we unpacked our clothes.

I very carefully unpacked several bottles of very special wine which I had brought for the rehearsal party. Leigh's father came up to inquire if everything was in order. He looked over at the wine, let out a low whistle followed by "Where did you get that? I thought I would never ever see an empty bottle, let alone a full one."

Smiling I followed his whistle with "I lucked out with a whole wine cellar and there are more where this came from for the reception if you wish."

"Do I wish?" was his only comment as he stared at the bottles.

Hanna and I were to host the rehearsal party on the evening before the wedding. We did not know what the good and bad restaurants were, so we relied on what Leigh's father recommended. He gave us a list of some local establishments. We went out exploring and chose one of the nicer places and gave them a down payment. After a few days of visiting, Hanna and I decided to let Wilhelm, Leigh and her parents spend some time without us. We rented a car and went off to Queenstown, the adventure capital of New Zealand.

Queenstown has a large number of good treks located close by.

I had gotten information on several of the treks. We had done a lot of the treks in Austria so we decided that we would start on the most famous of all, the Milford Track.

There are two ways to do the Milford Track, the first being sleeping in the DOC huts and the second being a guided trek staying in lodges. We chose to do the latter although it was considerably more expensive but much more civilized. We had to carry our own day pack and the rest of our gear was carried to the lodges for us. When we got to the lodge our food was ready for us and a warm comfortable bed was available for sleeping. The trek was totally amazing. It was definitely the most awe-inspiring walk we had ever done. Around every corner and over every hill was scenery unlike anything anywhere else in the world. Even in the rain the photography was amazing. It was not hard to understand why it was called "the most beautiful trek in the world."

Now that we had gotten our legs in shape we next tried the Routebourn Track but this time we had to carry all of our own gear including food and water. We stayed in the DOC huts and, although things were much more primitive, we had another amazing trek. New Zealand's treks must be able to hold their own with any other treks in the world.

We were gone the better part of two weeks before we returned to Christchurch. I decided to check out how our reception plans were progressing. The restaurant that we had chosen had a note on the door from the bailiff.

Oops!

We went back to Leigh's parents' house to get our list and to find out what had happened.

Leigh's father was totally embarrassed, especially when he found out we had given them a down payment for the party. He told us, "In New Zealand we operate on trust, down payments are never required."

Hanna and I then visited several other restaurants and finally settled on a small facility with a good wine cellar. The owner was very personable and when he found out what wine I had brought with me for the toasts his eyes became as big as saucers. "The only thing I ask is you leave me an empty bottle."

I replied, "I will even leave a glass for you to savor if you wish."

"Do I wish?" His beaming face told the rest of his story.

We discussed the menu for the evening and he presented several options.

Sitting back he smiled and said, "For a reasonable price I will cook the most amazing meal you have ever eaten. Leave it to me, just show up."

Hanna and I looked at each other and agreed. Somehow trust is a wonderful thing.

It was truly the most amazing dinner. We had wild boar, venison, elk, emu, beef, lamb and even a lowly chicken. The vegetables were superb and dessert was a pavlova to die for.

The whole meal was a life-memorable experience.

Leigh's father was astonished with the meal and its presentation. He was very knowledgeable about good food and told us he had never experienced anything like that before.

The toasts were short. Rumors circulated as to the value of the wine we were using. Some people actually requested a simple local wine for the toast because they believed the quality of the wine would be lost on them. Leigh, Wilhelm and all of the rest of the wedding party told us they thought it was the best party they had ever been to. Leigh's father openly wondered if the wedding reception would be as good.

The owner of the restaurant was predictably happy as he got all of the wine bottles, his own personal glass of wine and was able to show off his skills, to top it all off. Everybody enjoyed their evening.

The wedding was a rather grand affair. Wilhelm and Stefi were married in the Anglican cathedral right downtown in Christchurch. It was a beautiful church right on the square. We got to the church using horses and carriages. Some of the people used a special trolley car rented for the occasion. There was an old trolley line that traveled through that part of the city and it stopped right in front of the church. The trolley then made its trip to where the reception was and returned for more guests. The weather was bright and sunny, which, of course, added to the uniqueness of the wedding.

Hanna and I commented to each other on how we were now able to relax and watch the ceremony unfold. Our part had been completed the night before.

The speeches were limited because nobody could tell any stories on Wilhelm because he was new to everybody. That is until Stefi decided it was time for a roast and he got it from her. Everybody had many a laugh at Wilhelm's expense. She even told a couple of little tidbits that had Hanna shaking her head in wonder. She tugged my sleeve and told me if she had known at the time she would have slaughtered him.

The day after the wedding Wilhelm and Leigh returned, both beaming, and said good-bye to Stefi and Helmut as they were flying home. Stefi had another doctor's check up and Helmut had work at the office that was collecting and waiting for him.

Wilhelm and Leigh were going to stop in Thailand for several days before heading back to Vienna and the life of a young professional family.

Hanna and I planned to stay another couple of weeks before heading home. We had a couple of treks we wanted to do and some sightseeing which, of course, included the Farewell Spit and Golden Bay. The road over the pass to Golden Bay was something else again. I kept wondering why they did not put a tunnel through the mountain until I saw the river which started from nowhere at the side of the mountain and just flowed cold and strong into the sea.

We did the Abel Tasman Track but this time we did the trek the easy way. Rather than staying at the huts and carrying all of our gear we stayed at a beautiful bed-and-breakfast and used the water taxi to take us to our starting place and pick us up at the end of our day trek. The following day we did the same and the last day we walked back to the car and drove out.

We drove back south to Nelson, the main town of the area, overnighted at a nice hotel and then headed towards Christchurch, with a stop at Hanmer Springs. We wanted to sample the hot springs and soak out our stiff muscles from the treks. The next day we drove to Christchurch and spent our last two days there with Leigh's parents before we left to fly to Auckland. We overnighted in downtown Auckland and boarded an early flight to Singapore, where we spent two days before heading home.

Hanna and I talked all the way home about the wonderful time we had in New Zealand. The people were friendly and helpful in every way possible. The scenery in the country never seemed to end. We also talked about how happy we were that both the twins were now married and settling into their own lives. We were somewhat shocked to suddenly realize that we were going to be grandparents in the not too distant future. Were grandparents not old people? We certainly did not feel we were old.

Life was certainly complete.

When we arrived in Vienna, we stayed overnight with Stefi and Helmut before heading on to the lodge the next day. We did not move fast as jet lag and all those hours in a plane had taken their toll on our poor bodies. Helmut had arranged for the lodge to be opened and the heat on for our arrival.

We walked in, set our bags by the door, and continued into the sitting room, where we just sat down, looked at each other, and said that it was good to be home.

Chapter 37
At Home

It was great to be home. Hanna and I wandered around to see if everything was still in order. It was. We unpacked our things and put our newly purchased treasures in the appropriate display areas. Most of our photographs had already been developed so I took the last couple of rolls down to the village to the photo shop and got them processed. Hanna puttered around in the house and I went out to the garage to work on one of the cars. When we bought the property I made sure the cars that were on the property were included. There were actually three old automobiles in very good condition. One was an old Auto Union race car, one was an old Mercedes and the other was a Messerschmitt. The Messerschmitt was the most interesting as it was a three-wheel car with two seats, one in front of the other. The entry was through the top, by opening a side-hinged canopy. The battery was flat and I had put it on charge since the late morning. I got it running, ran into the lodge and got Hanna so we could go for a ride. She thought I was crazy but still went with me down to the village.

Our days were filled with house and garden projects, car projects, treks, photography, wine collecting, some construction projects and what ever else fit our fancy.

Stefi and Helmut finally had their first beautiful little girl and added two more as the years went on. Wilhelm and Leigh moved to New Zealand with their baby boy as Leigh eventually became very homesick. Wilhelm, with some assistance, passed the bar exams for New Zealand and went to work for a law firm in Auckland. He became quite involved in land development downtown. They had another child so we were now the proud grandparents of five grandchildren.

Hanna and I now spent our summers in Austria and our winters in New Zealand. From time to time everybody came to Silverthorne Lodge, our home, near Vienna. Hanna and I purchased a large property near Nelson, New Zealand and started a vineyard on it. We had obtained a quantity of vines from Europe and now the vines were mature enough to produce sufficient quantities of grapes for a decent amount of wine. We had several people whom we employed full time and they managed and worked the vineyard. We were always around for the picking season so were able to keep track of things. Our staff were so dedicated to their jobs that we kept them on all year. We paid them a much higher than average salary and believed it was money well spent.

Life was grand.

The morning sun was shining through the window casting its rays across a very traditionally decorated room. The room was located in the back of a very old lodge overlooking a small valley in the foothills of the mountains in Austria. A light scent of mountain flowers was wafting in the window and I lay there in bed with my arm around the most wonderful person in the world. I wondered how, after so many years and so many turns of fate, we had finally arrived at what could only be simply described as happiness.

The solitude was broken by a rumbling sound that seemed to shake the whole building. Hanna and I looked at each other and started to laugh. She jumped out of bed, grabbed her robe, and ran for the bathroom. I tucked my head under the bedding and curled into a ball as the door burst open. Five little grandchildren charged in jumping on the bed to get us to come downstairs for breakfast. I was covered in scrambling, yelling kids and in a weird voice answered them with "There's nobody under here but the lump in the bed."

*

DESTINY OF A WAR VETERAN

by Sal Atlantis Phoenix

Destiny of a War Veteran depicts the life of a conscientious veteran. The subject matter of the story is serious and tends towards the realistic side of the aftermath of war. The story is about the analysis of the human soul lost in fantasy and in reality, about submission and rebellion, and about philosophy and tyranny. The story is vivid with images, and complex and rich in characters. It is an intriguing tale that defines the socio-political scenarios.

Vietnam War veteran Joe is tempted to participate in Middle Eastern and international politics, compelled with insinuated illusion of establishing freedom and democracy. The subsequent effects of the human tragedies engulfed from the political scenarios devastate him, and he seeks refuge beyond the realm of humanity.

Paperback, 188 pages
5.5" x 8.5"
ISBN 1-4241-8005-8

About the author:

Sal Atlantis Phoenix, a veteran of life and a conscientious citizen, is a playwright and fiction writer. His lifelong experience convinced him that "…with all its sham, drudgery and broken dreams, it is still a beautiful world. Be careful. Strive to be happy."

THE ASSASSIN WHO LOVED HER

by Janet M. Henderson

In *The Assassin Who Loved Her*, journalist Jennifer Long wants two things: to become a great writer and to fall in love. Her dreams come true when she writes about a serial killer called the Assassin who stalks, threatens, and torments her for exposing his motives in the media.

Tim, the pilot, brings Jennifer financial security. Jason, the actor, brings her fame and fortune. John, the former FBI agent, brings her protection and intrigue. But Jennifer must survive murder, deceit, heartache, and grief before she finds true love, happiness, triumph, and relief.

Paperback, 276 pages
6" x 9"
ISBN 1-60610-424-1

From Chicago, to Washington, to Hollywood, to Portugal, Jennifer fights for her life and career. Her story will make you laugh and cry. It'll make you believe in love. It'll make you hope and pray she wins. With a fairytale beginning and a Hollywood ending, it has everything a good novel should have! Read it and love it!

About the author:

Janet M. Henderson teaches English in the City Colleges of Chicago. She was born in Chicago and, as the daughter of a U.S. Marine, grew up in Virginia, North Carolina, California and Hawaii. Her first novel, *Lunch with Cassie*, received excellent reviews from Writer's Digest. She lives in Chicago.

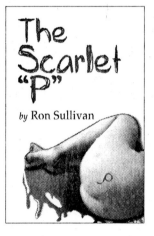